# Silverwood

## By

## Amber Reifsteck

ISBN: 9781798246399

Primary Category: Fiction / Fantasy / General

Summary: After a dark force of Shadow demons is awoken,
a secretive sorceress enlists the help of a reluctant
swordsman.

Language: English

Country of Publication: United States

# Contents

# Silverwood

## By

### Amber Reifsteck

# Chapter One

# THE DARKENING SKY

"Guardians! Guardians!" the shepherdess screamed as loudly as she could, running into the Temple of Aurora. The Guardians of Light and the temple dwellers met the shepherdess as she climbed the stairs.

"Guardians," the shepherdess panted, "the moon is gone!" A murmur of fear rolled through the temple and the Guardians exchanged nervous glances. Without a word they filed out onto the balcony to gaze into the night.

As true as the shepherdess had said, the sky above the land of Argentum was black as pitch, illuminated only by the cold glow of the glittering, white stars. The three Guardians stood silent and motionless, not wanting to believe their own eyes. They looked into the west where the second of Argentum's five moons had set.

The third moon should have risen in the east by now, but it was nowhere to be found. The sky was empty, the darkness was coming and no one could do anything to stop it. Fear began to fill the room.

"The Shadows, the Shadows," people whispered, not daring to raise their voices lest the Shadows hear them. None of them had ever seen a night without the moon, for in Argentum, the moon always shone brightly across the land.

More than three hundred years earlier, a group of sorcerers had captured the light of the sun and broken it into five moons. As soon as one moon began to set, another would begin to rise, ensuring that there was always a comforting silver light across the land to protect the people from the Shadows. But now one of the moons was gone, leaving just a swath of darkness in its place.

It would only be a matter of time before the Shadows realized that the moon had vanished, and if the moon stayed gone, the Shadows would leave their valley. Once outside of their valley, they would have free reign so long as the absence of the moon remained. The Shadows could consume anyone unlucky enough to cross their path. The Shadows were a force no one could stand against and they knew it.

"To the Lumidian immediately," Kelgar commanded. Notelcea and Enira nodded, following the old man as he hobbled up staircase after staircase until he reached the seventh tier of the temple. Together the three Guardians fixed their eyes upon the form of the Lumidian.

The Lumidian was the device that held the captured power of the sun. It was the Lumidian that distributed the sun's light among the five moons of the world. It had never failed. The device consisted of a large, glowing pedestal positioned in the very center of the temple's seventh tier. The sun crystal, the largest of six crystals, sat at the center of the pedestal, orbited by the five silver moonstones that floated through the air. But as the Guardians gazed upon the Lumidian that evening, they saw with certainty that one of the crystals was missing. Where the stone that represented the third moon should have hovered, there was now only open space.

"Selene has gone dark," said Kelgar, naming the third moon. The light of the Lumidian's remaining crystals cast an unworldly glow upon his wizened face.

"But how could the moon have gone dark?" breathed Enira in fear.

Enira was the youngest of the three Guardians, still being in her twenties, and still a bit new to the ways of the Guardians of Light. Despite her training, the young girl's slender frame trembled in what could not be mistaken for anything other than fear. Her blond hair sparkled all the more, as though trying to make its own light in the darkness.

"The moon has gone dark because it is no longer there," said Kelgar. "This is a fact that none would wish to believe, but whether we choose to believe it or not, the fact still remains. The third moon has gone dark because it has been destroyed."

Enira gasped. Kelgar might as well have told them that the world was ending because his words carried the same weight. If something could snuff out one moon, what was to stop it from striking another?

Selene was one of the late moons; the moon that rose while most people were sleeping. Few people would realize its absence immediately. Sooner or later, however, people were going to notice, and when that happened, panic would spread throughout the land. Such would only make the darkness stronger, for the Shadows fed upon fear.

"But that's not possible," Enira protested, the prospect being too terrible to believe. "The power of the Lumidian prevents the moons from destroying themselves. Someone would have had to steal the crystal and none but the Guardians are allowed to enter the seventh tier. If someone had come into this level of the temple we would have known. No one could do that. It must mean something else."

"It can mean only one thing," said Notelcea, the third Guardian speaking at last. "The Keeper of Darkness has infiltrated the temple."

Though a well-seasoned Guardian of Light, Notelcea had never lost her youthful appearance. Her hair was brown as ever, her skin was smooth as silk, and her body had all the energy of a youthful maiden. Because of this, Notelcea rarely spoke, letting Kelgar be the purveyor of wise words. She knew that wisdom was more easily believed when it was spoken by an elder, and Kelgar had the appearance of a wise old man. When Notelcea did choose to speak, however, the other Guardians saw fit to listen.

"The Keeper!" Enira choked. "Do you really believe the Keeper of Darkness has penetrated the Temple of Aurora?"

"I think there can be no other explanation. It will not be long before the Keeper of Darkness emerges from the valley and all the Shadows shall follow." Notelcea's blue eyes glowed like a sapphire flame, enhancing her fresh-faced appearance.

Even Notelcea didn't completely understand the reasons for her prolonged youth, and she wasn't sure she wanted to understand. She had a strong suspicion that it had something to do with the vanishing moon, though she couldn't say exactly what. The events of the evening had frightened her perhaps more than anyone else because she had been a Guardian longer than anyone else.

She knew it could not be a mere coincidence that the stolen moon just happened to be Selene. That particular moon had always been weaker than the others, almost since the beginning of the Lumidian itself. Most people had attributed it to a discrepancy in the construction of the Lumidian, but as the suspected mistake had never been found, it had eventually been ignored. It never seemed to hurt the light of the moon, however, it simply left it a bit misshapen on one side, like that of a moon which rises two days after the full. There was only one person in the world who knew why Selene was misshapen and that person had never spoken of it.

Notelcea sighed as she stared at the vacant space where Selene's crystal should have been floating. She knew something was happening, but she would not disclose more than she already had. Talk of the Keeper was worry enough and Notelcea knew that no good would come of panicking the temple dwellers, not when there was so much important work that had to be done. Notelcea had her suspicions, and she could only hope she was wrong.

"I am in agreement, Notelcea," said Kelgar. "I cannot begin to imagine how the Keeper of Darkness could have broken through our boundaries of light, but the Keeper has had hundreds of years to plan this with little else to think about."

"The Keeper has been striving to break free of the Valley of Shadows since it was first exiled there," Notelcea reaffirmed.

Enira was practically shaking as she listened. Notelcea slipped a comforting hand over the young woman's shoulder. Enira had only taken up the position of Guardian little more than a month ago. Before Enira, a ninety-four year old man had held the position of the third Guardian of Light, but when he died quietly in his sleep, Enira had taken his place. She had been raised in the Temple of Aurora with the other potential Guardians of the future.

When one of the Guardians passed on, it was the duty of one of the potentials to take their place, ensuring that there would always be three Guardians, just as there had been since the creation of the Lumidian. None of Enira's training or temple life had readied her for the events that were now in motion, however, and she was finding it difficult to compose herself. The Shadows had never been a threat during her life, or even the lives of her parents, but now they were a very real peril and Enira was little prepared to deal with them.

"For too long we have ignored the Keeper of Darkness and its Shadows, believing ourselves and our powers to be superior," said Kelgar. "Tonight we have been proven otherwise. We can ignore this threat no longer. We must undo what the Keeper has done. We must rouse the moon that the Keeper has darkened and we must make it whole. We have long known that Selene has been misshapen since before we were born, and we know that whatever caused that defect is what allowed the Keeper to silence Selene's light this evening. Now that the Keeper has taken Selene, it has a window open to the Lumidian. Who can say how fast the Keeper can work or how complete its plan is. We can only hope to stop it before it silences the lights of the world forever."

"What do you suggest, Kelgar?" asked Enira, desperate for anything that would seem to cast hope on the dreary situation.

"I suggest that we go immediately, Notelcea and I, for there is not a moment to lose," Kelgar replied.

"Me?" Notelcea's eyes locked with Kelgar's. "And what is it that you would suggest I do?"

"Go to the Hall of Records in the royal city beneath the king's palace."

"Kelgar, I know the information that lies within those records. There is no knowledge in them that I do not already possess," Notelcea protested.

"There is always something in the records that we do not know, Notelcea. That library holds the history of the world. I know that you were a Guardian long before I came to the temple, but–"

"What?" Enira whispered in shock. "Kelgar, how could Notelcea have been a Guardian before you? You're ancient."

Notelcea shook her head. "Kelgar is not as old as he appears. A childhood encounter with the Shadows left him much scarred and aged him before his time. He is hardly more than fifty."

Kelgar nodded. "And Notelcea is not as young as you may believe. She was already a Guardian before I came to take my place."

It was all new information to Enira. It was a rule of the temple that no one spoke of the previous Guardians who had passed on. Their names were not to be recorded or spoken after their deaths, for fear it would cause inequity among the ranks. The Guardians were all meant to be equal, for when they took up the position, they relinquished their personal identities and became merely the Guardians. The position of the Guardians was meant to be remembered and revered, not the people who filled that position. As such, the Guardians almost never spoke of those before them.

"We have no time to dwell upon this now, Enira," said Kelgar. He turned back to Notelcea. "Despite your age, even you could not know everything in those records, for they extend to the beginning of this very temple. There may be secrets in there that we need to know, perhaps secrets concerning the construction of the Lumidian that will point out its weakness. We are the Guardians and only we are allowed to access that information, but even we do not know the names of the first Guardians, the Guardians who captured the sun for us all."

"You as well as I do that we do not speak of the Guardians who have gone before us," Notelcea chided.

"Yes, I know, but now we may have to. Go to the records and see what you might find."

"I tell you with certainly that there will be nothing in those records that I do not already know, but I shall go if it will satisfy your curiosity."

"It will."

"And what then will you do?"

"I shall find the gypsy."

"The gypsy who dwells in Silverwood?"

Kelgar nodded and Notelcea narrowed her eyes. It was rumored that Kelgar had been raised by the woodland gypsy and that such had been a factor in his selection for the position of Guardian. It was a rumor that Kelgar had neither confirmed nor denied, but at the moment, it was certainly making Notelcea curious.

"What can you hope to find from the gypsy woman?" asked Notelcea.

"Answers," said Kelgar simply.

Notelcea shook her head. "You are nearly crippled. Let me find the gypsy while you stay here to protect the temple."

"She is a gypsy, Notelcea. She moves throughout Silverwood, not remaining long in one place. You could never find her yourself. I will go to Mordrelina the gypsy and seek my answers. You must go to the Hall of Records and whilst there you must alert the king to what has happened as well. Enira will remain here to guard the temple."

"Me?" Enira squeaked.

Kelgar nodded. "You are young, but you are still a Guardian and you have the power of the Guardians." He fingered the silver moon pendant that hung from Enira's neck. "If you mind what you have learned, then the temple will be protected."

"Are you sure I am ready for this?"

Kelgar nodded. "Advise the others in the temple to begin making candles and many of them. Have them sent to all the homes in Argentum and beyond, for soon anyone caught in the dark will be taken by the Shadows. It is nearly five hours until Maan, the forth moon, rises. Let us hope the world can hold out that long."

The three Guardians marched back down the stairs and out to the balcony once again. The sky was just as dark as it had been when they left. Kelgar looked at Notelcea. "We leave as soon as Maan rises."

Notelcea nodded gazing up at the sky once again. A weighty covering of clouds began to roll in, something that hadn't happened in hundreds of years, and a chilly wind blew from the west. Notelcea turned toward it, feeling it weave its airy fingers through her hair, and she knew the Keeper had sent it.

"Aecleton," she breathed.

# Chapter Two

## RESTLESS AMBITIONS

Raede Bremmin slowly made his way down the darkened steps of the palace, heading toward the kitchens. Due to a natural insomnia he was often awake while the others in the palace slept. In his own belief, it was due in no small part to the fact that he had lost the crown of Argentum, a crown that should have rightfully been his. He'd never slept well since then.

Raede was a dreamer and a conniver, spending many a sleepless night hatching plan after plan. Some were worthy of tucking away for later use, and some came in streaks where each was as useless as the next. But worthy or useless they continued to come, one right after another.

Raede spent many of his waking hours and nearly all of his few sleeping hours, dreaming of what might have been or what might still be. As was bound to happen, the incessant strategizing and wakeful nights often left him hungry during the late hours, so he had recently taken to haunting the kitchens, devouring whatever was left from the day's meals.

As Raede made his way down to the kitchens that evening, he glanced out one of the open windows on the stairwell to gaze over Argentum, the kingdom that he still felt belonged to him. He was surprised to find it pitch black across the land outside. He could barely make out the line of trees in the palace gardens and the familiar hills had all but vanished. It was dark, very dark, and in a land where the moons were always full, the darkness was anything but ordinary.

Raede leaned further out the window and perceived a sky choked with clouds far too substantial to be the normal rain clouds of Argentum. They blocked out everything, limiting Raede's vision across the land. The familiar light of the moon was nowhere to be seen.

Raede quickened his pace down the stairs, abandoning his trip to kitchens for the time being. Instead he raced out the palace's grand entrance in search of Herric, the night watchman. Raede found the soldier in his usual place as though nothing were amiss.

"Herric," called Raede. "Where is the moon?"

"I don't know, sir," Herric replied. "Lua, the second moon, set shortly after I began my watch, but the third never rose. It has been nearly two hours since the covering of clouds rolled in and I've seen not a glimmer of Selene."

Raede fixed his piercing brown eyes on the clouds covering the world. They were the thickest he'd ever seen in his lifetime. Even so, he should have been able to see the faint glow of the moon beneath them, but there was nothing. The moon was truly gone.

Raede stretched himself to his full height, looking as noble as ever standing there in the darkness of the palace's steps while he contemplated the situation. His square jaw was firmly set and his chestnut hair blew in the unusually strong westerly wind. Though he'd lost the crown, Raede still wore his hair in the manner of a king, cut off at his shoulders and sporting a line of short bangs across his forehead. The king of Argentum had never ordered Raede to change his hair, and while that secretly pleased Raede, it also made him view the king as a very weak man for failing to enforce the laws of his own kingdom.

"What are your thoughts on the matter, Lord Raede?" asked Herric anxiously.

"I think that Aecleton has at last found a way to breach the boundaries of the shadow world," Raede replied.

Herric nodded. "Those were my thoughts as well, sir, though I didn't want to admit them aloud. It is very unpleasant thinking that the Keeper of Darkness may be here within Argentum."

"Does this frighten you Herric?"

Herric nodded. "It does indeed, My Lord, though it is not for myself that I fear, but rather for my wife and children. I expect that they are home even now, sleeping peacefully, completely unaware of what has happened."

Raede nodded. "The Shadows have not left the Valley in almost three hundred years. It will take them some time to find their way back to Argentum. You will have warned your family by then."

"What are your orders, sir?"

Raede did not answer right away. He was still staring at the vacant sky with perhaps a bit of a twinkle in his eyes. Ever the optimist, where others saw only fear, Raede saw opportunity. His glass was always half full, no matter what the occasion. He quietly bided his time playing the role of submissive adviser, but all the while making his own deductions about a given situation. He could find what he considered *the good* in any circumstance, and he always kept a sharp eye open for anything he could use to further himself on his own quest for redemption.

"When are you to be relieved Herric?"

"An hour and a half from now," Herric replied.

"And who is to relieve you?"

"Meclellon."

Raede raised a hand to his chin. "He is here in the palace now isn't he?"

"Yes sir. He came in before Lua set," said Herric.

"Tell him he is to relieve you now, then go and wake my brother. King Laede will need to know what has happened."

"Yes, My Lord." Herric bowed and hurried away to do as Raede had bade him.

Raede reveled in the moment of silence, embracing the gloom of the evening. Herric was frightened and he was looking to Raede for guidance. It made Raede feel important; it made him feel big. It was a feeling he'd rarely felt on many occasions in his life.

Raede had been small-framed as a child and that form had never changed as he'd gotten older. Even now he retained his slim body, almost to the point of finding that it inconvenienced him in its weakness. He'd always tried to make himself appear bigger and more powerful than he was, but to no avail. No matter how much he ate or how hard he worked, he stayed small as ever, a pathetic figure of a man who came second to everything…even the crown. What Raede lacked in physical strength, however, he more than made up for with mental cunning.

Raede had a mind that worked like no other in Argentum. If anyone in the palace court had a question, it was well known that Raede could probably answer it. He was the king's senior defense adviser, a task well suited to someone who had been fighting a personal battle for most of the forty-eight years of his life. He knew that under the present state of affairs the king would soon call upon his wisdom, but this would not be like any other defense the king had been faced with. This time it would not be a fight with unruly citizens or foreign invaders; this would be a fight against shadow itself. Raede knew the king would never be able to win it alone.

Raede would be only too happy to provide the king with essential information about the events of the evening. He'd learned long ago that flies were drawn to honey more quickly than vinegar, and flies were exactly what the members of the court were. Mindless little insects hovering around their king as though their lives depended upon it. Each one seeking to appear more courageous, more wise, or more valuable than the next. Their entire lives were spent putting on airs for a man who'd received the crown by mere chance that the spirits had given him the imposing form than Raede had always desired.

It wasn't Raede's fault that the spirits had made him a small man and he didn't feel he should have to pay for their mistake. He knew he was worth far more than the other insects of the palace. He truly did have value and the king would never be able to do without him. Oh yes, he would advise the king on all matters necessary, because the people would need someone to look to now. They would need someone wise, someone who could answer their questions, someone who could make them feel safe. It would be Raede whom the people would look to now. He grinned. He'd been waiting for an opportunity like this for a very long time.

"Good evening, Lord Raede," came Meclellon's voice.

"Good evening, Meclellon," said Raede turning toward the guard. "Does the night appear different now than it did when you arrived at the palace?"

Meclellon resisted the temptation to gasp in surprise as he noticed the darkened night around him. "It does, sir," he replied, "for Lua has set, the sky has become clouded, and as far as I can tell, Selene has not yet risen."

Raede nodded. "Then you see what Herric and I have seen as well. It is an ill tiding, Meclellon, and I may require your help very soon."

"It is my duty to protect the palace, sir, even from the Shadows. I will do whatever I can."

"You are brave, Meclellon, but swords cannot fight the Shadows. I fear this darkness may have been caused by the Guardians."

"The Guardians of Light? Their one duty is to protect us *from* the darkness. Why would they remove the light?"

Raede could hear the idealism in Meclellon's voice. It was obvious that the soldier bore the great respect that the presence of the Guardians commanded. Perhaps there was even a bit of admiration there. In any event, Raede decided to change the subject. There was work to be done and Meclellon would have to help…whether he knew it or not.

"It is simply that I'm worried an accident may have occurred there," Raede replied switching tactics. "We shall have to send someone to the Temple of Aurora to learn what has happened, but for now I have a different task for you. A task to protect the people of Argentum."

"I am at your service," said Meclellon, always ready to undertake a noble assignment.

"First go to the cellar and gather as many torches as you can find. Dole them out to all the guards of the evening watch, telling them what we believe has happened. When you have finished, wake the kitchen maids."

"The kitchen maids, My Lord?"

"Yes. Tell them to begin constructing more torches immediately. If Selene's absence is to continue, torches will be our only salvation in the coming nights. When you have completed that task, rouse two of the horsemen and have them ride immediately to the Temple of Aurora to find out why the sky has gone dark. Then return here and take your place on the night watch."

"Of course," said Meclellon making to leave. "What of Herric, sir?"

"I have given Herric orders of his own. He is waking the king even as we speak, but his watch is over for the evening. When you have done what I've asked of you, return here, but be sure you bear a torch. It would not do to fall prey to the

Shadows."

Meclellon nodded as Herric had done and ran off to fulfill Raede's orders. Raede watched him intently. The man was a true noble, perhaps too much of one. He was an unmarried man with no family to be concerned about and nothing but his own glory to strive for. Like any true noble, however, Meclellon cared little for his own glory, wanting only glory for the kingdom he served. Herric was a different story.

While Herric did have a very good heart and a kind disposition, he also had attachments. A wife and three children was not something a man would wish to lose. Some men would do anything for love of their families…or for fear of losing them. Fear was dangerous thing, but it could also be a powerful ally, for fear could transform a man. All his ideals could be shattered in one gripping moment. Herric was standing at such a crossroads, and with just the right amount of pressure, the soldier might prove to be very pliable.

Herric reemerged from the palace a few minutes later. "I have done as you asked, Lord Raede."

"Well done, Herric. Did the king send you with any messages?"

"No, sir. It was the bedroom guard who awoke the king. I did not actually speak to him."

"No matter," said Raede. "If the king wishes my counsel, he need only ask."

Herric nodded, but he still seemed anxious.

"There is nothing to be concerned about, Herric, for I do not fear the night."

"Nor I, sir, but I admit I still fear for my family."

Raede nodded in understanding. "How far away does your home lie?"

"At the far end of Argentum, on the outskirts of Silverwood."

Raede rubbed his chin thoughtfully for a moment. "Then you must go, Herric."

"Go?"

"Yes, there is not a moment to lose, for Silverwood is west of Argentum and the Shadows will reach the forest long before they enter our city. I have sent Meclellon on an errand, but he will soon return to take his place on the watch. You are free to go. Take as many torches as you can carry and return to your home.

Tell your family of tonight's events. Leave them torches and bid them make more, or bring your entire family into Argentum where you might keep watch over them and be sure they are safe."

"It will take me several days, Lord Raede."

"I know, but you have my permission. I will take the burden of blame if the king protests. Every man has a right to warn his family."

"Thank you, My Lord," Herric breathed in relief. "Thank you."

Raede merely nodded in reply, knowing that Herric was his. He had given Herric the much-desired opportunity to protect his family, and now Herric would follow Raede anywhere. Raede stifled a grin. With Herric at his side, Meclellon would soon see fit to fall in line. Raede would bide his time until then, letting his familiar quiet disposition calm everyone in the palace. He would appear to silence their fears, but all the while secretly fan the flames. The wheels in his head were rapidly turning, but he kept his outside demeanor just as tranquil as it had always been. It was something he'd been practicing for decades and it had never failed him yet.

"I will try to return as quickly as I can," said Herric.

"Whenever you can, Herric. I would never expect a man to sacrifice his own family for his kingdom. Go."

Herric nodded and turned to leave. Just as he ducked inside the palace he paused and looked back at Raede. "You are a very wise man, sir," he said and then he was gone.

Raede glanced at up the cloud-encrusted sky once more and smiled. "I know."

# Chapter Three

## THE GYPSY IN THE WOOD

Kelgar watched as Lua slipped below the horizon and Selene refused to rise for the third night in a row. He balled up his fist tightly, closing his eyes in deep concentration, then quickly released the hand. A ball of white light glowed upon his open palm. He was in Silverwood now and the assortment of trees was the only thing standing between him and the Valley of Shadows. If Aecleton, the Keeper of Darkness, left the valley, the forest would be the first place attacked. Kelgar's ball of light would be the one thing protecting him.

It had taken Kelgar two days to reach Silverwood on foot. The borders of Argentum were not as well guarded as they used to be and Kelgar had found little trouble slipping beyond them unnoticed. He'd always been well practiced in stealth anyway.

He was cloaked from head to toe in black. He'd abandoned his white Guardian robes before leaving the temple, choosing peasant garb that he felt would make him less conspicuous. The people of the land were frightened enough as it was and the sight of a Guardian outside the Temple of Aurora would only increase their uneasiness. They would know the Guardians were searching for answers as well. That was something the Guardians could not let the people know, for utter chaos would follow such a confession.

Kelgar glanced around the now darkened forest. The patches of silver moonbeams had set with Lua and his own palm light was the only source of illumination in the black woodland. He knew he was getting close to the gypsy. It was not that she left any signs; he just always instinctively knew where to find her, no matter where she was.

"Mordrelina?" he called feeling the gypsy was near.

"I wondered how long it would be before you turned up here," a cracked and gravelly voice spoke in the darkness. Kelgar turned around and watched as the gypsy stepped into range of his light, her ragged clothing more tattered than ever.

"Then you know?" asked Kelgar, blowing on his palm to lessen the light a bit.

"Just because I spend my life in the woods doesn't make me oblivious to what's happening in the rest of the world. Who would know better than I when a moon disappears?" She pushed a strand of gray hair back into her unruly chignon. Her almond eyes looked almost black staring out from her wrinkled face in the dim light. "I taught you how to read the stars. Do you think I have forgotten how to do so myself?"

"No," said Kelgar quietly, waiting to see if the gypsy would grant him an audience.

"It has been many years, Kelgar," she said at last.

"I know," Kelgar admitted, "and I'm sorry."

"So am I," said the gypsy.

Kelgar relaxed knowing that she was giving him permission to speak freely at last.

"I've come for your wisdom, Mordrelina," Kelgar explained.

"I thought as much," Mordrelina replied. She touched the white glow on Kelgar's hand as though testing to see if it was real. "Your power has grown stronger in your absence."

"It is not my power," Kelgar corrected. "It is the power they gave me when I was made a Guardian." He fingered the moon pendant that hung from his neck.

Mordrelina nodded. "Come."

Kelgar followed the gypsy through the trees back to her tent. It was the same deerskin dwelling that he had been raised in and it brought a familiar comfort in the dark forest.

"Your home looks well," he said, sidestepping the gypsy's campfire to run his hand across the smooth leather of the tent.

"Yes," the gypsy agreed, "when one considers that every third night or so I roll it up and move to a new place in the forest." She pointed to a patch of ground not far from the tent where the plants had been cut and the earth was trampled every which way. "Raede's men have been in the forest gathering tarkweed," she explained.

"Tarkweed!" Kelgar gasped. "Are you sure?"

"Yes," the gypsy nodded. "Perhaps now you can forgive me for what I did to you."

Kelgar sank to the ground, leaning his back against a tree. "I forgave you a long time ago, Mordrelina," he sighed. "I've just been too proud to admit it. How could I begrudge the woman who took me in and raised me as a son when my own family abandoned me?"

"Then why did you take so long to come back?" the gypsy demanded. "It's been over thirty years."

"It was my own stubbornness that prevented me from doing so. I didn't know how to say I was sorry. It's just that…it was difficult for me. I was only seventeen and I looked like I was forty. I should have been making love to women who thought I was old enough to be their father. They were repulsed by me and I didn't know how to deal with that. I was too arrogant to apologize, so I left."

"And I am sorry that you had to. I never meant for your appearance to be aged before its time." Mordrelina stroked the earth beneath her fingers. "That was a side effect I had not foreseen."

Kelgar laughed lightly. "You would have done it anyway, even if you had known."

The gypsy smiled back. "Yes, I would have. I knew it was something that had to be, for I had seen it in the stars. I knew that someday the experiment would serve you well, even though I didn't understand how at the time. But now with the events that are currently under way, I think we both know why the stars gave me warning."

Kelgar nodded. "Do you think it will really come to that?"

"I think it already has. It is not Laede that sent the men to the forest and my sticks tell me that the king will not sit much longer upon his throne. Raede is no fool. He's had many years with nothing else to do but think."

"A potentially dangerous pastime."

"Indeed," the gypsy agreed. "That ill-timed side effect of your past may now be your greatest ally, for who would suspect a shriveled old man?"

"If Raede is smart enough to be gathering tarkweed, he may suspect me sooner than we think. The Guardians know I'm younger than I look."

"Yes, but there's no reason for them to tell anyone else. Besides, they don't know why you look like an old man do they?"

Kelgar shook his head. "No, they don't. Notelcea still believes I had a childhood encounter with the Shadows that gave me this appearance. I don't think she's even certain whether you raised me, though she'll find out soon enough."

"Where is Notelcea now?"

"I sent her to the palace library to read the ancient texts."

"A pointless excursion."

"Yes, but I didn't want her following me. She's older than I am and can overrule my decisions. I didn't need that now. Besides, it would be difficult to talk openly if she were here."

Mordrelina touched a bug that was crawling across the ground. It waggled in a form of dance before ascending to the air. "Are you sure Notelcea went to the library?"

Kelgar looked up quickly. "Why do you ask?"

"We all know it is a pointless journey and she does not seem to be one who would waste her time with it."

"You know something, I can see it, but per usual you'll not tell me straight out. You're still playing mind games with your student."

"My student has not been here in many years to play mind games with," she smiled. "I am only saying that your faith in Notelcea may be misplaced. You are planning to send her against Aecleton aren't you?"

Kelgar shook his head. "I never could hide my thoughts from you, Mordrelina."

Mordrelina smiled. "A mother always knows what her son is thinking. But I warn you, Notelcea may not have as much power against Aecleton as you hope. She is older than you and has more experience in games. She may be playing with your mind as much as you are with hers. Don't forget, she no more appears her age than you do."

Kelgar smirked. "Just don't tell me that you did to her what you did to me and she ended up looking like that, while I ended up looking like this. If so, I truly couldn't forgive you."

"No, I did not raise Notelcea, nor has she ever seen me. But if she does not have the power that you hope, your plan will fail."

"That's why I came to you," Kelgar confessed.

The gypsy nodded. "Come back to the fire." Kelgar followed the gypsy and sat down beside her while the flames burned next to them. "What do you need to know?"

Kelgar bit his lip. "It looks like Aecleton, but is it really?"

The gypsy picked up a mirror, tilting it this way and that until at last she nodded. "Yes, Aecleton is the moon swallower."

"Where does he get his power?"

The gypsy shook a handful of acorns and tossed them onto the mirror. She seemed surprised by what she saw. "From the light?"

"From the light! How could the Keeper of Darkness, or any of the Shadows for that matter, obtain power from the light?"

"Aecleton is different from the other Shadows. Aecleton is not as old, but bears far more power. For every moon that vanishes, its power is converted to darkness increasing Aecleton's strength."

"So Selene's power, now belongs to Aecleton?"

"Yes."

"But how is that possible? How did he manage to get hold of Selene in the first place?"

"That is complicated. Even I cannot see the full answer."

"And you wouldn't tell me if you did."

Mordrelina looked up at Kelgar. "I only tell people what they are ready to hear. The signs tell me there are things that must be learned before either of us can fully understand this."

"Then tell me what you do know about it?"

"I know that Aecleton was born bearing a piece of Selene," said the gypsy.

"The misshapen moon," Kelgar breathed. "That's why it has never been completely round. Aecleton had it from the start, from the very beginning of the Lumidian!"

"Aecleton has been playing the world for fools for a long time."

Kelgar rubbed his forehead. The new information was complicating matters a bit, and there was still something he needed to know. "Who were my parents, Mordrelina?"

"I don't know, Kelgar. You were not the first child of nobles that was abandoned to save the parents' reputations and you'll certainly not be the last. Had I known who your mother was, I would have had you nursed by her instead of the wild sow. The nobles abandon their children to protect themselves. I don't know who your parents were."

"But you can find out."

"Why do you want to know?" asked Mordrelina.

"If what we fear is true then I have work to do and I want to make sure that I'm not about to kill my brother."

The gypsy smiled. "Will it matter?"

Kelgar smiled back. "No, but it will make me feel better if I'm not."

The gypsy conceded. "Give me your pendant."

"Mind you don't break it. Remember, I don't own it. I'm just a Guardian."

The gypsy nodded, taking the pendant as Kelgar handed it to her. She twisted the rope it hung on and held it over the fire, watching the light flicker across it as it unwound.

"What do you see?" asked Kelgar, watching the gypsy intently.

"I see Laede," said Mordrelina.

Kelgar sighed leaning his head back against the tent. He had feared that.

"And his father," the gypsy added.

"What?" Kelgar sat up straight.

"You are the son of Laede's aunt and a man who appears to be a woodcutter. He died many years ago and is of little consequence."

"Then I am Laede's cousin?"

"Yes, does that displease you?"

"Well, it makes my task easier, as I'm not his brother," he breathed in relief. "Tell me about Raede."

"He's a man of limitless ambitions," said Mordrelina, handing back Kelgar's pendant. "The night Selene disappeared he sent men to Silverwood to gather tarkweed."

"He's waiting for the Shadows isn't he?"

"Yes. He will unleash the blow he has been holding since he lost the crown."

Kelgar shook his head in frustration. "I don't have time to warn Laede do I?"

"No," whispered the gypsy. She looked up at the sky. "The Shadows are coming."

Kelgar looked up at the sky as well and saw that the thick covering of clouds had rolled in again, but this time there was something else. He couldn't quite put a name on it. It was more of a feeling than a vision. There was a penetrating coldness threatening to grasp his heart and that was when he knew.

"The Shadows have left the valley," he whispered.

Mordrelina nodded. Kelgar had never seen the Shadows. They had been confined to the valley for hundreds of years, but now they were riding the skies above him and it made his heart clench. He knew they were looking for victims, anyone they could catch unawares without a light. Kelgar slipped his pendant back over his head and relit the white glow in his palm, knowing he would need it in a moment. He looked back toward Argentum.

"If Raede is gathering tarkweed, it can only mean one thing," said Kelgar.

The gypsy solemnly nodded. "Yes."

"I must return to the Temple of Aurora," said Kelgar. He rose making ready to leave. As he did, he glanced at the gypsy who still sat by the fire. "I am sorry I left you, Mordrelina."

The gypsy met his eyes. "I'm sorry that what I did made you leave."

# Chapter Four

# THE RECKONING

The Shadows had come at last. Raede held tightly to his candle as they made their presence known throughout Argentum, scouring the land with their dark forms. Only the previous night the Shadows had swept in during the nearly five hours of darkness and taken a man who'd been unfortunate enough to be caught without a torch. Now the Shadows had again returned and Raede perceived that his time had come.

This was the moment Raede had been waiting for. This was the opportunity he'd recognized two nights earlier when Selene first failed to rise. All his many years of planning and relentless scheming had been building toward this one moment, and now it was here at last.

Raede began to walk toward his brother's room, a coveted packet of white power hidden beneath his green tunic. Laede had been nothing but trouble to Raede from the moment his babyhood form first sprang into the world. It was time to put an end to the misery. It was time for Raede to reclaim what was his, and who better to help him than Aecleton, the master of the Shadows.

There would be no need for knives or poison. Such approaches often left the user easily identified. The obvious suspect was always the last person who had visited the king. But Raede was smarter than that. He had no intention of using methods that would single him out as Laede's murderer, not when there was something so much easier and far more difficult to trace. Raede would use the Shadows themselves. He would allow them to strike the king in such a manner that no one would ever suspect Raede, the brother who had always served the king so faithfully.

Raede made his way down the stone steps, still holding tightly to his candle. Everyone in the palace had taken to carrying some form of firelight since the disappearance of Selene. It was the only way to ensure protection from the Shadows. Raede knew that the king had his own candle as well. It was the only thing that stood between him and a gruesome death should the light happen to go out. The question was, how to make it do exactly that.

The evening watchmen were standing outside the king's door as usual. They were both holding torches for their own protection. "Good evening, Lord Raede," said the watchmen.

"Good evening," Raede replied smoothly. "Is my brother in his chambers?"

"Yes, My Lord," replied one of the watchmen. "He's only just entered them."

"Good, good," said Raede, "then he'll not yet be asleep. I must speak with him."

"Of course, sir." The watchmen stood aside and allowed Raede to enter the king's room. Raede entered and the door closed behind him. Now it was just Raede and his brother in the room.

"Who is it?" called Laede from somewhere in the room.

"Who is the only member of the court that calls on you at all hours without first being announced?" Raede responded with a question.

"Raede," the king breathed, "I should have known."

"Yes, you should have," Raede agreed, spying his brother. Beneath his mat of red hair, Laede's pasty face looked more ghostlike than usual. He sat in a chair beside his enormous bed, reading scrolls about the Lumidian in hopes of discerning a solution to the current problem facing the land. His own candle sat upon the nightstand within arm's reach, so it would be easy to pick up should the Shadows decide to pay a visit to the palace. It was upon that candle that Raede's attention was deeply focused. It left dark shadows on the king's weary face and Raede knew it would not take his powder long to work its will.

"What is it this time? Have you come to lecture me again, brother?"

"Lecture the king of Argentum?" Raede feigned shock. "Never."

"Oh yes, never," Laede replied sarcastically.

As the younger of the two, Laede had been listening to his brother's lectures since before he was king. Laede's taking the crown had never dampened Raede's words. Laede generally took his brother's advice into consideration, however, for Raede did indeed possess a certain wisdom that seemed to be lacking among the other members of the court.

"I expect you've come with advisement then?"

"Yes," said Raede, "but first let us have something in the way of a drink."

"A drink?"

"You have objections to the idea? As it is, we will not sleep until Maan rises."

The king shrugged. "This is true." He stood up and stretched. "Very well, you gather the glasses, I shall gather the wine." Laede turned away and headed toward the closet which always contained his private stash of wine.

Raede grinned darkly watching the king turn his back. He wasted no time in snatching two goblets from a nearby shelf and carefully setting them upon the table. Checking to be sure the king wasn't looking, Raede quickly pulled out the packet that had been hidden in his tunic and dumped the contents into Laede's empty cup. He shook the glass to settle the white power then hurriedly stuffed the empty pack back into his tunic. He knew Laede would never notice in the dim light.

"There are better years," said Laede, returning with a dusty bottle of wine, "but this should do for a simple discussion."

"Yes, it should," Raede agreed, watching as Laede filled both goblets.

"To Argentum," said Laede, raising his glass.

Raede smiled and nodded. "To Argentum," he toasted.

"And now to the matter at hand," said Laede after draining his glass. "What have you come to talk about?"

"The Guardians," said Raede. "Your rider informed us that only the youngest remains at the temple. Enira, I believe she is called."

"Yes, they said the elder Guardians have gone to find answers."

"Which must mean they know little more than we do."

Laede nodded. "Yes, but that is something that must remain between us. I cannot image the panic that would ensue if the people knew that the Guardians had lost control of the light."

"Where have the elder Guardians gone?"

"You heard the rider as well as I did, Raede. Enira would not divulge the elders' locations to anyone but me. As I have not yet been to the temple, I don't know where they are."

Laede was beginning to look very sleepy. Raede fought back a smile.

"We should find out as soon as possible," said Raede.

The king nodded, fighting to stay awake. "Raede, perhaps we could continue this discussion in a few hours? I'm really more tired than I had realized."

"Of course, Laede. I'll just put away the wine."

"Thank you, Raede."

"You're welcome, brother."

Raede made sure to take his time gathering up the wine bottle and the glasses. He slowly walked to the wine closet and gently set the bottle back in its place, listening as the king laid down upon his bed. Raede smiled his darkest smile. He shelved the glasses and quietly walked back to the king's side.

Laede was fast asleep. Raede's drug had done its work well. The king's candle still burned on the nightstand, but Laede was not awake to know. Raede drew a chair up next his brother's bed. He leaned in close and began whispering the speech he had wanted to give for so many years.

"The Shadows will soon take you, brother, but before they do, know this; Argentum is mine. You were nothing but a curse to me since the day you were born. Father always favored you because you were bigger and stronger. You could hunt and fish better than I. You were far more the sportsman. Father loved you so much that he even gave you what always should have been mine; the crown of Argentum."

Raede rubbed his tongue over lips as his poisoned words poured into his brother's ears. "The crown always passes to the elder child. As first-born I was in line to receive it, but father saw fit to deny me of it, simply because you were stronger in body. But there are other forms of strength. There is strength of mind. My body may be small, but my mind is stronger than any."

Laede lay unmoving in his sleep. The drug Raede had given him was very potent. Raede didn't even know if the king could hear him, but he didn't care. He would say his piece and depart.

"The people of city are sheep. They need a strong shepherd, not someone who would rule with the soft touch that you use. If you want respect you must demand it and you my dear brother never have. You never even executed those who have tried to assassinate you over the years. Father chose you because you looked strong, but you ruled with a weak hand. You will rule no more.

"For too long I have asked myself what would have happened had I been stronger? What would have happened if I tried harder to court father's favor? What would have happened if you had never been born at all? But now I realize there can be no what-ifs, for there is only *what is*. Now *what is* shall be what I say. You took my crown and now I will take your city. Goodbye, Laede, my unwanted brother."

Raede took a breath and blew out the candle beside his brother's bed. Laede under the influence of the sleeping potion had no knowledge of Raede's actions and could do nothing to stop them. The effects of the drug would last almost a half hour more. Raede knew his brother would not have time to relight the candle before the Shadows arrived.

Carefully holding his own candle, Raede arose and made for the door. He did not give his brother another look. As far as Raede was concerned, the king was already dead. He smiled at the thought and exited the room.

"Lord Raede," the watchmen acknowledged as he stepped out of the king's bedroom.

"Gentlemen," Raede nodded in reply. "Long discussions encourage my appetite," he said. "If my brother should request me tonight, I'll be in the kitchens instead of my chambers."

The watchmen smiled. Raede's midnight kitchen visits were well known throughout the palace. "Still pinching late evening meals, My Lord?" one of the watchmen mused.

"As much now as ever," Raede smiled.

He left the watchmen and made his way down to the kitchen to enjoy a long awaited victory meal. He would sit in the solace of his food while he awaited the king's forthcoming death. After that he would have little time to eat, for Argentum would be his, and he would have all the responsibilities of the king. His blood pulsed with satisfaction at the thought.

Raede did not have to wait long. He was only on his second leg of turkey when he heard the screams sounding from three floors above. It began with the shrieks of the king, followed quickly by the sound of the watchmen.

Alerted by the king's screams, the watchmen threw open the door to his room, both holding tightly to their torches. They entered just in time to see the wispy forms of the Shadows slipping out through the darkened walls. The king's screams were carried in their wake and when they were gone, all that remained was silence. The candles were out and Laede's body was gone, taken by the Shadows. The two watchmen were frozen in place.

Several other members of the palace, roused by the king's screams, ran in behind the watchmen. "We heard the screams," said a page. "What is it?"

"Go to the kitchens," one of the watchmen instructed the page. "Inform Lord Raede that he is needed…the king is dead." The watchman's voice shook as he spoke. "Taken by the Shadows."

The page gulped. He cast a quick glance around the dark room hoping the watchman was simply mistaken, but it was true. The king was nowhere to be seen. The page turned on his heel and ran down the stairs toward the kitchens.

Raede heard the feet of the page as they pounded down the steps and he sat with baited breath until the door to the kitchens burst open. "Lord Bremmin, come at once! Your brother has been murdered!"

"What!" Raede jumped to his feet, dropping his turkey leg as though he'd been too surprised to hold onto it. He'd spent the last several minutes practicing for this very moment.

"Taken by the Shadows, My Lord."

"It can't be true!" Raede dashed past the page, running up the stairs to his brother's empty bedchamber. The watchmen still stood within and a large crowd had gathered at the door, all wondering what had happened.

Raede pushed his way through the crowd until he reached the watchmen. "What happened here?" asked Raede, feigning disbelief.

"The Shadows have taken the king, My Lord. He is dead," the watchmen replied.

"Dead? No, it can't be true. No!" Raede sank to the floor as though he were utterly beside himself.

After a moment one of the watchmen asked, "What are your orders, sir?"

"My orders?" asked Raede.

"My Lord, with your brother dead you are the king now," said the watchman. "We look to you for guidance."

"I wasn't expecting this," Raede lied. "I shall need a few moments to collect myself."

"Of course, Lord Raede." The watchmen bowed and left the room, shutting the door behind the new king. Raede smiled gleefully as he held his own candle. He had done it; he had killed the king at last and the Shadows had taken the blame.

"You have done well, Raede," said a voice from behind.

Raede turned to see who had managed to creep into his midst unannounced. He saw a shriveled old man standing in the doorway, holding a candle.

"Leingella," Raede breathed, smiling fondly at his old tutor. Leingella had played more of a hand in Raede's upbringing than Raede's own father. Raede's father had always been far too concerned with Laede. Leingella had been the one constant in Raede's life.

Leingella was his tutor, his mentor, his only friend. Leingella had been, in essence, Raede's true father after Laede was born. Raede prided himself on having received his own intelligence through Leingella's careful guidance. Leingella had long sympathized with Raede's plight. He cared for Raede like a son and had never been pleased when Raede's crown had been given to the youngest brother. It wasn't proper tradition and it had been unfair to Raede.

"It is done," said Raede, "my brother will bear what is mine no more."

"And what of the Guardians?" asked Leingella. He was not a warrior, but neither was he a fool. He always looked at a situation from every angle. He wanted to be sure his treasured pupil had done the same.

"While you may fool the people of Argentum, you might not be able to fool the Guardians," Leingella continued. "They are the Keepers of the Light and we don't know how far their influence extends. They may know what you have done."

"I have already put the solution into action," said Raede. "The young Guardian is the only one left in the temple now. It does leave me certain options."

Leingella nodded at his student's wisdom. "Yes, and a frightened public is more easily controlled. They will be too busy looking for your protection to balk at your taking of the throne."

Raede narrowed his dark eyes. "Yes, and when this is finished, there will be peace throughout my land."

"You shall rule over it all, as you always should have." Leingella licked his lips. "You are certain your plan is intact?"

Raede nodded. "I hold Herric within my palm and Meclellon will follow now that I am king. The patrols returned from the forest this very evening. You are sure about the tarkweed?"

"I have heard the tale many times and I've no reason to doubt it. When do you leave?"

A contented sigh rippled through Raede's body. "In two days. We make for the temple at moonrise."

# Chapter Five

# ANGER

A dark and cloaked figure glided purposefully through the misty groves of Silverwood. The rising moon shone eerily off the fog as the phantom silently slithered through the trees. She walked alone in the solemn darkness of the night.

Her name was Lismella, but there were few who knew it and fewer still who truly knew the woman herself. She preferred it that way. Secrecy was as much a part of her as the blood within her veins. Betraying that secrecy was something that could never be done. That secrecy had been a part of her for most of her life and she could not afford to lose it now. Doing so could be fatal.

It was raining as Lismella carefully tramped the rugged, woodland paths of Silverwood. She'd been forced to take the long way to the forest due to a great many circumstances out of her control. She could not risk being seen by anyone, least of all by Kelgar, the elderly Guardian of Light whom she knew was making his own way through Silverwood. Her mission was far too important to be interrupted by the Guardians. The Guardians didn't know what she knew. They didn't understand the secrets hidden in the rain.

It was a strong rain, not the kind that normally fell in Silverwood. This was a rain sent by Aecleton during the dark hours of Selene's absence to remind everyone that the Shadows were rising. Before Selene's disappearance, rain was something that fell frequently, but it came lightly from a paper-thin veil of clouds that was never thick enough to obscure the light of the moon. Since the Keeper of Darkness had gained control of Selene, however, the rains had grown stronger and the clouds had grown thicker.

For five days Selene had failed to rise and now the king of Argentum was dead. Rumor of his demise had spread through the land like wildfire, but Lismella knew it had been no accident. The Shadows were strong, but they were not yet strong enough to extinguish fire. Someone had outright murdered the king; Lismella just didn't know who yet. The death of the king had greatly complicated matters and Lismella's already short timetable had become even more rushed.

She was looking for someone, though even she didn't really know who. It was not so much a person for whom she was searching, but rather an idea, a feeling, a virtue. It was something she couldn't put a finger on, but she would know it when she saw it. She needed to find a person who contained within them the courage that she herself had once lacked. She needed to find someone who would not make the same mistake she had made so many years ago. And she had to find that person soon. The fate of her entire plan might lie with that sole choice. She knew she must choose wisely.

The rain lessened as Maan rose higher and Aecleton's hold over the land was released for the time being. Lismella couldn't see the Shadows, but she could feel them as they dissipated, slithering back to their valley to hide from the rising moon. A veil of cloudy vapor filled the void in the wake of the Shadows' departure and Silverwood gleamed like the metal of its namesake. Lismella knew she was getting close.

The trees through which Lismella walked suddenly gave way and she found herself within a clearing still flecked with the drops of Aecleton's passing rain. A small group of outlanders, composed of people who appeared to be mostly rebels and thieves, stood in a circle playing games of swordsmanship. And there in the midst of that circle, Lismella saw him, the person for whom she had been searching.

His name was Ericahs, Lismella knew that much. She had been questioning the surrounding villages and they had all told her to seek out the one with such a name. She had done so with faint hope and much doubt that he would truly be the person she desired. Seeing him now, however, all her doubts had vanished. Ericahs was exactly the person she had been searching for.

He did not embody the courage for which Lismella had been hunting, but he harbored something that might be of far greater use; anger. Lismella could see a deep anger in Ericahs' very veins. There was rebellion in his every movement. He would bow to no one and nothing, least of all to fear. Ericahs had no fear of death, that much was clear. He almost seemed to wish for it, testing the fates to see how close he could come to it without actually being killed. Where the others in the circle fought well, but carefully, Ericahs was reckless.

Though much shorter than his opponent, Ericahs fought twice as fiercely. His strong arms wielded his sword like a man who didn't care, like a man who'd once had everything, but had it no more. Like a man who had nothing left to lose. He was filled with hate for all forms of authority or power and he was defiant in every sense of the word. He was looking for trouble and Lismella knew she could give it to him. His anger would become her weapon. He was perfect.

"Ericahs," Lismella called.

Ericahs looked up in surprise at the sound of his own name being called by the mysterious woman. He stopped fighting and turned to stare at Lismella. He tried to appear indifferent, but he could not help being secretly intrigued. There was truly something out of the ordinary about her.

Most would have quaked beneath the stare of her cold blue eyes, but Ericahs was fascinated by it. He almost wanted to know more about the strange woman, but he would not allow himself to appear too eager. He'd spent the last several years of his life forcing himself to control his own emotions. He wasn't going to give into them now.

"I am Ericahs," he said plainly.

"I know," Lismella replied.

She could see as well as anyone Ericahs' spiteful heart and his powerful hate, but that was what he wanted people to see. Lismella did not have the eyes of a commoner, however, and she could see through Ericahs like transparent water. She could see the things he didn't want anyone to see, the things he didn't even want to see about himself. She could see that there was still one thing that greatly frightened this hardened warrior. He was deeply afraid of being afraid.

"And how might you know that?" Ericahs asked smoothly. He shoved a stray lock of brown hair off his sweaty forehead.

"Because your eyes betray something of your past. There is a mark upon them that can mean only one thing," said Lismella almost at a whisper. "You have seen the Shadows."

Ericahs' stocky form stiffened and Lismella could see his carefully controlled emotions beginning to rise. "And so what if I have?" He shot defiantly.

"Then you are the Ericahs I am looking for."

"Why would you be looking for me?"

"I'm looking for one with the heart of a warrior," she replied enigmatically.

Ericahs pursed his lips, shrugging his shoulders nonchalantly. "I think you're looking for the wrong person. I only fight when there's money involved. I've no interest in being your warrior, so why don't you run along back to whatever hole you crawled out of." He looked around with a rueful grin. "This is Silverwood. This is where people go when they don't want to be found or when they want to find those who have gone into hiding. I'm not looking for those who have gone into hiding. I simply don't want to be found by anyone, including you."

Lismella nodded. "That's why I know I'm looking for you, Ericahs."

Ericahs stood there sizing her up. There was something in her words that he could not quite place. It was something that had to be read between the lines. What she said and what she was thinking were not necessarily the same thing. There was a tone like poisoned honey in her voice; sweet but deadly.

She bore no torch, no barrier between herself and the darkness. Ericahs could not help but wonder if she was trying to show defiance to the Keeper itself. She was either braver than she looked, or very stupid. If she did not fear the darkness, Ericahs even entertained the possibility that perhaps she was the cause of it. Either way, he sensed that she could not be trusted.

"What makes you think I'm the one you're looking for?" asked Ericahs. "What makes you think I have this heart of a warrior?"

"I don't think you have it yet, but I think you could if you let me show you how to find it."

Ericahs narrowed his eyes, and Lismella observed them closely, looking into the man's soul. He was not very old yet, probably still in his late twenties, but he had seen much during his years. His own loathing was eating away at him. The villagers had told Lismella as much. There was a deep scar buried in Ericahs' heart and Lismella knew that she would have to reopen that wound before the end. It was the only way to shape her warrior. Once she had finished her work on him, Lismella knew he would be unstoppable. She simply had to keep him from the Guardians.

"You live by your sword?" asked Lismella, referring to the money Ericahs had just won.

"Yes, and someday I'll die upon the sword," Ericahs replied, his green eyes snapping with fire.

"Only if you're lucky," Lismella countered. "Only if something else doesn't happen to you first. The Keeper of Darkness has awoken from its three hundred year slumber and the Shadows are running rampant at every disappearance of Selene. The Shadows have already taken the king of Argentum. They could help themselves to anyone in Silverwood."

"And what would you know about it?"

"I know that not many people can withstand an attack by the Shadows, but you seem brave…"

"Courage makes a sword fast; that is how I live."

"…and angry." Lismella finished her observation.

"Maybe my anger is what keeps me alive."

"Maybe you're angry *because* you're alive," Lismella countered, "and someone else isn't."

"Maybe you and I are done talking to one another." Ericahs turned to walk away.

"Maybe I can give you what you want," Lismella called after him.

Ericahs stopped. "What?"

Lismella stepped toward Ericahs. "All I need is your help, Ericahs, and then I shall help you fulfill your heart's greatest desire. I know that you hate the Keeper."

"I don't need your help."

"But I need yours," said Lismella, "and you may need my help more than you think."

"No I don't. If I ever meet the Keeper, I'll kill him, even if it kills me to do so."

Lismella shook her head. "A mere sword won't kill Aecleton, Ericahs. You don't know how to defeat your enemy, but I do."

"What miracle do you possess then?"

"Knowledge."

"Knowledge?"

"Yes, Ericahs, I know more than you may think, more than any may think, about the workings of the dark side of the world. Even the Keeper has its weaknesses."

"The Guardians have been unable to bring back the moon. Why are you so confident that you'll be able to help me destroy Aecleton if I help you?"

"Because I can show you what even the Guardians cannot. I can tell you things that no one in the Temple of Aurora has ever heard. I can teach you how to use the Keeper's own weakness against it."

Ericahs stared at her skeptically. She could not be more than in her mid thirties. It seemed very young to have such immense knowledge. "Why should I believe a word that you say? I don't even know you. How could you know so much about the Keeper of Darkness when even the Guardians do not?"

"I have my ways," Lismella replied. "The Guardians are wise, but even they are not all-knowing. This is far too important to leave to them. I am the only one who bears the secrets to defeat Aecleton, but I can't do it alone. I need someone to help me. Someone with a determined heart. Someone like you."

"Why don't you just go to the Guardians yourself and share your knowledge with them. Why don't you ask them to help you?"

"The Guardians would never believe what I would tell them. If by some chance they did believe me, they would have me executed on the spot for what I would reveal. They would fear what I would tell them, and then they would fall prey to that fear. The Keeper would take them without warning, for their own fear would feed the Shadows and bring about their demise." Lismella sighed. "I keep this information from the Guardians to protect them as much as anything. They must stay alive or the Shadows will take us all."

"So why me? I'm a fair swordsman, but that is nothing special in Silverwood.

Swordsmen are to be had in plenty here. Why are you choosing me? I'm just an outlander; I'm not a hero."

"That's why I need you," Lismella replied. "A hero cares too much for the people around him. You don't. You don't even care for yourself anymore. There is fire in your eyes. You are nearly fearless and you are exactly what I need."

"Suppose I decide not to help you. Suppose I decide to just run you through with my sword right now."

"You won't."

"So certain are you?"

"I've done nothing to threaten you. You're not going to slay an innocent woman," said Lismella fearlessly, "especially not when you're so curious as to what I have to offer you."

To prove her wrong, Ericahs quickly drew his sword and pointed it at the woman. "You don't know me," he growled through clenched teeth.

Lismella didn't flinch. Instead she walked toward Ericahs until his outstretched sword was pressed up against her body. She knew Ericahs was just using the sword to try and prove that no one was in control of him. So if his greatest fear involved losing control, then Lismella would let him believe he was still in control. Consequently, she would be the one to gain control of her new-found prodigy.

"I don't have to know you Ericahs; I can read you like an open book. That arrogant front you put up may work well with other people, but it can't fool me, boy. You do want to hear what I have to say. You want to know if I can really help you. Your entire being is filled with anger and hate. You are motivated by revenge and you will do almost anything to get it, even if it involves helping me. Now if I am wrong, then push your sword through my body here and be done with it, but if I am right, then stop this foolishness. Give in to your true feelings and listen to my proposition."

Ericahs wavered. Lismella was right. She was exactly right, more than even Ericahs himself had realized. He did want revenge. He'd wanted it most of his life. All the time he spent training himself with a sword, all the illegal acts he had committed, all his insubordinate workings, they had all been drawing toward a single purpose. He wanted revenge, revenge against almost everyone and everything in the world.

He wanted revenge against the Shadows. He wanted revenge for all the things in his life that had been taken from him. He wanted revenge for all the things in his life that had been given to him. He wanted revenge for life itself, for having ever been born at all. Revenge was precisely what he wanted and he truly was curious to know if Lismella could give it to him.

Ericahs slowly lowered his sword. "Who are you?" he asked.

"I am Lismella," she replied, "and I have only one question to ask you. Are you afraid of the dark?"

## Chapter Six

## FRIENDS AND ENEMIES

Raede slowly approached the pegs at the far side of his brother's room. He carefully took up the king's red mantle in his hands and fastened it around his shoulders. Then he picked up the crown and set it upon his own head knowing that after forty-eight years of living, he had at last attained what should always have been his. He stood for a moment admiring the feel of his own appearance. He'd waited his whole life for this moment.

Raede could hear a crowd gathering outside the palace and he smiled knowing they had come to hear his sage advice. Meclellon would be arriving at any moment to announce to the new king that the people had assembled. As he waited, Raede sliced a few pieces of tarkweed into small bits and placed them into a tiny box. Leingella had told Raede to always keep a supply of the herb near him and who was Raede to argue with the knowledge of a great sorcerer like Leingella?

A knock sounded at the door. Raede sheathed his knife and put the small box of tarkweed in his pocket. "Enter," he said.

Meclellon stepped into the room. "My Lord," he said bowing his head to his new king.

"Is Leingella waiting outside?" asked Raede.

"Yes, My Lord," Meclellon replied. "The high residents of the city have gathered as you requested and Herric has returned as well."

"Then it is time. Gather your men, Meclellon. We must make for the Temple of Aurora. Either something terrible has befallen the Guardians or they have sold the secrets of the light to the Keeper of Darkness. In either case, your men will be needed. I expect the supply of tarkweed is protected?"

"Yes, we have kept it safe, My Lord."

"Very good, Meclellon. If the Guardians have failed, the tarkweed may be our only protection against Aecleton."

"I know little of such matters, Sire, but I trust that you do."

"Before my brother's death, it was my job know much about many matters, Meclellon. I know that tarkweed may protect us when all else fails. You would have no need to bear such knowledge, but nonetheless, you serve your country well."

"I live only for my king and country, Sire."

"Then go and gather the men. We leave as soon as I address the people. But first, ask Leingella to join me."

"Yes, My Lord." Meclellon bowed and scurried away.

There was little that could stop Raede now. He was so close to obtaining everything his heart desired. No one would dare challenge the new king openly, none but the Guardians of Light, and Raede would deal with them soon enough. But before he addressed the people, he needed to speak with his old master.

The hinges creaked as Leingella's form emerged from the hall. "You look well, Raede," he said, noting his pupil's kingly regalia. "It suits you."

Raede grinned broadly, rubbing his hands over his recently acquired cloak. "Indeed it does."

"Everything is going according to your plans then?"

"Yes," Raede nodded. "I will address the people, striking fear into their hearts, and then I shall ride for the Temple of Aurora."

"Just beware the other Guardians. You don't know where the elder two are and thus you don't know what they may doing in secret. Or what they may be learning."

"I don't think it matters either way, for soon I shall turn the people against them and no one will believe the Guardians no matter what they find."

"Yes, but if they find out too much too soon, they could try to challenge your claim to the throne."

Raede glanced around the room and shook his head. "No, I wouldn't let that happen. The kingdom is mine now and there are none who can ever take it from me again."

"So long as you take care that the Guardians never learn the truth about Laede's death."

"They won't," Raede assured him, "you have taught me better than that."

Leingella smiled and nodded in thanks for the praise.

"In truth you have taught me everything I know. You taught me how to hone my patience, how to bide my time. You taught me to trust no one. You taught me how to behave like a king until I could actually become one. And now here I am. You have served me well these many years, Leingella. You have been a lifelong friend." Raede smiled at his teacher and turned away, staring out the window at the kingdom that was now his.

"And if there's one lesson you've taught me above all else," he continued, "it's that enemies are dangerous but friends are deadly." Raede suddenly spun around, burying a dagger into the sorcerer's gut, "Because you never see them coming until it's too late." He leaned into Leingella, hugging the man closely to drive the knife deeper into his flesh. "You taught me well," he said softly into the sorcerer's ear.

Leingella shook and gasped as Raede twisted the blade in his stomach.

"Thank you for all your wisdoms, my teacher," Raede whispered, "but I think perhaps it is time we parted ways." He shoved the sorcerer to the ground, watching with smug satisfaction as blood oozed from the wound in the man's belly.

"Did you truly think I was such a fool?" Raede hissed. "Friends are deadly you said and who could be more deadly than you, my friend, the man who raised me. You think I don't know why you wanted me upon the throne? It takes a schemer to spot another and it occurred to me that if I could scheme against my own brother, why wouldn't someone be just as likely to scheme against me…someone like you. As long you were serving my purpose, of course, I kept you at my side, but now that I have nearly everything, I think you've worn out your usefulness.

"Did you really believe I would let you use me as your puppet? You of all people should have known better. Or have you simply forgotten your own teachings, my master?" Raede smiled darkly. "You told me to follow my own mind and let no man control me, and so I have taken that teaching to heart." He used the bottom of Leingella's robe to wipe the blood from his dagger. "Not even you will control me."

Raede rose and walked away, leaving Leingella dying on the ground, not even giving him so much as a second look. He sheathed his knife as he left and shut the door behind him. It was time to address his new kingdom.

It was true, Raede was in a way playing with fire as he plotted against both the Guardians of Light and the Keeper of Darkness, but ambition knows no bounds. If there was one thing Raede was confident of, it was that he could manipulate both the light and the darkness with equal success. At present he stood between them, perfectly poised to pit one against the other. And when all was over, Raede would be the only one left standing.

Everything was proceeding smoothly according to Raede's plan. He had already killed his brother and taken the throne for himself. He was just moments away from convincing his populace to turn suspicions against the Guardians. The only thing left would be to gain control of the Keeper itself and use it to keep fear within the hearts of the people. And if one or two of his subjects ended up dead in the process, then so be it.

Raede had already murdered in cold blood, without even blinking, the man who had raised him. Why should he hesitate to sacrifice a few commoners in his quest to gain what was rightfully his? Besides a few missing villagers might help keep the people in a state of constant fear and make them all the more controllable.

Raede made his way out to the balcony walking slowly, stretching himself to his full height in order to display his majesty. He gazed down below at the crowd of frightened Argentum residents who had gathered to hear their new king's words. They moved like the waves in some large ocean and their torches glittered like diamonds against the dark of night.

Raede could feel the people's terror already. He smiled. It would make his transition to ruler more peaceful. Where his brother had always feared inciting the people's panic, Raede embraced the opportunity with open arms. Raede wanted the people to be afraid. He wanted the darkness to terrify them, for then they would look to him. He would save them from the Shadows and they would hail him a hero. And with the Guardians out of the way, no one would doubt a king who was a hero.

"My fellow people of Argentum," Raede bellowed, "I'll not lie to you, for the rumors are true. The king is dead; taken by the Shadows."

Murmurs of dread rippled through the crowd. They all knew the king was dead and they had even heard it was by the doing of the Shadows, but in their hearts none of them had wanted to believe it. Listening to their new king confirm it, however, they knew their hearts could not deny the truth any longer. They silently listened to Raede, hanging on his every word.

Raede continued. "It is with a very heavy heart that I accept this duty as your king. I mourn my brother's death more than anyone else, but we cannot allow his death to have been in vain. That would be a disrespect to his memory."

Raede paused for breath, letting his words sink in. "I will not rest until I find who is responsible for the events that allowed the Shadows to take my only brother from me. I fear that something terrible has happened in the Temple of Aurora that allowed the Keeper to swallow the light of Selene. After three hundred years the Guardians have somehow lost control of the light."

Raede pointed to Maan rising above the city. "Not all hope has been gone astray in this darkness, however, for even now the other moons still rise. We are not yet defeated by the Keeper and his ways of evil. Even now, my men are preparing the horses. When I leave you it will be to ride to the Temple of Aurora and learn what has become of the magic that once protected us from these shadow demons.

"We will find a way to reverse the damage the Keeper has done. Until then, however, hold your torches close, my people, for the Shadows give no warning when they appear in the night. The loss of our king, my own dear brother, is proof of that. I give my promise to do everything within my power to protect you all." Raede bowed his head and backed away into the palace, leaving the people to think on his last words.

It was done. Raede knew the people would follow his word anywhere. Silently he returned to his new chambers, taking care to make sure no one else had come with him. He slipped in through the closed door, carrying his candle before him. He let its light trail along the floor until it reflected off the glassy surface of a small jewel. Raede smiled, bending down to retrieve it. He'd been looking for this.

Raede fingered the gem. It was all that remained of his former master. It looked harmless enough, but the tiny gem lying where Leingella's body had previously been was far more valuable than its appearance would suggest. It was a truth stone, an essence crystal that bore the remaining residue of the sorcerer's magic. Raede had learned long ago that these crystals always appeared when a sorcerer died. He also knew they contained magic that would be of great use to him.

He smiled as he rolled the crystal around in his hand. Perhaps his former teacher had not completely ceased to be of use. Raede could use Leingella's essence crystal to his own advantage should he require it. He slipped it into his tunic for safekeeping and turned to the matter at hand. The ride to the temple was about to begin.

The Guardians of the Light did not yet know that Laede had been murdered, only that he was dead. Raede was no fool, however. He knew it would only be a matter of time before the Guardians realized the truth about Laede's death, and when they did, they would turn the people against Raede. That was something he simply couldn't have. He had to quell the Guardians' rumors before they even began to utter them. He had to discredit the Guardians before they tried to discredit him.

"We are ready, Sire," said Meclellon entering the room.

Raede looked at the empty space where Leingella's dead body had lain just a short time before and he felt the truth stone inside his pocket. He nodded. "Let us go."

# Chapter Seven

# THE BESIEGING

There was a gentle breeze blowing on the warm air as the night watchman stared out from his perch atop the Temple of Aurora. He held closely to his torch as his eyes scanned the dark horizons below. The sky was clear and the watchman breathed a short sigh of relief as he saw Maan climbing higher into the sky. He knew the Keeper of Darkness had not yet succeeded in taking that moon at least.

The watchman's eye was suddenly caught by movement to the south. It was too far away for the watchman to discern what or who, but it was movement just the same. This struck the watchman as odd. It was unusual for anyone to be out at so late an hour. In Argentum most people were sleeping while the light of Selene and Maan covered the land. And with the recent disappearance of Selene, even fewer people left their homes before Maan's journey across the sky was at least half over. The watchman stared closely wondering who it could be at such a dark time.

He saw the horses before he heard them, as they drew closer and slowly came into view. They went at a snail's pace, ambling up the long path to the Temple of Aurora. The riders were alert, but relaxed as they held their horses' reins. The entire procession was so calm that there appeared to be no reason for alarm, but appearances can be deceiving, for this was no ordinary royal procession. It was not simply a pleasant visit to the Guardians' temple. This was a visit of great purpose and only its leader truly knew what that purpose was as he smiled darkly at the white temple.

The watchman mistook that smile as a sign of friendship; there was no reason for him to think otherwise. He could not see into the leader's heart as he watched the horses drawing near. He could not read the true intentions that lay behind his new king's false smile. He did not know the terrible plans that Raede harbored deep within his blackened heart. The watchman only knew that the king himself was making his way to the temple and he had no doubt come to speak with the Guardians.

"Lord Raede approaches," the watchman yelled into the temple.

There was a brief scurrying in response to his calls. This was the first time that the new king had visited the Temple of Aurora and everyone wanted Raede's first impression to be a good one. One of the apprentices quickly alerted Enira.

"My Lady," said the apprentice, "the watchman has just informed us that our new king is approaching."

"Lord Raede?" asked Enira.

"Yes, My Lady, he comes even now."

"Thank you," said Enira nodding and rising to her feet.

Though she was young and inexperienced, Enira was still the senior Guardian at the temple now that Kelgar and Notelcea had left. She knew Raede was coming to speak to her about the disappearance of the moon. She had little knowledge about the Keeper of Darkness, but she would share all that she knew. She would be grateful for the king's interpretation as well, considering he had been Laede's most trusted adviser before recently taking up the crown himself.

Enira took a deep breath to compose herself and headed for the temple's door. She wanted to meet Raede upon his entrance. It would not do to have a king at the temple without a Guardian of the Light to greet him.

Enira stood in the doorway watching as the king dismounted, followed by several highly ranked men of the royal army. They regally marched up the steps of the temple. Despite Raede's naturally small stature, no one could deny now that he looked mighty in the royal cloak. His walk had become a confident swagger and his form was almost imposing. It was as if taking the crown had given strength to his physical body.

"Lord Raede," Enira bowed her head at the king's approach. "We are honored by your presence in the temple, Highness."

Raede nodded, pleased with his subject's respect. "Thank you, young Guardian."

"I was sorry to learn of your brother's death," said Enira.

"As were we all," replied Raede, "but this no time to dwell on matters than cannot be changed. I've come to talk about the matter at hand."

"You've come to speak about the darkness."

"I have," Raede nodded. "I need to know how to best protect my people. I need to know what the Guardians know."

"Of course, My Lord," said Enira, not sure if she even had the authority to give Raede all the answers he might want. She could only hope that he wouldn't ask her for information that wasn't hers to give. "Let us sit."

Enira led Raede to a tiny alcove not far from the door. There was a small, round table with two chairs in the very center of the floor, but the rest of the room was empty. Raede followed smoothly, knowing he would have no trouble in the temple. He could see that the young Guardian was unsure of herself. She was alone and afraid in a very large world.

Enira and Raede took their places on either side of the table. Raede's men stood not far behind and Enira was flanked by one of the young apprentices of the Temple of Aurora. Enira didn't know why, but she felt on edge, as though her intuition were trying to give her warning. She turned to the apprentice behind her. "Milessandra, would you bring the king and I a pot of tea?"

The apprentice named Milessandra nodded and skipped away.

Enira returned her attention to the king. "What have you to come to ask, My Lord?"

"First, what has happened?" asked Raede. "Why has Selene gone dark?"

"Even we in the temple do not know for certain," answered Enira. "The moon was here one night and gone the next, taking with it all its light." She gazed out a westward window toward the Keeper's stronghold. "We believe, however, that Aecleton has at last left the Valley of the Shadows."

"But how can that be possible?" asked Raede, feigning ignorance. "How, after so many years, has the Keeper of Darkness only now learned how to steal the light of the moon?"

"We don't know. We can only assume that the Keeper has been plotting this for three hundred years and has only recently found a way to put those plans into action."

Raede smiled inwardly. He was no stranger to harboring plans. He knew how the Keeper thought. He was not going to tell that to Enira, however.

"I do not pretend to know what the Guardians know," said Raede carefully, "but it did not escape my attention that Aecleton just happened to take the misshapen moon. Is this merely a coincidence?"

"We don't believe so, Lord Raede. We think the Keeper took Selene specifically because it was the weakest of the moons, and thus was the easiest light to steal."

"And why was Selene the weakest of the moons to begin with? History tells us that the light of the sun was captured by the Lumidian to be divided equally among the five moons. Yet, Selene has never been completely full."

"I don't know. None of us do. Selene has been weak for as long as any of us can remember. We don't know what caused it to be so, but perhaps the Keeper took part in it. If so, it would explain how he has managed to take the moon now."

Raede relaxed himself. He could see that Enira truly knew nothing. "You know the people of Argentum are quite frightened by this occurrence."

"Of course," Enira replied, "as well they should be. A stolen moon is not a matter to be taken lightly."

"No, indeed it is not," Raede agreed. "Panic can cause people to do strange things. Even now the people are beginning to fall victim to their fears. Some of them believe that perhaps the Guardians are slipping, that you are losing control of the light."

Enira made no reply. She herself had wondered the same thing, though she would never admit it to the other Guardians. She had speculated that perhaps after three hundred years of peace, the Guardians had been lulled into a false sense of security. Perhaps they had let down their guard allowing Aecleton to swoop into the void where they should have been protecting the light.

Enira knew that she herself had never given much thought to the Keeper before Selene's disappearance, other than what she'd learned about the history of darkness during her training. It was possible that the other Guardians had been equally lax. Perhaps even the teachers had become too lenient with the information they were passing onto the younger generations, thus leaving them ill prepared to deal with a foe as cunning as the Keeper. No matter what the reason, however, there was no proof yet that the fault lay with the Guardians and Enira was not going to be the first to suggest it.

"A few of the more terrified people even blame the Guardians outright," Raede continued smoothly, "accusing you of being in league with Aecleton himself. Of course I know such foolish notions could not possibly be true."

"Of course not," Enira burst out quickly. "The idea that the Guardians of the Light would even think of helping Aecleton is utterly ridiculous. The Keeper of Darkness stands enemy to everything we are sworn to protect."

"Yes, I am very aware of this, but sadly that it not always enough. Often all that truly matters is what a deluded public will allow themselves to hold as truth. If they believe strongly enough in something, it does in fact become true to them in their own minds." Raede was just having fun with Enira now, skillfully toying with her mind as well as the minds of his men.

They could see the young Guardian's steadily rising anxiety, her racing nerves, and the perspiration that was beginning to appear upon her brow. She was quite in contrast to their own king, whose composure always remained calm and relaxed, even in the face of great adversity. If either of them were going to look guilty of anything, it would not be Raede.

"I was told that the elder Guardians left the temple just after Selene was taken," said Raede. "Have they returned yet?"

"No, My Lord." Enira was walking right into Raede's trap and she didn't even know it.

"I would greatly like to speak with them. It's possible that you, being so new to the rank of Guardian, do not know as much about the present situation as the others."

"I know as much about the light as either of them, Sire."

"Or so you believe. It is a possibility that the elder Guardians have not told you everything. Perhaps they still have some secrets yet to be revealed."

Enira opened her mouth, but merely stumbled over her words. "I-I don't think they would keep anything from me during such a...such an important time."

Even she didn't truly believe her own words, however, and she knew Raede wouldn't either. She didn't want to confess it, but she knew Raede was raising a valid point. Enira had, after all, only just learned the truth about the ages of the elder Guardians. She could not help but wonder if maybe they were keeping other secrets from her as well. It was, in fact, a bit insulting thinking that perhaps they didn't deem her worthy enough to disclose to her all the information they themselves were privy to. Enira hoped Raede was mistaken.

Raede's heart gave a flutter of victory. The inexperienced Guardian had taken the bait. "Perhaps you are right, but I think it would be best if I was to hear it from your fellow Guardians themselves. I was told that you would disclose the reasons for their absence only to the king, and here I am."

"Of course. Kelgar went on a mission for the temple, to search for...for information that might help us," Enira replied carefully. "Notelcea is doing the same in the palace library."

"I assure you there were no Guardians in the palace library when I departed," said Raede.

Either Enira was outright lying to him or Notelcea was truly keeping secrets from the young Guardian. Either scenario presented a fine opportunity for Raede to use in his manipulation.

"Perhaps you simply did not notice her," Enira explained. "We knew the public would be frightened and did not want to alert them any sooner than necessary, so Notelcea would not have been dressed as a Guardian."

"I say again, young one, there were no Guardians in the palace library, for someone would have told me if anyone at all had been there. Perhaps the elders did not feel compelled to disclose their true whereabouts to you. What mission has Kelgar gone on?"

"He-he has gone to seek information," Enira stuttered, growing more nervous by the minute.

"Yes, you said that," Raede replied. He leaned toward the table bringing his face closer to Enira's. "Where?"

Enira could feel her chest heaving as the king pressed himself toward her. There was something not quite right about the whole situation. The entire world lay in peril, but Raede was calm, too calm for comfort. Something deep inside of Enira knew she could not tell him where Kelgar had gone.

"I am not at liberty to say," Enira replied.

"What?"

"I was sworn to secrecy before he left."

"Reveal his location, Guardian."

"I can't."

"Tell me."

"No." Enira was beginning to grow defensive. She was sure now that something was amiss. Raede was concentrating far too much on finding the other Guardians.

"Do you honestly refuse your king's order?"

"Yes!" Enira jumped to her feet.

"Then you are guilty of treason."

Meclellon moved in so fast Enira barely had time to react. His sword flashed from his sheath as he slid toward her, grabbing her wrist.

"How dare you," Enira was appalled as she pulled her hand out of his grasp. "I am a Guardian of the Light!"

"But that does not make you above your king." Meclellon reached for her again, but this time Enira was ready.

"Adula!" she shouted casting a brilliant beam of light toward Meclellon, the force of which sent him flying back against the wall.

The other men drew their blades and Enira turned toward them. "Stay back," she warned. One of the men disregarded her warnings and lunged at her. "Blemyn," she whispered pulling her arms down in front of her. The man crashed into a sold wall of light and fell backward unconscious.

Raede suddenly captured Enira's wrist from behind with a long green rope. The Guardian spun around tossing a chair toward him. He ducked to avoid it, dropping the rope that was wound around Enira's wrist. Enira raised her hand at

Raede.

"Delimus!" She cried.

Nothing happened.

"Adula!" she bellowed.

Still nothing. Enira was stunned. This was the first time her magic had ever failed to perform and she needed it now more than ever. A cold wave of panic swept over her. She was powerless, completely at the mercy of the men in the room.

Meclellon, having regained his wits, quickly seized her during the brief lull in magic. He held her tightly, crushing her ribcage with his muscular arms. Raede stood up grinning at the scene with sadistic pleasure. He picked up the free end of the rope that was still attached to Enira's wrist.

Slowly Raede stalked toward Enira as she struggled futilely in Meclellon's vice-like grasp. Raede tightly twisted the remaining rope around Enira's wrists, cruelly grinding them together as he did. She clenched her teeth to keep from crying out, but Raede could see the pain and the fear in her eyes.

He smiled. "Did you think I would let the Guardians defy me without contestation? I came prepared, my dear, knowing what might lay at hand. You will pay the price for your temple's betrayal." Raede looked at Meclellon "Take her to the Lumidian."

# Chapter Eight

# DEVIATION

Notelcea gathered her thoughts, contemplating making contact with Kelgar. She had not gone to the library, nor did she have any future intentions of going. There was nothing to be learned in those books that she did not already know. She knew far more than the books ever would. This was something Kelgar did not understand.

Notelcea would not justify her actions to him, however. Despite Kelgar's aged looks, Notelcea was still the ranking Guardian of the Temple of Aurora. She would make her own decisions about the present situation and would not stand for Kelgar trying to order her to the library. It was a pointless excursion anyway and Kelgar must know that as well.

Notelcea could not be sure why Kelgar had so greatly insisted upon sending her to the library, but she had a feeling he was simply using it as a diversion. What he was hiding she could not say, nor did she care to take the time to try and find out. There were more important things at stake now.

One moon was already gone and Notelcea knew it would only be a matter of time before another was taken. Notelcea did carry something of great value, however. She carried a secret, a very great secret. A secret she had carried the better part of her life. She was not about to divulge that secret to anyone just yet, but she knew it would soon come into play. Until then she had to proceed with her newly hatched plan.

Still, she felt she should at least give some sort of word to Kelgar that she had deviated. The last thing she needed was for him to come looking for her in the library. There was too much information within those books. While she herself already knew most everything in the library, there were still many secrets of the world that Kelgar had not yet learned. And at least for the time being, perhaps it was best to leave those secrets buried.

Notelcea looked around. She could not communicate with Kelgar just now, but soon she would make the effort. She simply had to wait for right moment.

# Chapter Nine

## THE GUARDIAN IN THE DARKNESS

Kelgar ran through the woods swiftly and silently, reminiscing back to the days when skulking about unseen had been a part of his life. He had not been the privileged child that most of the residents of the Temple of Aurora started out as. Long before he was granted the magic of the Guardians, learning how to melt into dark corners had been his way of living. His childhood street skills were serving him well now as he darted in and out of the trees like an unseen phantom.

Kelgar knew that any effort to save Laede was futile. The king would be dead long before Kelgar ever made it back to palace if he wasn't dead already. There might still be time to stop Raede, however. Kelgar knew well enough what Raede was planning. No one went about idly gathering tarkweed unless they planned to wage a battle, and Kelgar knew that was exactly what Raede planned to do.

Raede had obviously been waiting for an opportunity such as the return of the Shadows. Now that they had come, Kelgar knew that Raede would be hesitant to banish the demons back to their valley. Raede would use the chaos produced by the Shadows to achieve his own ends. He might even soon try to strike a bargain with the Keeper of Darkness itself. Kelgar knew Raede was no fool, but he was arrogant. That pride would be his downfall.

Raede would believe enough in himself to think he could control the Shadows and perhaps even the Keeper. If he tried to bargain with the Keeper, however, Raede would unleash a force more powerful than even he could possibly imagine. If Raede tried to bargain with the Keeper, he would need more than tarkweed to save him from the evil it would create.

Most importantly, Kelgar was worried about Notelcea. He had sent her to the palace library, and if she had actually gone there, she would be right in the path of Raede's rampage. Raede was helping the Shadows and any friend of the Shadows was an enemy of the light. The Guardians would be chief on Raede's list of people to strip of their power. They were the only ones who could stand up against him. If Notelcea was in the library, Raede would take her by surprise using his manipulative charm until he held the senior Guardian as his prisoner.

Kelgar quickened his pace. His black cape was tousled by the wind as he watched two men making their way through the forest. Kelgar stopped for a moment to examine them. Years of practice had given him hawk-like eyes even in the darkness. He could see they bore the royal crest. Obviously they had been sent by Raede with orders to gather more tarkweed or to search for the missing Guardians.

Kelgar smiled ruefully in the darkness. He held no light while they tightly clasped their torches. If they had in fact been sent to find him, they would never see him through the blackness. He slunk closer to hear what they were saying.

"I don't like standing out here with nothing between ourselves and the Shadows but a few torches," said one man.

"Nor I," said the second man, "but I'm equally unreceptive to the idea of defying the king's orders."

"At least a king kills you with a sword," the first man continued. "It is said that people taken by the Shadows don't even die. They actually become the Shadows, part of the demonic force that destroys everything in its path."

"This isn't a subject I'm keen on discussing while we stand alone here in Silverwood."

"Does hiding from the truth change it? Rumor has it that even the Guardians don't know what's happened; that they've lost control of the light."

"I know. I have a cousin who is an apprentice at the temple and she told me that the two elder Guardians have left and no one knows where they are."

"The cowards have probably gone to save themselves and leave us prey to the Keeper of Darkness."

Kelgar shook his head. He could hear the fear in their voices. It was the very thing he and the other Guardians had hoped to prevent by not immediately announcing the disappearance of Selene. Listening to the men of the royal army, however, Kelgar knew that the Guardians had failed in that task, for the men were clearly afraid.

Fear was a dangerous thing. It was more contagious than a disease. The men were afraid that the Guardians had lost of control of the light, and ironically, such a worry would bring about the very event that the men feared. Their fear would give power to the Shadows. The more power the Shadows gained, the less control the Guardians would have over the light, until at last, it would be gone.

It was time to return to the palace. The Guardians had to regain control of the light before the panic spread too far. Kelgar crept past the royal guards completely unseen and took off through the woods again. Maan was already setting and Ngame was beginning to rise by time the cold stones of the palace came into view, glittering in its light.

The palace was quiet, too quiet to be any ordinary night at the royal house. Something was wrong. There was not so much as a night watchman to be seen guarding the palace that housed the king of all Argentum. It bore the echoing mark of the Shadows and Kelgar feared he was already too late. He softly made his way to the castle, prowling the edge of the walls until he came to a tiny servants' door. Seeing no one around to stop him, Kelgar slipped through it, allowing it close quietly behind him. He gazed around letting his eyes adjust to the thick darkness.

It smelled dank and empty as though this quarter of the castle had been abandoned for years, but Kelgar's ears gave away the truth. It was not completely deserted, for he could hear footsteps coming down the stairs. He ducked behind a wall and pulled a long knife from the sheath at his side, fingering it tensely as he listened to the servant coming closer. Kelgar waited until a hand emerged from the side of the wall and then he pounced, pinning the unfortunate servant's neck beneath his dagger.

"Tell me where the king is and I may even let you live," Kelgar growled, deepening his voice in effort to hide his identity.

"Lord Raede has gone to the Temple of Aurora to seek the Guardians' counsel," said the man, quaking beneath Kelgar's violent stare and cold steel blade.

"Lord Raede? Where is the true king?" asked Kelgar, knowing full well what the answer would be.

"Laede was taken by the Shadows several nights ago," the man whispered hoarsely. "Raede assumed the throne shortly after."

"Where is Notelcea?"

"Who?"

"The Guardian of the Light. She came to search the library for the legends of the Keeper. Where has she gone?"

"I'm not permitted to enter the library. I cannot say whether the Guardian or anyone else might be there."

"Then tell me what guidance Raede plans to seek from the Guardians."

"I don't know, sir."

Kelgar tightened the blade against the man's neck.

"I swear it to you on my life," the man pleaded. "On the life of my wife and my three daughters, I don't know. I'm just the kitchen man. I clean up the table after the royals have had their meals. I-I scrub the floors when the hall is empty. I've never even been in the same room as the king. I'm just a lowly servant and I swear I don't know anything about matters of the court."

"Very well," said Kelgar removing the knife from the man's neck. "If you love your family, you'll remain silent about this meeting. Breathe a word about my presence here and I promise you, you'll wish the spirits had never given you lips."

It was an idle threat, for Kelgar would never harm an innocent, but the servant had no way of knowing that. He swallowed and nodded, taking Kelgar's warning to heart. Kelgar resheathed his dagger and glided away, leaving the traumatized servant alone in the hall. He simply hoped the man wouldn't recognize him as one of the Guardians. If the people were afraid now, their terror would be doubled if they thought the Guardians were going around threatening people with knives.

Kelgar made straight for the library and pushed open the door, not even bothering to check if anyone was watching. He had to find Notelcea and there was not a moment to lose. If Laede was already dead then it would just be a matter of time before Raede declared war, however sweetly he might disguise it, on the

Guardians. There was no way that the Shadows could have taken Laede by themselves. He had clearly been murdered and all fingers pointed to Raede.

Kelgar sighed knowing the twisted new king was probably already on his way to wreak havoc at the Temple of Aurora. He now greatly regretted leaving Enira alone. She was so young and inexperienced that he doubted she would be able to defend herself, let alone the entire temple, against a man of Raede's cunning intelligence. Raede's tarkweed alone would be enough to stop Enira in her tracks.

Kelgar halted in the doorway of the library, not even wanting to image the terrible things Raede would do to the young Guardian if she held her tongue. "I am sorry, Enira," he whispered and stepped into the darkness of the library.

There were no torches burning among the long rows of books and the smell within was musty. It didn't appear as though anyone had bothered the hall of study in several months. "Notelcea?" Kelgar whispered into the empty room.

There came no reply.

"Notelcea, it's Kelgar," he called more loudly.

Still the room remained silent.

"Notelcea!"

The only reply Kelgar received was the echo of his own voice. The room was empty. Notelcea wasn't there.

"Where could she be?" Kelgar whispered to himself.

He wondered if she had already been taken prisoner by Raede or if she had simply never gone to library in the first place, just as the gypsy had warned. The question remained, however, if Notelcea wasn't at the library, then where was she?

Kelgar shook his head. He didn't have time to dwell on it, for he was sure that all would reveal itself in due time. For now he had to return to the Temple of Aurora and hopefully get to Enira before Raede betrayed her too. It was time to end it.

Sneaking out of the palace, Kelgar took the opportunity to steal the horse of a man who had gone to relieve himself. It was not exactly Guardian behavior, but it couldn't be helped. Time was of the essence and lives lay in the balance. If sneaking into palaces, pretending to threaten servants and borrowing horses without permission were necessary to save lives then so be it.

Kelgar rode hard, only stopping the horse when the spiked form of the Temple of Aurora came into view. It stood stark and foreboding in the fading moonlight. He quickly dismounted and sent the horse running back toward the palace. He crept the rest of the way to the temple on foot, taking care not to be noticed.

Kelgar could see that Raede was inside, for his army stood at the door, guarding the temple. Raede had almost certainly already taken Enira prisoner as well, for the men at the door were not merely standing casually, they were armed and ready. Kelgar suspected they were waiting for himself and Notelcea to return.

He grinned ruefully. He'd been raised by the Silverwood Gypsy; he had no intentions of going that quietly. Still, there were too many of Raede's men in the temple for Kelgar to try and fight them all on his own. Even with the magic of Guardians, he knew he could not control them all. He could not risk the possibility that someone would use Enira as a hostage to make Kelgar lay down his magic. And then there was still Raede.

Kelgar was not a simpleton. He knew as well as anyone that Raede had been as good as raised by the sorcerer Leingella. Whatever magic Leingella had taught Raede, it was sure to be far more powerful than the folk magic Kelgar had learned at the hand of the gypsy. However, while Leingella's magical teachings may have been more powerful, the gypsy's were no doubt more practical. She had not stopped at merely teaching her son simple magic. She had taught him life skills as well, skills whose value had never truly dawned on Kelgar until now.

He thought back to his days of hunting. When a man is hunting wolves with one arrow, he doesn't just randomly shoot into the center of the pack; he picks off the animals one at time when they stray from the others. That was what Kelgar had to do. He would pick off Raede's men one at a time.

Scurrying around to the backside of the temple, Kelgar rubbed his hands along the stonework until he found what he was looking for. There beneath his hands lay a tiny crack in the wall. He pushed his weight against it and a secret door opened. He quietly stepped through it, pushing it closed behind him.

Thump! Something came out of the darkness striking Kelgar in the back of his head. The force of it knocked him to the ground and he fell in an ungraceful heap. Just before the blackness washed over him, Kelgar briefly perceived two feet walking toward him. Before he could make out any more of his attacker, he slipped into unconsciousness.

## Chapter Ten

## REBELLION

"Again!" Lismella shouted.

Ericahs stood bent over, supporting himself with his hands on his knees. He raised his head to look at the woman who was being relentless in her training of him.

"Give me a moment," he panted wiping the sweat from his brow with his forearm.

"Again!" Lismella commanded, refusing to back down.

"We've been at this for hours!" Ericahs shot back raising himself to his full height. "You're pushing me too hard. I need a rest."

"I'll decide when you rest," said Lismella. "We don't have time to waste. The Keeper is plotting its next move as we stand here bantering. It could take another moon at any moment. You're a fighter, now act like one."

"I fight with a sword not with the light magic that you're attempting to beat me to death with."

Lismella stepped toward Ericahs. "But this what you need to learn, because only light will defeat the Keeper of Darkness. Your sword is useless against the Shadows."

"I don't have the amount of energy this requires!"

"That's why I'm teaching you, and the only way you're going to grow stronger is by repetition. Just as you strengthen your arms to wield a sword, you must now strengthen your mind to wield this power. Focus your energy, concentrate on your task."

"I need a break," Ericahs hissed.

Lismella reacted quickly, catching Ericahs by the head and driving him to the ground. He fell hard as he had not been expecting her attack. She held the point of Ericahs' own sword toward him.

"We don't have time for you to take a break! The Keeper of Darkness is growing stronger at every moment. More people are being taken by the Shadows every night and you're here moaning about how tired you are? You don't have time to rest and I don't have time to fight with you like a pouting child!" She flipped the sword around, offering the hilt to Ericahs. "You have the spirit to argue with me, now use that spirit to drive this magic. From what I've heard, Guardians of the Light train for at least twenty years. You have only days."

"Then get a Guardian!" Ericahs shouted, grabbing the sword and rising to his feet. "Find someone else to be your slave. I'm finished with you. I have the great fortune of being my own master. I belong to no man or woman. You can't just walk into my life and then think you have the right to control it. What do you know of the Guardians anyway? How do I know you're not just using me as a pawn to try and steal their magic?"

"Without me the Guardians will never succeed. I know that I don't have time to find someone else and train them as I have done with you for the past several days. I know that if you walk away from me now, you will be responsible for the death of everyone when the Shadows succeed in overrunning the land." Lismella looked toward Argentum. "They have already succeeded in taking the king. There is no telling who might be next."

Ericahs snorted in disdain. "The king should be dead. He was worthless as a ruler and worthless as a man. I don't feel any sorrow at his death and I'm surprised you do. You don't seem to be one who would revere a king."

"I respect his position," said Lismella firmly.

"And what about Raede? Do you respect him as well?"

"The brother who took Laede's place is not a king. He is a scheming murderer."

"And was Laede any more?"

"Yes, he was a king. I think he tried to do what was best for his people. He may not always have been right, but he did the best he could with the knowledge he had. Even if you don't like him, it's the duty of his subjects to respect his position."

"It's not my duty. I never swore my loyalty to Laede. He was never my king."

"Whether you like it or not, he is the king of everyone in Argentum."

Ericahs looked straight into Lismella's eyes. "I live in Silverwood, not Argentum." He turned and walked away.

"Ericahs!" Lismella called after him. "Ericahs!"

Ericahs didn't stop, he just kept on walking. Lismella sighed. She had chosen Ericahs specifically for his rebellious spirit, but she hadn't anticipated that he would be quite this stubborn. She needed Ericahs far more than he needed her, but she couldn't let him know that. She looked into the trees behind her. Perhaps there was still something that could make Ericahs see reason.

Lismella waited until Ericahs had taken time to cool his anger and then she approached him. "Ericahs," she called.

"What?" he answered grudgingly.

"Come with me. I want to show you something, something you need to see."

"And what is that?" asked Ericahs, not moving.

"You have to see it with your own eyes," Lismella pressed.

"You can tell me now or I'm not coming."

"Just for once do as I say!" Lismella was beginning to lose patience. "If you channeled the amount of energy you use to fight me into your training, you would be unstoppable. Must you always be so stubborn?"

"I didn't ask to be here! Can I help it if I'm angry now?"

"You're not angry at me," Lismella retorted, "you only think you are. You're targeting me with your rage because you're so filled with hate that you can't even remember what made you angry in the first place. You've simply fallen to hating everyone."

"What makes you always think you know so much about me?"

"Enough to know that you hate Aecleton and that hate is the only reason you ever agreed to come with me in the first place." Lismella moved in closer. "What was it, Ericahs? What did the Keeper do to you?"

Ericahs turned away. "It doesn't matter. It was long ago."

"And your heart still bears the mark of its scar. It does matter to you, Ericahs; I can see it. It matters very deeply to you. It defines you, Ericahs. Before you can be ready, you will have to face that again."

"I don't need to face it again," Ericahs protested. "Once was enough to make me as ready as I'll ever be."

Lismella shook her head and stepped toward Ericahs. "You're not ready until I say you're ready. Now come with me. If what I show you displeases you, you are free to leave at any moment, but I think you will change your mind when you see it."

Ericahs made no reply, but neither did he argue. He turned and silently followed Lismella, stalking after her in the darkness. Lismella said no more, grateful to have him obeying at last.

"How far are we going?" asked Ericahs at last, after walking for what seemed like hours.

"Just a bit farther now," said Lismella.

No sooner had she spoken the words when the trees immediately opened into a large clearing which seemed to be lit by something other than moonlight. The trees around the clearing were so thick, they almost formed a fence and there in the midst of that clearing was what Lismella had come for.

"This is it, Ericahs," she said.

"This is what?" he asked.

"This is where the Lumidian was built."

Even a man as stubborn and unemotional as Ericahs could not help but gape in awe as he stood in the presence of the Lumidian's place of creation. What the sorcerers had done hundreds of years earlier was probably the greatest display of magic in history, probably the greatest the world would ever see. And here stood Ericahs, in the midst of that clearing.

"How can you be sure this is where the Lumidian was built?" Ericahs asked at last, not daring to raise his voice above a whisper. "That was over three hundred years ago and only the Guardians of Light have access to the history texts of the palace library."

"There are more places than the palace library to learn the secrets of the world," Lismella replied mysteriously. "But believe me when I tell you, it was indeed this place, this place and no other where the Lumidian came into being. This is where the first Guardians captured the sun so its light would be forever dispersed among the moons. It was meant to banish the Shadows, but it could not destroy them completely. It only restricted them to the Valley of the Shadows until Aecleton joined their power. With Aecleton behind them, it was only a matter of time before the Shadows regained hold of the land. And now that day is coming."

"So why did you bring me here? Is the Lumidian's place of creation supposed to endow me with some great power to defeat Aecleton?"

"No. The Lumidian is leagues from here now, nestled in the highest tier of the Temple of Aurora, and it took all its power with it. I brought you here for something else."

"What?"

"The prophecy."

Ericahs squinted his eyes. "What prophecy?"

"The one that says only you can destroy the Keeper of Darkness."

"What?" he asked in disbelief.

"See for yourself." Lismella pointed toward the rock in the very center of the clearing. It was all that remained to mark the spot where the Lumidian had come into being.

Ericahs slowly walked over to it, debating between wanting to know and wanting to turn away in defiance. Curiosity got the better of him and his feet made their own decision carrying him toward the rock. He walked around it to face the front. The carved letters of the prophecy stared out harshly from the rock, their words etched in impenetrable stone. Even Ericahs could not pretend away their existence as he read the message in the light of his torch. He bent closer to read what it said.

*The outlaw from the silver wood, who lives life by the sword, lost something to the darkness and bears no love for the world. But this warrior shall be the one to strike the heart of the Shadows. His anger shall save the world.*

Ericahs couldn't believe it, but there it was as real as the rock upon which it was carved. It was a prophecy about himself that no amount of wishing against could wipe from the stone. Lismella observed the realization in his eyes and softly walked up behind the shocked man.

"You see, Ericahs, this is why the world needs you," said Lismella.

Ericahs recovered from his initial shock and began to think more rationally. "This prophecy doesn't bear my name. It could be about anyone."

"You know that's not true," Lismella countered. "While you can choose to ignore my words, you cannot deny what you see before you carven in stone. This prophecy clearly names you, no matter how much you might try to deny it."

"I don't believe that."

"Yes you do. You believe it even if you won't admit it, and perhaps that's enough, enough to give you the motivation to learn what I am trying to teach you. You have read it for yourself and deep in your heart you know the prophecy is true. I have the secrets to destroy Aecleton, but only you can deliver the fatal blow, for you have the anger to save the world.

"You were right when you said your anger keeps you alive, for it does and it can save us all. You have the spirit, but you must learn to control your anger, to focus it against the Keeper where it is meant to be. Do not let your anger be directed upon the entire world simply because you despise Aecleton. Do not let your hatred consume you."

"It already did," said Ericahs, "a long time ago." Ericahs looked at his sword, feeling the same hollow anger he had felt so many years before. He glanced at Lismella. "I will try harder."

Lismella gave him a tiny smile. She could see the change within him and she knew that he was at last ready to learn. It was remarkable how just a few words etched on a piece of stone could have such a profound effect upon a person.

"We begin anew tomorrow," said Lismella. "Tonight you shall rest."

Ericahs nodded and began to walk away. Lismella made to follow him, but stopped for a moment. Ericahs was too lost in thought to notice, but Lismella carefully returned to the stone. She stood over it for a moment, reading the words of the prophecy one last time. She glanced at Ericahs for a moment and then she let out a long, slow breath, blowing on the carven sentences. They melted away like sand in the wind, revealing nothing but the smooth surface of the rock where the prophecy had sat only a few minutes before.

Lismella turned and followed Ericahs.

# Chapter Eleven

## EMOTIONS

Ericahs slept an unpeaceful slumber. His troubled mind wandered restlessly through the night. His thoughts no longer seemed his own, for they were being pulled, as though by some outside force, back to a night twenty years earlier. It was a night of great significance to Ericahs, for it was a night that had changed the course of his future forever.

Donya and her two sons walked along the steep ridge beside the Valley of Shadows. The moon was high in the sky and its light bathed the land in a comforting glow, yet the three travelers held their torches tightly in hand as they scurried along the cliff. No matter how many torches they bore, and no matter how bright the light of the moon was, the edge of the Valley of Shadows was still not a place to linger.

It was the stronghold of the demons and it was a possibility that in the midst of their own territory, they might have the power to snuff out the light of a torch. It was unwise to journey so close to the Valley of the Shadows. Donya knew that as well as anyone, but she had no choice. She held tightly to her berry basket; the valuable prize that she'd risked nearing the Shadows to obtain.

"Hurry, my boys, hurry," Donya urged her sons. "We mustn't linger here long."

The boys quickened their pace, knowing as well as their mother the danger that lay within the valley. But hurried feet are often the most unsteady, scampering along as they wait for the inevitable accident to occur. The unsteadiness of Donya's sons was intensified by the fear they felt at passing so close to the Valley of Shadows. The two combined were nothing short of a recipe for disaster.

Perhaps it was indeed Petrya's unsteady feet, or perhaps it was the Shadows themselves, reaching their dark, slippery fingers out from the confines of their valley if only for a moment. It all happened too fast to know for sure. One moment the boy was running as quickly as he could past the valley and the next he was slipping down in the rocky crevasse itself.

"Petrya!" Donya screamed as her youngest son's form disappeared over the cliff.

Petrya gave no answer, but there was a small groan from the bottom of the valley. Donya leaned over as far as she dared, holding her own torch so tightly that her knuckles were white.

"Petrya!" Shouted Donya's second son running toward the cliff.

"Back, Ericahs!" His mother shouted. "Stay away from the cliff!"

Ericahs did as he was told, breathing hard as he watched his mother peer into the Valley of Shadows. The moon was full and bright overhead, as it always was, but it gave no comfort. Even its silver light could not penetrate the depths of the demon chasm into which Petrya had fallen. He had lost his torch during his fall and now lay at the bottom of the valley alone and defenseless. It did not take the Shadows long to become aware of his presence.

They had been seething for fresh meat for ages and now a boy lay within their midst. They swarmed upon him hungrily, attracted to the innocent fear within him. They capitalized on that fear, latching onto it, making it grow within the child until it overtook him completely.

"Petrya!" Donya screamed. "Petrya run! Run!"

But it was too late, the Shadows were already taking him, transforming all the life within him into nothingness. The black cloud of fear that the Shadows had been growing inside of the child burst from every point of his body, tearing his entire being apart until there was nothing left. Until he was no more than a wisp. Until he had become part of the Shadows themselves.

The screams Petrya made as the Shadows ripped through him were the most bloodcurdling sounds Donya had ever heard. They were worsened by the fact that it was her own son making them. Donya could never have described those chilling sounds with any words in any language known to man. They were sounds she would never forget.

"Mother!" Ericahs screamed hearing his brother below and beginning to run toward the valley.

"Don't look at it!" Donya shouted grabbing the boy and turning him away from the view of the Shadows.

She shielded her son, covering his eyes, but there was no one to shield Donya as she bore witness to the horror of watching her own child be consumed by the wraith-like demons. She painfully watched the blackness engulfing the child until he was gone. Only his screams lingered long after his body was gone, the last remnant of his life echoing on the wind.

Donya knew that she could not save Petrya. Efforts to do so would be futile, but the motherly instinct within her soul would have made her cast herself into that valley no matter how useless her attempts to save him were. The only thing that stopped her was the son she still held tightly in her arms.

She could not abandon one son to save another who was already doomed, so she sat there helplessly as Petrya was taken from the world. She shielded her son from watching his brother's death, but there was nothing to stem the flow of tears that poured down her cheeks as she watched Petrya be destroyed. Just before everything became silent, Donya let out one final cry to her son.

"Petrya!"

Ericahs awoke with a start, panting, covered in sweat as he recalled the nightmare he'd just had.

"Visions of death?" asked Lismella calmly.

Ericahs looked over and saw her staring intently at him. "How did you know?"

"You were screaming in your sleep," said Lismella. "Who is Petrya?"

Ericahs hesitated a moment before answering, not sure he wanted to reopen that particular wound.

"He was my younger brother. The Shadows took him many years ago." Ericahs stood up. "I haven't dreamed about it since I was child, and yet I've dreamed of it almost every night since meeting you."

"It's the Keeper of Darkness calling to you, Ericahs. Aecleton is somehow aware that you've begun training in the ways of the light. Aecleton knows well enough of the prophecy. These dreams are likely meant to frighten you away from your resolve to destroy the Shadows."

"But why send me dreams of my brother's death?" asked Ericahs. "Won't that only increase my desire to destroy them?"

"The Shadows have only one weapon, preying upon the fears of others. That is what they are trying to do to you."

"But I don't fear the Shadows."

"No," Lismella agreed. She stepped toward Ericahs dropping her voice. "You're not afraid of *them*, but you are afraid of *being afraid* of them." Lismella watched Ericahs' face change as the firelight flickered across it and she could see that her assumption was correct. "You saw someone taken by the Shadows, yes, but you also saw something else. You saw someone driven to madness with fear, and that type of consuming fear is what frightens you most of all. Who was it, Ericahs? Who was it that you saw lose their grasp on reality?"

"My mother," said Ericahs slowly. "When we were children, Raede advised the king to put up the boundaries around Argentum and implement a road tax. It was already forbidden to hunt the king's game in Argentum, so my mother had to hunt in Silverwood if we wanted to eat. It was easy enough to get out of Argentum, but we had to pay the toll to reenter the city. The problem was that my father had died years earlier and we had no money. We could never afford to pay the king's road tax."

"Why didn't your family just stay in Silverwood?" asked Notelcea.

Ericahs met her eyes. "You've been here. It's a lawless land. My mother knew it was no place to raise a family; it was barely even a place to hunt. We'd been robbed of our game more than once while hunting in Silverwood. But we didn't have any choice. If we'd ever been caught hunting the king's game in Argentum, my mother probably would have been executed on the spot."

"So she avoided that danger by choosing another perilous road?"

"Yes," Ericahs nodded. "She would take us to the far meadows beside the

Valley of the Shadows to gather painge berries. It was the only place to find them in any quantity because it was far enough out that few people went there. Due to their rarity they were valuable enough that we could always trade them for passage back into Argentum. Naturally it was still dangerous being so close to the valley. One night Petrya lost his footing and slipped in."

Ericahs turned away. He was telling Lismella the story, but he would not allow himself to relive the pain. He remained emotionally detached from the words he spoke. "His screams were horrible, but we couldn't do anything to save him as the Shadows feasted upon him. My mother made sure I didn't look, but I could still hear Petrya's pleas for help. I knew my mother could too.

"I don't know if you've ever seen anyone taken by the Shadows, but my mother did. She watched them take her own son and she couldn't even try to help him. I think she felt guilty for ever taking us with her, so close to danger. That was what ate away at her most of all. She was never the same after that. The Shadows continued to torment her with dreams and visions so strong that they finally drove her to insanity. I tried to take care of her, but she just kept drifting further and further from me, fighting with demons that only she could see. And then one day," Ericahs finally turned back toward Lismella, "she was gone. The visions tortured her to death. It was as though the Shadows had killed her without even touching her."

"So what did you do?"

Ericahs sighed. "Whatever I could to survive. I became a thief. I was only nine and I was alone in the world. What else could I do? I didn't even know how to hunt that well yet, so I began to steal anything I could get my hands on. Once I started, it just became a way of life."

Ericahs sat down next to the fire. He'd never told anyone so much about his life, but strangely enough, he didn't even want to stop. It felt good for once to be able to let his guard down and just release everything to someone who was actually willing to listen.

"I've been in the dungeons of the Argentum palace more than once," he confessed, "that was where I learned to fight. It was a different world in the dungeons. Down there it was either kill or be killed. So once again I adapted to my situation and I taught myself what I needed to know to survive.

"The first time I was sent to the dungeons for stealing I was eleven. Two years later I found myself there yet again. When I was freed, I picked up a sword and I hardened my heart against the world, using the fighting skills I had developed in the dungeons. I found that I could live by my sword, fighting for money. Because of what I'd learned in the dungeons, I was naturally very good at it. It meant I'd never have to steal again. I didn't even have to kill anyone to win. I only ended up in the dungeons once more after that, but that was the last time."

Lismella thought for a moment before answering. "I can see why those dreams are something you want to remain buried. I wish you didn't have to face them again, but you must. I know I'm repeating myself, but at some point you will have to face your one fear. You will have to go the Valley of the Shadows and relieve yourself of the fear that you might be afraid. It's the only way you can stop your dreams. It's the only way you can make yourself truly ready to meet Aecleton."

Ericahs shook his head in protest. "Aecleton took everything from me. He killed my family and stole my life when I was forced to become a thief. The desire for revenge is truly the only thing that drives me. I swore I'd never go back to that valley, and so I won't. Aecleton will come to us. I already have all the rage I need to give strength to my fighting. I am ready."

"I already told you, Ericahs, you're not ready until I say you're ready. Yes, you have rage, but it's misplaced. You are so angry now, you don't even remember who you were mad at in the first place."

"Aecleton," Ericahs replied quickly.

"Yes," Lismella nodded. "Much of your hate is directed toward the Keeper of Darkness, and rightly so, but who else? Who hurt you more than anyone? Look deep inside your heart and ask yourself who you're really angry at."

Ericahs' answer was almost a whisper. "Myself," he said.

"Why?"

"Because I survived." Ericahs sighed, turning away once again. "Because all three of us were on that valley ridge and I lived while they didn't. Even before I had to fend for myself, I was a mischief-maker. Petrya was the good child and yet he was the one that died." He turned back toward Lismella searching for wisdom. "Why did they take him? He was innocent. How can the Shadows take someone who is innocent?"

"No one is innocent, Ericahs. Everyone has a dark side."

Ericahs shook his head. "No. Petrya was only seven. He hadn't lived long enough to develop a dark side."

"Everyone has a dark side," Lismella repeated, "though some are darker than others." Lismella began rubbing her hands together, using them to demonstrate her words. "There are only two real emotions in the world; fear and love. All other emotions stem from these two. Hate, anger, joy, hope, sadness. When the surface on these emotions is scratched away, they all come from one of two bases; love or fear. A person's light half is made of love. A person's dark half is made up of fear.

"The emotions of fear and love are more powerful than all the magics of the world combined, for all things are done in the name of fear or love. Sometimes people will kill or steal or do unspeakable things, but all these things are simply because somewhere deep inside people are afraid of something. Sometimes it is the fear of losing the ones they love, sometimes it is the fear of being powerless. But whatever it is, dark actions always come from fear. Even a seven year old is not immune to fear. Even your brother had a dark side though he hadn't lived long enough to give into it, for a dark side is simply fear.

"That is how the Shadows take people. They find that black spot of fear within a person, no matter how tiny it might be. They grab hold of it, expanding it and making it grow until it overtakes the person entirely. They are consumed by their own darkness."

"So the Shadows are trying to reignite my fear to destroy me?" asked Ericahs.

"No," Lismella replied quickly. "No. Aecleton knows you're different. Your dark side gives strength to your light. You are not afraid of dying, therefore you are waging war against Aecleton more out of love for the ones you already lost, rather than out of fear of losing something else. The Shadows are sending you these dreams in hopes of distracting your mind to keep you at bay." Lismella looked toward the west.

"Well they're going to have to do better than that," said Ericahs. "A few dreams aren't going to frighten me. And despite how it might disappoint you, they're not going to make me go to the valley just because you think I need to prove something to myself."

"That is up to you. It is an enemy only you can face."

"I'm going to get more wood for the fire," said Ericahs, ignoring Lismella's last words.

He wanted to be alone for a moment, so he began to walk away. When he was far enough out of the firelight, he turned around to look at Lismella, her form glowing in the light of the flames. He had expected her to be trying to sleep, but what he saw was something else entirely.

Her white gown glowed in the night as she reached into the recesses of her cloak lying upon the ground. She withdrew a small packet and glided toward Ericahs' belongings. She carefully pulled open his pack and took out his water gourd. Without even hesitating, she dumped the powdery white contents of the packet into Ericahs' water, shaking it to ensure everything was mixed well. Then she folded up the empty packet and returned to her spot by the fire.

# Chapter Twelve

# PRISIONER

Enira stood alone in the Lumidian room, her hands tightly bound to the roof beams, with only the dim glow of the Lumidian to keep her company. It had been several hours since Meclellon had dragged her kicking and screaming through the halls of the Temple of Aurora. She still had no idea why her magic had failed her.

Several of the young temple residents had tried to help Enira, but only halfheartedly. They found themselves wondering whether they should help a Guardian or obey a king. It didn't matter anyway, for they too had been quickly subdued by Raede's magic and now Enira was alone and helpless.

Enira tried to stretch her wrists. She had long ago lost feeling in her fingers and now the numbness was spreading down her arms. She knew there was only one reason she was still alive. Raede needed her magic and he needed her knowledge. He wanted to use her to find the other Guardians so he could control their magic as well. Enira would never betray the other Guardians, however. She would die first. She could only hope that the other Guardians wouldn't walk into Raede's trap as she had, or all would be lost.

Footsteps sounded on the stairwell and Enira's heart jilted. She knew it was Raede coming to try and extract information from her at last.

"Hello, Enira," he said striding toward her. Enira back away as far as her arms would allow. "I apologize for leaving you by yourself so long, but I'm afraid I had other matters to tend to before I could share in your company here." He sighed in mock exhaustion. "The work of a king is never finished you know."

"You're not the king," Enira spat back.

Raede looked at her. "Oh that's where you're mistaken." He slunk closer to the Guardian. "You may not feel that I *deserve* to be king, but I am king just the same," he leaned in close to Enira and whispered, "no matter how I acquired my throne."

Enira turned her head away.

Raede smiled. "What's the matter, young Guardian? Wondering why your magic isn't working?" He nodded to himself. "Yes, my master Leingella wondered that as well," he put his hand under Enira chin, forcing her to look forward, "right after I killed him."

Enira couldn't hold back a small gasp, knowing that she was probably next on Raede's list of victims.

"This," Raede said pointing to the ropes that held Enira's wrists, "is tarkweed. It only grows in Silverwood, but that is not what makes it so remarkable. What is special about this plain little plant is its ability to tame the magic powers of any sorcerer, even a Guardian. And as I found with Leingella, if you stab a sorcerer with a blade that has been cutting tarkweed, they can't even use their magic to heal the wound."

Raede look out the window. Lua was setting and the land was growing dark. "It seems it's time to light the torches. We don't want the Shadows getting at you," he said setting fire to the wall candles on either side of Enira, "at least not yet."

Enira's blood ran cold. The thought of being murdered by Raede was one thing, but the thought of being left to the Shadows was another. "Why are you doing this, Raede? Why are you helping the Shadows? They want to take the world and the Guardians of the Light are the only ones who can stop them."

"The world?" Raede Scoffed. "The Shadows can have the world; all I want is Argentum. All I want is what is mine. You see little Guardian, you have it backward. I am not helping the Shadows; they are helping me. They gave me back my kingdom. Why would I want anyone to stop them? Why fight for a kingdom when you can have it given to you?"

"Raede! The darkness will destroy you!"

Raede shook his head knowingly, playing with the flames of the candles. "No. You see, darkness is only something to fear if you don't know how to control it."

"You can't control it."

"Why not? I've managed to control you." Raede glided around the room as he spoke, his movements theatrically demonstrating his words. He finally halted on the far side of the Lumidian and looked over at his prisoner. The light of the Lumidian made his eyes glow eerily as he laid out his plan to Enira.

"Fear is the greatest weapon anyone can have." The king licked his lips, hungry with ambition. "You don't know how long I have waited for this day, the day when I would regain everything my father made me forfeit to a younger brother. I was the firstborn child, but my father always liked Laede better. My father saw that Laede was bigger and stronger in body than I would ever be, so he broke tradition and passed the crown to my younger brother instead of to me, the rightful heir. Since that day I have wanted nothing more than to take back what was mine. Now the Shadows are helping me to do exactly that.

"The people are terrified. The sheep are looking for a shepherd, and when the Guardians fail to appease their expectations, who will step in to help? It will be I, the new king, still grieving the loss of his brother, who will risk his own life to banish the Shadows back their valley and save the people of Argentum."

"You mean you're doing all this, helping the Shadows, just so you can be the hero that saves the world?" Enira asked in disbelief.

"In part, yes. After all my years of waiting, I deserve an easy rule. No rebellion will come between me and my throne, for who would raise rebellion against the one who would save the world? Besides, the Shadows are helping me remove you from your high place. The Guardians' reign of glory and power is at an end. It will be I, and not the Guardians, who vanquishes these demon foes, avenge our dear lost king and return peace to the land. There will be no more brooding group of light sorcerers to have higher authority than the king. My word as king will be absolute, just as it should be. The people will bow before me in devotion."

"The people are not as foolish as you think. It won't work."

"It has already has. The people's faith in the Guardians is beginning to waver and soon it will be gone. They will turn their weary gaze from you and see me standing with open arms to protect them. Your display this evening only furthered my standing with my men, because it was you who defied me. You betrayed your king. You broke their hearts and shattered their world for you betrayed everything they had been taught to believe. And perhaps their lack of faith in your power is well-founded. You are a Guardian of the Light, but you could not even stand up to me, a mortal man." He leaned in and whispered into Enira's ear. "If you cannot stand up to me, what makes you think you can stand up to the Shadows?"

Enira felt a shiver run up her spine as Raede's icy cold voice penetrated her ears. "What makes you think *you* can?" Enira whispered back, though her voice was soft out of fear rather than malice. "The Shadows aren't human, Raede. You can't bargain with them. You can't reason with them. They are a force without a mind. You won't be able to keep Argentum if they take the world."

Raede fingered the moon pendant around Enira's neck. "This is where your power stems from isn't it?" He pulled the pendant until the string broke and he looked at it greedily in his hand.

"It doesn't work like that. You can't just use a pendant to create magic. It's used to channel the magic within us, magic that belongs only to those trained in the arts of the Guardians."

"Yes, but you forget one thing, my confident little Guardian," the king grinned sinisterly, "I am not a common man. Perhaps you've not heard the rumors, but I was raised by a sorcerer. It is a shame that Leingella couldn't live to see me, his dear student, reach what I am now attaining. Sadly even the ones we love most sometimes meet an untimely death."

"An untimely death at your own hand."

"Yes, well, I never said that untimely wasn't convenient for me."

Raede held Enira's pendant aloft and began weaving a spell, chanting in tones that Enira had never heard. White light issued from the pendant coating every room in the temple until the entire structure was sealed by a white light. Now there would be no one entering in or out of the temple without Raede's permission. Enira gasped in surprise.

"You didn't really think the Guardians were the only ones with magic did you? I know sorcerers who bear power you couldn't begin to dream of, powers that the other Guardians would scarcely breathe a word of to you. Many of these powers have been taught to me and I know where to find more."

"It doesn't matter what you do Raede," said Enira recovering herself, "no matter how much power you have. You can't turn one pendant against another. They all have equal magic. Kelgar and Notelcea will be able to walk right through the seal you've put on the temple. That little necklace won't give you the glory you're seeking because one pendant alone is hardly strong enough to defeat Aecleton. You would need all three, and even then you might not succeed."

"I know. That's why you're going to help me?"

"What?"

"You're going to tell me where the other Guardians are."

"Never," Enira hissed.

Raede slapped her across the face with the back of his hand, drawing blood from her lip. "Tell me where they are."

Enira made no reply.

Raede hit her again, harder this time. It was all she could do to remain silent against the pain.

"You know you've been abandoned by them, Enira," said Raede playing with her mind again. "Why are you protecting people who left you to my torment?"

"They left me to guard the Temple of Aurora," said Enira feeling the warm stream of blood trickle down her face.

"Yes, and you failed deeply at that, didn't you? Do you really think they're going to bother coming back to help someone who couldn't even do the one task they left her with?" Raede gently wiped the blood from Enira's mouth. "Do you really think they planned to come back at all?"

Enira cringed under Raede's touch. There's was more poison in that gesture than there had been in his strikes.

"Kelgar and Notelcea aren't cowards," said Enira. "If they've not yet come back, then they've a very good reason for it."

"Yes, and perhaps that reason is that they know there is no hope. Perhaps they have gone to save themselves and left you here to die."

"Play your mind games with someone else," Enira panted. "You're not going to destroy my faith in the Guardians."

Raede hit Enira again. This time she could not hold back her cry of pain and Raede took joy in it.

"Just tell me where they are, Enira. Tell me where the other Guardians have gone. You have my word that they'll never know it was you who betrayed them. I'll tell them you fought gallantly to save us all before the Shadows overcame you."

Enira swallowed, taking a moment to catch her breath. "So you can lead them into your trap too?" Her voice quaked as she spoke.

"Where are they, Enira?"

Enira's answer was no more than a whisper. "I'll never tell you."

"Oh," Raede smiled, "I think you will." He reached into his pocket and extracted the tiny crystal he had placed there before leaving his palace.

"Do you know what happens when a sorcerer dies?" he asked holding up the crystal. "Their body melts away until only the residue of their magic is left in its place. All the magic that was ever within them shrinks down, compacting upon itself until it becomes hard and forms a single crystal; an essence crystal. The crystal itself is the essence of the sorcerer's magic, but it is more commonly known by the name of a truth stone."

Raede held the crystal to Enira's face. "Do you know why they call it a truth stone?"

Enira shivered and closed her eyes. She had never seen a truth stone, but she knew well enough where its named derived.

"Because when dissolved in water, it forms a powerful truth draft," said Raede, not waiting for the Guardian to answer, "which can make anyone confess everything they know...whether they want to or not."

Enira opened her eyes, watching as Raede dropped the stone into a flask of water. It fizzled and foamed white making crackling noises as it disintegrated and then the water was calm. Enira struggled futilely against her bonds as the king approached her. Raede looked at Enira, holding tightly to the potion. He grabbed her by the neck, forcing her head back and set the flask to her mouth.

"And now," he growled, "I think it is time to discuss the missing Guardians." He poured the burning potion down her throat.

# Chapter Thirteen

## TRUTH

Very, very slowly the room came into view as Kelgar awakened. The first bit of sensation he recognized was that of the throbbing pain in his head followed by the very quick shuffling of someone else in the room. Kelgar opened his eyes to see a young woman whom he recognized as one of the residents of the temple. She had a very concerned look on her face as she watched Kelgar come to his senses.

"I suppose you had a good reason for using my head as an anvil?" asked Kelgar sarcastically.

"I-I'm sorry," the woman stammered. "I thought you were one of them."

"That's alright," said Kelgar sitting up. He rubbed his head painfully. "That's a powerful hit you've got there."

"Well, I think the cauldron did most of the damage," she smiled, referring to the small cast-iron pot that lay nearby.

"Even so, I think you might have a future in temple defense," said Kelgar in jest. "Have you ever considered a position as temple guard? You seem to have a natural gift for it."

"How bad is it?"

"Well, I'll live," said Kelgar still holding his head, "but let's just say I'd rather not repeat the incident." Kelgar sized her up for a moment. "You're one of the apprentices aren't you?"

"Yes," the woman nodded. "Milessandra. I work in the kitchens."

"Good, you can help me." Kelgar looked around.

"With what?"

"With taking back our temple."

"You know that Raede's taken over then?"

Kelgar looked at her and grinned. "Why do you think I came in this door? I hadn't expected anyone would be here."

"Enira sent me here after Raede entered the palace."

"You mean Raede knows about this door?" asked Kelgar in alarm.

"No, no. Enira told me to bring a pot of tea for her and the king, which of course is not at all in tradition. I knew she must be telling me to hide and to protect everything I could in the temple. While she conversed with Raede, I crept to the seventh tier and removed anything that Raede might try to corrupt. The only thing I couldn't take with me was the Lumidian, though I assure you I would have if I could have. After that, I brought everything down here and have been hiding ever since."

Kelgar looked at her blankly. "You figured all that out from Enira telling you to bring them a pot of tea?"

"Enira's my cousin," Milessandra explained. "We can nearly read one another's minds we know each other so well."

"Well thank the spirits for that." He glanced up the stairs. "Have you been into the temple since you hid down here?"

"Yes, several times. I didn't want anyone to realize I was missing and go searching through the temple."

"Wise thinking. Where is Enira now?"

"Raede is holding her prisoner in the seventh tier."

"The Lumidian room," Kelgar sighed. "No doubt he plans to try and extract information from her."

"He can't can he?" asked Milessandra in concern. "Isn't her magic too strong?"

Kelgar shook his head. "I'm afraid I can't give you any reassuring words. Raede has magic of his own, and there is something more." Kelgar's mind drifted back to what the gypsy had told him in the woods. "Raede knows the one weakness of the Guardians, the weakness of all sorcerers; tarkweed."

"Tarkweed?"

"It's a plant that grows in Silverwood. Raede's men have been collecting it. It mutes the power of sorcerers and that is no doubt how Raede managed to capture Enira."

"But isn't there anything we can do?"

"Yes, but I don't want to make any rash moves. Enira isn't in any immediate danger, so I don't want to act without thinking or she might end up in the middle. Besides, as long as Raede doesn't know that I'm here, I'd like to learn exactly what he's planning to do."

Kelgar reached into his robe and extracted two white crystals. He held one in his right hand while staring thoughtfully at the stone lying in his left.

"Everyone in the temple will recognize me as a Guardian if I go marching out there, but you're not likely to be seen as suspicious." He sighed and looked at Milessandra. "Do you think you could find a way to get this crystal into the seventh tier without Raede noticing?"

"I can try," said Milessandra. She took the crystal in her hands. "How close do you need it?"

Kelgar raised an eyebrow. "Don't put yourself in danger. As long as the crystal is in the room I'll be able to see, and more importantly hear, anything that is happening within."

Milessandra nodded. "I'll do my best."

Kelgar smiled. "I can't ask for more than that." He watched as Milessandra turned away and crept barefoot up the stairs.

It was a tense few minutes as Kelgar waited in the darkness. The stone floors were thick enough that he could not even hear the people walking above his head. He had no idea where Milessandra was, how close she had gotten to Raede, or if she would even come back alive. He could only stand and wait, hoping that he had not been foolish enough to send an innocent young girl to her death.

Kelgar's hands began to sweat as time slipped away. It seemed to be taking the girl a long time. Too long. He wondered if something had gone wrong. Raede was not easily fooled, for he'd spent too many years learning how to think. Kelgar just was beginning to contemplate going to find Milessandra, when a figure entered the room. Kelgar breathed a sigh of relief. It was Milessandra.

"You succeed?" said Kelgar.

"Yes," she nodded keeping the left side of her face out of view. Kelgar noticed it immediately and grabbed her chin turning her face so he could see it. A long streak of blood ran down from her head.

Kelgar sighed. "What happened?"

"I don't think the king liked his tea," said Milessandra trying to make light of the situation. Kelgar didn't smile so she sobered. "Let's just say Raede's not the most charming gentleman I've ever met. He threw me against the wall for disturbing him."

"I'm sorry," said Kelgar. "I should not have sent you into that lion's den."

"Well, what were you going to do? Go yourself? You'd have been caught three steps out of this room and then where would we be? Honestly I'm all right. Raede may be ruthless, but I think my younger sister can hit harder than he can."

Kelgar finally gave a small smile, knowing that Milessandra wasn't hurt, despite the blood on her face.

"Very well then, let us see if this truly works." He began rubbing the crystal between his fingers, watching as a white light in the center of it slowly grew until the entire crystal was glowing. He gazed into it and could see everything that was happening in the seventh tier.

There was Raede standing in the Lumidian room, holding Enira prisoner.

"The truth draught should be starting to take effect, my dear," said Raede stepping in close to Enira. "So now I think it is time for you to tell me where the other Guardians have gone."

"Notelcea went to the palace library," said Enira unable to resist the power of the truth draught.

Raede shook his head. "There was no one there. Either she lied to you, or you are mistaken."

"Kelgar sent her there," Enira insisted, "though she seemed as though she didn't truly wish to go. I just learned that she is the high Guardian of the Temple of Aurora, not Kelgar, so I suppose she does not have to follow anyone's orders but her own."

"And where did Kelgar go?"

"He went to find the gypsy."

"The gypsy?" asked Raede.

"The Silverwood Gypsy. She is wise and powerful and may know better than anyone how to stop the Shadows."

"Where does she live?"

"I don't think anyone knows for sure," said Enira. "She moves from place to place. That is why Kelgar is the only one who could find her."

"What magic does she possess?"

"I don't know. It's old magic, the sort that is rarely taught now."

Raede looked at Enira's moon pendant. "If I attain all three of the moon pendants, will I have the power to send the Shadows back to the valley."

"I cannot say. Even the Guardians don't know how Aecleton has stolen the moon. Without knowing that, we cannot know how to prevent the Keeper of Darkness from taking the rest of the moons. The pendants increase our magic, but if we are not focusing the magic on the right problem, it may not be worth anything."

"Can the magic I was taught be channeled through the pendants?"

"Yes," said Enira.

Raede smiled. He called to Meclellon who had been standing outside, but not within earshot.

"Take a patrol to Silverwood," said Raede, "and find the woman they call the Silverwood Gypsy."

"She is notoriously difficult to locate, My Lord," said Meclellon.

Raede nodded. "Yes, so I've heard, but find her. The Guardian Kelgar will be with her. Take the tarkweed and bring him to me alive."

"Yes, Sire," said Meclellon. "And what of the gypsy?"

"From what the young Guardian has told me, the gypsy is leading the conspiracy with the Guardians. Kill her."

Kelgar breathed hard as he watched and listened to the conversation through his crystal. "Mordrelina," he gasped. He turned to Milessandra. "I can head them off as soon as they reach the outskirts. There will be few enough that I should have little trouble subduing them."

"What about Enira?" Milessandra protested.

Kelgar sighed not liking the decision he had to make. He gazed through his crystal at the unfortunate Guardian who lay at the mercy of Raede. Kelgar decided against revealing his relationship with the gypsy. Few people understood her, so she had developed the unsavory reputation that always follows things of a mysterious nature, despite the fact that none of it was true. People tend to believe rumors, however, and Kelgar was sure young Milessandra wouldn't understand.

Instead he whispered, "They want the Guardians alive. Enira may not be comfortable, but she will be safe until I return."

"You mean you're just going to leave her there?"

"There are many important matters you don't understand and I've not the time to explain them now. They won't kill Enira, at least not yet. She's too valuable to them. But if I can stop the patrol going to Silverwood, then Raede will have a few less men at his beckon."

"Kelgar!" Milessandra was shocked. "Listen to your own words! You're leaving an innocent woman in Raede's clutches. You think they won't kill her, but you've no way of knowing that for sure. Saving the Guardians is far more important than killing a few of Raede's men. They're going to Silverwood where they'll be no threat to us for quite some time. Here and now is the true danger. Raede has Enira and the Guardians are more important than anyone right now. Your magic will save the world, but only if the three of you are alive. How can you risk the life of a Guardian? How can you risk the fate of the world?"

"Milessandra, I'm not risking Enira's life. I'm saving it. I'm only one man and I've only so much magic. If I go bursting in there now, assuming Raede's guards don't kill me on the spot, Raede will use Enira against me. Right now he doesn't know I'm here in the Temple of Aurora, but if he finds out, he will use Enira's life as a bargaining chip to make me do what he wants. And if I don't, he will surely kill her. Trying to save Enira now will only end with her dead. I can't save her without Notelcea's help, but I can stop the band going to kill the gypsy."

It was the truth, but he knew it wasn't what Milessandra wanted to hear.

Kelgar turned to leave, but Milessandra grabbed his shoulder. "Kelgar, please don't abandon Enira."

"What goes on here?" a voice demanded from the top of the staircase.

Kelgar and Milessandra looked up to see one of Raede's men staring down at them. Apparently Milessandra had been followed.

"I've captured a Guardian," said Milessandra quickly. She pushed Kelgar to the floor to emphasize her point and put her foot on his chest, holding him to the ground. "He snuck in here to try and stop King Raede from restoring order to the land."

The man nodded thoughtfully. "Well done, little maiden. There is more to you than meets the eye." He stepped closer to examine the prize Milessandra was offering him. He smiled at the subdued Guardian. "Tarkweed I expect?"

Milessandra grinned. "No."

She quickly stepped away from Kelgar, ducking as Kelgar threw the man against the wall with a strong beam of light. He fell to the ground unconscious.

"Well done," said Milessandra.

"Thank you," nodded Kelgar. "You as well."

Milessandra smiled. "Just doing my part to help the Guardians."

Kelgar nodded. "Thank you." He paused for a moment. "Bring me a candle."

"A candle?" asked Milessandra. She had been expecting a more difficult task.

"It's the only way to find a Guardian," Kelgar sighed. "If I am to save Enira, I need to find Notelcea."

Milessandra bit her lip for a moment before replying. "What if Notelcea doesn't want to be found?"

# Chapter Fourteen

## ANCIENT MAGIC

Ericahs lay in the darkness pretending to rest, but not a wink of sleep crept over his eyes. He was watching Lismella with the intense gaze of a hawk, following her every move. He knew there was more going on than what Lismella was telling him. One way or another, he was going to find out what.

He had drank none of the water in which he'd seen Lismella mixing the powder, though he had emptied the container when she turned her back. He wanted her to believe he was under its influence, whatever it was. Observing Lismella now, he could see that his ruse was working.

Lismella carefully rose from the fire, not even bothering to check if Ericahs was awake or alive. She wandered almost out of reach of the firelight and turned her back to Ericahs. He couldn't see what she was doing, but he surmised by her movements that it was probably some kind of magic. Then she began to speak. Her voice started out low and rose to a loud roar that echoed through the night.

"Eie-Eigah-Eigah Ha-Eigah Halia-Eigah Tila Halia!" She finished with a shout.

Ericahs was suspicious but intrigued. Lismella was clearly a sorceress of some type. While she didn't seem to hold anything against Ericahs personally, she certainly had large plans whirling around in that innocent looking head of hers. Ericahs could only wonder if he was being unwittingly used to help Lismella gain her own ends. He watched as she came back to the fire.

Lismella did not lay down to sleep as Ericahs had expected. Instead she began to rummage through Ericahs' belongings. She didn't seem the type of person who would rob him, so he couldn't imagine what she was doing. He half contemplated sitting up to let her know he was watching her, but he thought the better of it. He was far too interested in finding out what she was up to.

Lismella kept digging until she found Ericahs' sword. She held it gingerly and brought it back to her side of the fire. She inspected it carefully as though looking for any defects. After being seemingly satisfied that there were none, she rose with the sword in her hands. Judging by her stance and her clumsy movements, Ericahs could tell she was not a swordswoman. Still he had no intentions of startling her while she held his sword and he held nothing.

Lismella swung the sword through the dark sky a few times, eyeing up the blade.

"He has lived by this all his life," she said to herself as she lowered the sword, "perhaps he cannot be separated from it."

Lismella sat down once more and crossed her legs. She held the sword horizontally across her upturned palms and then she began a strange chant.

> *"Out of the darkness comes the light,*
> *A glimmer of hope amidst the night,*
> *To remove what's wrong and return what's right,*
> *To bring back the peace after the fight."*

Lismella turned the sword vertical and chanted again, but louder this time.

> *"Mighty weapon heed the call,*
> *Sacrifice none, but sacrifice all,*
> *Upon the throne in the mighty hall,*
> *Until at last darkness shall fall."*

Lismella held the sword high into the air and this time her chant was almost a shout.

*"Power of day I call upon you,*
*Amidst the darkness to run through,*
*Gather strength for what you must do*
*Make again one what now is two!"*

The sword in Lismella's hands began to glow. It started dull, but continued to increase until its radiance was brilliant. Ericahs' sword almost looked as though it was on fire, as bright as it had been the day it was forged. He held in a gasp of surprise, waiting until the glow of the sword finally died down. The light subsided and Lismella returned the sword to Ericahs' side, all the while unaware that he had lain awake the entire time.

As Lismella turned around to make her way back to her own side of the fire, Ericahs stole a glance at his sword. The blade lay there quietly, looking as it should, but Ericahs did not trust it. Though its outward appearance was normal, Ericahs was no fool. He knew he had just seen Lismella weave a powerful spell into his sword. When Lismella sat down, Ericahs took the opportunity and sat up.

"What were you doing?" he asked.

Though usually skilled at cloaking her emotions, Lismella's surprise at seeing Ericahs sit up was evident. "What are you doing–" she began.

"Alive?" Ericahs suggested before she could finish.

"Awake," Lismella corrected, ignoring his accusatory tone.

"What were you doing?" Ericahs repeated. "What were you doing to my sword?"

"You saw me then?"

"Yes," Ericahs replied, "I saw everything."

Lismella sighed. "Well then I assume you have probably deduced that I am a sorceress. You would be correct in that assumption, for I have magic that is beyond most people's comprehension. You just witnessed me using it on your blade."

"I gathered as much, but why?"

"I told you before that you could not kill the Shadows with a sword, but I think I may have been mistaken. I realized that the sword is such a part of you, it might be the only way for you to face the Shadows. Of course no ordinary sword was going to stand up against Aecleton."

"So you put magic within it?"

"Yes."

"What sort of magic?"

"It's long and complicated, but it will give you the power you need."

"Is it the same type of magic the Guardians of the Light use?"

Lismella gave a small laugh as if she felt the magic of the Guardians to be inferior to her own. "Far from it, Ericahs. There are not many who could perform that spell, for much of the ancient knowledge has been lost. There are so few now who remember the magic of old."

"Why?"

"I don't know, Ericahs. I have often wondered that myself. Perhaps with the coming of the Lumidian, people were content to let the Guardians bear the magic to protect them. Perhaps they no longer felt it necessary to pass down ancient spells when the Guardians had so much new magic of their own. Whatever the reason, the magic I just displayed is very rare now."

Ericahs nodded in suspicion. "And is knowledge of poison part of that ancient magic of which you speak?"

"What are you talking about?"

"I saw your white powder," Ericahs explained. "Why are you trying to kill me?"

Ericahs knew full well that Lismella hadn't been trying to kill him. He was simply hoping that by being blunt, he would back her into a corner where she might reveal her true motives for drugging him.

"If I wanted to kill you," said Lismella, "you'd already be dead."

"Then what were you trying to do to me?"

"It doesn't matter, for clearly it didn't work."

"I didn't drink it this evening because I saw you putting powder in my water. What was it?"

"I told you it doesn't matter."

"Tell me, Lismella. I have a right to know."

"Ericahs, isn't it obvious?" asked Lismella. "It was a sleeping powder."

"A sleeping powder?" It suddenly made perfect sense to Ericahs as he heard her explanation. This had been the first night in several that he had not been exhausted. He surmised she must have been drugging him since she'd first met him.

"Where did you get it?" he asked.

"I am a sorceress, Ericahs. Enchanted powders are not something that the magically inclined find difficult to come by."

"But why, Lismella? Why? Why bother to train me and put magic in my sword only to numb my wits with a sleeping potion?"

Lismella took a breath, unsure how much she wanted to reveal. "Because this situation is deeper than anything you could possibly imagine. There are some things I cannot show you, things you are not meant to see, things that are for the eyes of magicians alone. I knew you were too stubborn to let me do that which I needed to do on my own, so I gave you the potion. It was the only way to keep you with me so I could continue to train you for the work you must do."

"Then what were you doing in the trees before you spelled my sword?"

Lismella looked at Ericahs sharply. "That is not your business. It does not involve you, and you've no need to know about it. The only knowledge you need is the knowledge I am willing to disclose to you, and that I already have."

"I'll make up my own mind about what I need to know. I'll not be your puppet to use for your own ends, Lismella."

"You can make up your own stubborn mind, but I'll not tell you anything I see unfit to reveal."

Ericahs fingered his sword. "Give me one good reason why I shouldn't run you through right now. One reason why I shouldn't have killed you the moment I met you."

"Because you know that if you try, I will make sure you spend the rest of your days as a slug crawling across the forest floor." Lismella said the words calmly, but Ericahs could hear in her undertones that it was not an idle threat. He released his grip on his sword as she continued. "And because you still need me to teach you how to stop Aecleton. If you kill me, I assure you the entire world will fall to the Shadows."

"Who are you really?" Ericahs demanded. "Tell me the truth."

"You want to know who I am, Ericahs? I'll tell you." Lismella sighed. "I am the last living person to have ever seen the sun."

# Chapter Fifteen

## SEDITION

"It's strange. I can't find Notelcea at all," said Kelgar looking into his candle, "almost as if something is intentionally shielding her from my search." He sighed and looked at Milessandra. "You may be right. Perhaps Notelcea does not want to be found."

"What is she hiding from?" asked Milessandra in wonder. "And what is she hiding from us?"

"I don't know," said Kelgar, "but I'm not entirely sure she's the one who is hiding."

"What do you mean?"

"Notelcea is eldest Guardian, and even if Raede truly doesn't know where she is, someone else might, someone with perhaps the same mindset as the king."

"I still don't understand."

"If someone wants to manipulate the present situation with the Shadows, the eldest Guardian would be their first choice. She would know more about the light than most, with the exception of perhaps the Silverwood Gypsy and some of the older townsfolk. That's why Raede wants to find her and I so badly, because we're older than Enira and thus have more knowledge."

The flame in Kelgar's candle suddenly began to flicker, weaving from side to side as if blown by some invisible draft, and yet there was none. The air was still.

"Kelgar, look," Milessandra whispered.

Kelgar watched the candle carefully, squinting his eyes as the flame grew smaller and smaller until it suddenly burst forth from its melted wax recesses in a blinding blue radiance. Milessandra gasped, stifling a scream, not knowing what was happening. Then as quickly as the light had appeared, it was suddenly gone.

"What was that!" Milessandra whispered harshly.

"It was Notelcea," Kelgar replied. "Or at least a signal from her."

"What does it mean?"

"It means she's still alive. Perhaps she is in hiding or perhaps she is danger. I cannot know for sure, but she knows I'm looking for her. She sent the blue light to tell me she is still alive."

Milessandra stared at the candle in Kelgar's hand. "Why didn't she tell you where she was?"

"Maybe she can't," Kelgar replied. "Perhaps that was the only spell she had time to send. It is possible that someone has taken her prisoner the same way Raede took Enira. Be that as it may, I don't know where she is and I don't know if I'm going to be able find where she is…at least not yet." He handed the candle to Milessandra and turned away.

"Wait, where are you going?"

"I have to stop Raede's men from killing the gypsy. Wait for me here. When I return we shall devise a plan to free Enira without getting her killed in the process. We will have to do it without Notelcea. Either she is hiding or she is already someone's prisoner. In any instance, she is not here to help us."

Milessandra looked sharply at Kelgar. "Maybe we should devise a plan now. I don't want them to kill the gypsy, but isn't her life and the escape of a few of Raede's men a fair price to trade for Enira's life?"

"This is beyond Guardians and fair trades, Milessandra."

"Kelgar! The gypsy can probably defend herself if her powers are as great as legend says. Besides, what is she to you? Just some crazy woman who lives alone in the woodlands and–"

"She's my mother, Milessandra!"

Milessandra stepped back. "What?"

"Well, not literally," Kelgar explained. "The gypsy did not physically give birth to me, but hers was the face I saw over my cradle. She raised me from the day I came into this world because the mother of my body had abandoned me."

"Who was that?"

Kelgar sighed. "That is a very long story, one that I don't have time to recount to you now."

Milessandra nodded. "Then I'm coming with you. I can help you."

Kelgar shook his head. "You'll not be able to leave the temple."

"Why not?"

"Raede has sealed the entire temple with magic from Enira's pendant."

Milessandra shook her head. "How can you know that?"

"I'm a Guardian, Milessandra, I can feel it when he uses one of the pendants. Enira told him he could channel his magic through her pendant and that was all he needed to know."

"Can you feel it when Notelcea uses hers?"

Kelgar nodded. "Yes, when she channels her magic through the pendant."

"What do you mean *her* magic?"

"Not all the Guardians were children of gypsies. Notelcea is a fair sorceress even without the magic of the Guardians. True sorcerers are something there are too few of today. Most of them are like Raede; twisted and corrupt."

"So how do you plan to get out of the temple then?"

Kelgar smiled. "Like water through sand." He fingered his own pendant. "Raede used a pendant to create the shield; I can use one to slip through it."

"Why don't you just use yours to take it down?"

Kelgar shook his head at her ridiculous notion. "I might at well shout aloud for all to hear. Taking down the shield he made would bring the same amount of attention and would be a quick way to place Enira in danger. I'll not take it down until we are actually ready to rescue Enira."

"What should I do while you're gone?" asked Milessandra.

"Just stay alive. Keep doing as you've been doing, making yourself seen enough, but not too much. I may need your help when I return."

Milessandra nodded. "How long will it take you to return with the gypsy?"

"It takes two days just to reach Silverwood on foot, and however long it may take me to find Mordrelina herself."

"Mordrelina?"

"The gypsy."

Milessandra looked toward the stairwell. "What if someone should happen to–"

Milessandra's words were suddenly cut off by the sound of trumpets. Even in the deep recesses of the secret room in which they stood, Milessandra and Kelgar knew it could be no other sound.

"The trumpets!" Milessandra breathed. "What could be happening?"

Kelgar shook his head. "I don't know."

He gazed into his crystal once more, but he could see nothing except the empty wall of the seventh tier. Something was wrong and he knew it. He looked at Milessandra not wanting to speak the worries on his mind.

"Enira's gone," he said.

"What do you mean gone?"

"She's no longer in the room with the crystal," said Kelgar. "They must have taken her somewhere else."

"Where?"

"I don't know," he admitted.

The trumpets sounded again, louder this time, despite the fact that they were outside of the temple. Milessandra looked up quickly, her fear beginning to show her face. She knew something was wrong just as Kelgar did.

"I'll see what I can find out," said Kelgar trying to reassure Milessandra. "Wait here. I'll be back in a moment."

Kelgar turned to the wall, carefully reopening the hidden door. He gingerly touched the invisible shield that Raede had surrounded the temple with. It did not so much as blink. Kelgar smiled knowing he would be completely unnoticed as he slid through Raede's shield.

Once outside Kelgar resumed his shadowy skulking, cautiously making his way around to the front of the temple. A crowd had gathered and Raede was out front. He appeared to be giving a speech, but Kelgar was too far away to hear the words. Ever so carefully, keeping to the darkest corners of the grounds, Kelgar crept as close as he dared. Once within earshot, Kelgar began to hear what Raede was saying to the gathering of people.

"Who can say how long the Guardians have been working against me," Raede bellowed. "Who can say how long they've been using their fine words to try and poison the people against the royals. They seek the power for themselves."

Kelgar looked at the crowd hanging on Raede's every word. He shook head. They were mere sheep following a shepherd, so easy fooled by Raede's charming lies.

"Not only have the Guardians lost control of the light," Raede continued, "but they may even be in league with the very demons who killed my brother! The shadow demons who stole our very king. Even now, the one Guardian who is still at the temple has outright defied me."

A murmur rippled through the crowd.

Raede raised his voice. "That is nothing less than sedition! If there is one thing we cannot afford in this time of chaos, it is sedition. Such will only succeed in giving the Shadows a stronger holding. We must work together and not fight amongst ourselves or we shall all fall prey to those dark creatures of night. The Guardians seem to think differently, however."

Raede signaled and one of his soldiers dragged Enira out into the open, her wrists tightly bound with what appeared to be tarkweed.

"This is the face of treason," said Raede pointing at Enira. "This is the face of the one would defy the king's own orders. Upon my arrival at the temple this young Guardian turned on me almost immediately. She tried to attack me with her sorceress ways while I was having a mere conversation with her."

It was all Kelgar could do to keep himself from attacking Raede at that very moment. He knew he couldn't, however, not as long as they had Enira. One false move by Kelgar, and Raede would surely kill the young Guardian.

"Even after we had subdued her, she still refused to give us information that would save Argentum. Apparently she feels that information is privy only to herself and the other Guardians. And those other Guardians have not shown their faces since the moon was first taken! The moment Selene disappeared, the elder Guardians fled the temple, disappearing into hiding. They took with them all their knowledge that might protect us, and even now are too coward to show themselves.

"I am a lenient lord, but the one thing I cannot withstand is betrayal. That is exactly what the Guardians have done. They have betrayed us all. Let it be known throughout the land that the Guardians are now outlaws seeking only to have us all destroyed by the Shadows. Let it also be known that whoever brings the other Guardians to us will be well rewarded. Together we shall bring them to justice and force them to give us their hidden knowledge so that we might not perish at the hand of Aecleton."

Raede's words seemed to get a thrill out of the crowd. Kelgar wasn't sure, but he thought he almost saw the beginning of a smile appearing at the corners of Raede's evil mouth.

Oblivious to Kelgar's presence, Raede concluded his speech. "And finally let it be known that we shall not tolerate anyone who seeks to help outlaws. The Guardians are now the enemy of the good people of Argentum. Should anyone help the Guardians in their plot to destroy us, we must consider them our enemies as well. We must work together, my people, so that we may survive these dark nights. Anyone found guilty of joining the Guardians in their sedition will be executed."

Raede nodded his head at one of his men. "It will begin with Enira."

The man Raede had motioned to nodded back and gave the signal to his waiting soldiers. They came out fully armed with their bows carried proudly, quivers ready to be used. Kelgar's heart jumped in his throat. He hadn't been expecting this move on Raede's part.

He had thought Raede would feel Enira too valuable to kill, but it now appeared he was wrong. Raede was going to kill Enira and her death seemed to be frightfully imminent. Whatever information Raede had hoped to glean from the young Guardian, he must have gotten it, for it now seemed that he felt her useless enough to be rid of.

Of course there was another possibility, but Kelgar didn't even want to think about it. He knew that Raede could simply be using Enira to flush out the remaining Guardians. Kelgar hadn't been wrong when he'd told Milessandra that Enira was valuable to Raede, he'd simply wrong in the manner of value. He had thought the value would be in Enira's knowledge of the light. But now he was realizing that nothing could be more valuable than a young Guardian to use as bait against the elder, more experienced Guardians.

Unfortunately Kelgar knew Raede's plan would probably work. Even if it was merely a ruse to draw out the other Guardians, Kelgar knew his own heart was too soft not to take the bait. He would have to show himself to save Enira and he was sure Notelcea would too. That was assuming Notelcea was even close enough in the vicinity to know what was going on.

Kelgar had received nothing more than a light flicker merely telling him that Notelcea was alive. It didn't tell him where she was or how long she'd been there. She could have sent that light flicker from the other side of the Valley of the Shadows for all Kelgar knew. It was one more reason Kelgar might have to reveal himself to Raede's requests. He might have to tell Raede the truth that no one knew where Notelcea was, if only to prevent Raede from harming Enira.

Kelgar looked straight at Raede and suddenly knew that it was no ruse. Kelgar couldn't believe what was happening. Raede was going to kill Enira. Raede was actually going to kill her that very moment. As quickly as he could without being seen, Kelgar charged back to the secret door, sliding through Raede's shield. Milessandra met him on the other side.

"What happened?" she asked.

"I think I have gravely underestimated Raede," Kelgar panted.

# Chapter Sixteen

## MORBID CONFESSIONS

It was Ericahs' turn to let his carefully guarded emotions show upon his face. He stared blankly at Lismella. "What?" He couldn't think of anything else say.

"I am only the only living person who has ever seen the sun," Lismella repeated. "And I am the only one who might know how to bring it back."

Ericahs shook his head. "That's impossible. The sun was lost hundreds of years ago. You would have to be at least–"

"Three hundred and sixty-six years old. The Guardians of the Light built the Lumidian three hundred and twenty-nine years ago. I was thirty-seven at the time and I've scarcely aged a day since then."

"Why? How?"

"I don't know, Ericahs. I've often wondered that myself. Perhaps in my workings with magic, a spell of some good fortune has found its way to maintain my appearance. All I do know is that even the Guardians don't have the knowledge I have, because they weren't there hundreds of years ago when the sun disappeared...I was."

"Then why wasn't it your name in the prophecy?"

"I'm not a warrior, I'm a sorceress. I have the knowledge; you have the sword."

Ericahs stood in silence for a moment. It was stretching well beyond the bounds of his imagination to believe that the apparently thirty-something woman sitting before him was in fact hundreds of years old. Not only that, she had actually seen the sun, something that had been gone so long the rest of the world could only wonder if it had ever been more than a legend to begin with. Ericahs' conscious mind didn't know how to believe her, but it also had no reason to doubt her. Everything she was telling him made sense, despite the fact that it was still completely illogical.

"You have truly seen the sun that is little more than a myth now?" Ericahs asked again.

Lismella nodded. "Yes, Ericahs, I was dancing in the light of the sun long before your grandparents' grandparents had even been born." She looked away through the trees as though remembering some distant memory.

Ericahs let out his breath still unable to take it all in. It was as if he was entering into the realm of some ancient mystery.

"What was it like before the night covered the land forever?" he asked at last. "What was it like before the Shadows?"

"The Shadows were always here, Ericahs." Lismella turned and looked at the man as though she was surprised he didn't already know. "They were here long before anyone can remember."

"What?" Ericahs shook his head in confusion. "But if that's true, how did they become so dangerous?"

"Aecleton has played a large role in their strength, and they grow stronger in the gathering darkness, but they were here long before the Lumidian." Lismella took a deep breath. "The Shadows are nothing more than reflections of our own deepest and darkest fears. The Shadows are fear itself, the fear that lies within us all. That is something that can never be destroyed, only controlled, until we learn how to let love overcome fear. There is no time before the Shadows for they were not created by the Lumidian. The Lumidian was created in effort to drive out the Shadows."

Ericahs was confused. "I admit I'm not a scholar, but I had always thought the Lumidian was created to save the light of a dying sun. To ensure that the world would not be completely covered in darkness. I thought that's how the Shadows were born."

Lismella shook her head. "The sun wasn't dying, Ericahs; we killed it."

"Why?"

"Because we were frightened people trying to erase the night. It was a dark time then, despite the sun's warm light. The Shadows had long been getting stronger. For hundreds of years before my time the strength of the Shadows would wax and wane with the fears of the people. Even then fear was a dangerous thing. If a person believes in their fear, it becomes real to them, and if it is real to them, it has the real power to harm them. Fear can drive a person to insanity or even kill them if they believe strongly enough in it. Once a person's fear subsides, however, the fear no longer holds power over them.

"Something more happened three hundred years ago; a series of events coincided that caused the world to change irreversibly. The queen who sat upon the throne at that time was a ruler not unlike Raede is now. She ruled cruelly, and with an iron fist. She preyed upon her people, keeping them in a state of fear in order to gain their submission. The queen was aware of the Shadows' presence. She would have people killed in secret and then the blame the Shadows in order to keep the citizens frightened and compliant. That is what gave the Shadows their great power.

"The more fear the people held, the stronger the Shadows became. The stronger the Shadows became, the more the people feared the Shadows. This in turn only gave the Shadows more strength. Fear breeds more fear and since the Shadows are fear themselves, it consequently created a stronger force of Shadows. Eventually even the royals found that they were not immune to the power of the Shadows. The people had let their fear grow until it was real enough to hold control over them.

"The nights became sheer terror. In those days the sun rose in the morning and set in the night, and then the world was enclosed in darkness for many hours until the sun rose again. The moon was only full once every thirty nights. The rest of the time the Shadows had free reign over the land. Only the completely fearless were protected from their torment."

"What do you mean the moon was only full once every thirty nights?"

Lismella smiled realizing that Ericahs was completely ignorant of the old world. After more than three hundred years of darkness, the old world was little more than legend now.

"The world was very different then, Ericahs," she explained. "You know the world as it is now. Now rain falls often from wispy clouds and crops can be sown whenever a farmer desires because, though they grow more slowly, they grow all year. In the old days, crops grew faster, but they had to be saved for the months when nothing would grow at all.

"We did not have five moons then. We had one sun that rose in the day, brighter than the five moons combined. It was so bright it could hurt your eyes to look at and would burn your skin red if you stayed out under its rays too long. But the lands grew dark each night as the sun slipped beneath the horizon. The moon would appear at night, but it was not always full. It would wax and wane over a repetitive cycle of near thirty days. There were thirteen full moons in a year.

"We had seasons then too, for everything we did revolved around the sun. The days were longest and warmest in summer and that was when the plants grew best. Midsummer's Eve was the longest day of the year. We would celebrate on that day, giving thanks for the hours of light that would protect us from the Shadows. Even now people still celebrate the day out of tradition, a distant memory of the forgotten past. In the season we called winter, the hours of darkness were longer than the hours of light. It was so cold that rain would fall from the sky as ice and cover the ground in white. You would be amazed to see how thick the clouds could grow then, even thicker than Aecleton can make them now."

Lismella sighed. "And of course in those days the Shadows had sway enough to comb the lands every single night. Only the full moon could keep them away and give us peace one out of every thirty days. That was how the idea for the Lumidian first came into being. There was no way to create more light, but the sorcerers of the land knew there might be a way to disperse the light of the sun more evenly. Instead of having bright light followed by utter darkness, they decided to break the light of the sun into five moons so the land would always be covered by a full moon's glow."

"And you saw it all happen?" asked Ericahs.

Lismella nodded. "Yes, I was there. I watched as the sun was darkened forever. All the sorcerers in the land were gathered together. There were one hundred and twenty-one sorcerers in all. They pulled down the sun into the magical Lumidian they had created to forever ensure moonlight in the land and banish the Shadows from our world.

"Of course the sorcerers could not completely destroy the Shadows. The demons were here long before we came, and no one could change that. But with our new-found source of constant illumination, the Shadows were relegated to a dark, cavernous valley beyond Silverwood."

"The Valley of the Shadows," Ericahs breathed.

Lismella nodded. "When it all was over, the wisest and most powerful among the sorcerers were chosen to be the Guardians of the Light. There were three at the beginning just as there are now. There are always three. They built the temple and named it Aurora to remind us all of what had been given up to ensure protection from the demons. We sacrificed the dawn because we feared the night."

"And were you one of them?" asked Ericahs. "Were you one of the hundred sorcerers who helped seal the sun in the Lumidian?"

"Yes, I was one of the many that night so long ago. Who can say now if it was a mistake? Darkness is a part of the world and perhaps we did more harm than good in trying to change that. Light and darkness are symbiotic, they need each other to survive. Dark shadows are made by light and light cannot live without darkness. That is the essence of light." Lismella dropped her voice almost to a whisper, as though reciting some long ago learned text. "Without darkness there can be no light, for there would be nothing to illuminate."

Ericahs had forgotten to breathe as he listened to her. The truth about the mysterious woman who had come out of nowhere to claim him as the world's savior was finally beginning to be revealed. He was certain that information she was now divulging was something that had not fallen on the ears of many in the last three hundred years.

"We tried to control the world and now the world fights to control us. We didn't understand it then, and humans fear most greatly that which they do not understand. If only we knew then that darkness is not always bad and neither is light always good." Her voice trailed off into the distance as though regretting some terrible action of the past.

"What do you mean?" asked Ericahs.

Lismella shook her head. "Nothing. It doesn't matter anymore."

Ericahs glanced up at the sky. A thin layer of clouds was rolling in as raindrops began to fall in the silence. It seemed so natural, as though it could never possibly harm anyone. With all the talk of Shadows and fear, Ericahs could not help but wonder if it were all simply an illusion. What if Aecleton was not a threat? What if people only perceived the Keeper of Darkness to be a danger?

"Even if Aecleton does destroy the light, we will still have torches and candles to protect ourselves," said Ericahs.

Lismella looked sharply at Ericahs. "No! Aecleton is not just some imagined fiend. Aecleton is real. Though courage is the one weapon that can be used against the Keeper, the power of the darkness is still there. The more moons that are taken, the stronger Aecleton and the Shadows become. If the Keeper manages to take all the moons, the darkness will be irreversible. In complete darkness, no amount of firelight will save you."

Ericahs jumped to his feet. "Then why don't you run to Guardians now and tell them what you know? Why don't you help them release the sun?"

"Ericahs, it took one hundred and twenty-one sorcerers with more power than you could ever imagine to capture the sun. Do you really believe that three Guardians and myself are going to be able to undo all that in one night? We changed the world, Ericahs. We changed the seasons; we changed everything. We can't just open the bottle and let the sun out. Releasing that much energy so quickly is more dangerous than you will ever know. It would probably rip the entire world apart. It's like a wine that has been fermenting for too long. When you remove the cork, it explodes out of its hold. Now envision that as an entire sun.

"As long as the Shadows are alive, releasing the sun would destroy the balance too quickly. And with the sun free, there would once again be almost thirty days in between full moons. Each night the Shadows would hunt people in the darkness. With Aecleton behind them, it would only be a short time before they managed to overrun everything. The Shadows must be stopped before we can even think of toppling the Lumidian."

"But I thought you said the Shadows were always here, so how could they be stopped?"

"It's possible that they can't be, but either way, Aecleton must be stopped or releasing the sun is pointless. And..." Lismella hesitated, "...and there is still one small glimmer of hope. You see when Aecleton rose from the darkness, it entwined itself with the Shadows. For better or for worse, Aecleton's fate is now irreversibly bound up with theirs. As long as Aecleton is part of the Shadows, what happens to one will in turn befall the other. The Keeper draws strength from the Shadows and the Shadows draw strength from the Keeper. Because Aecleton can feed upon light, the Shadows have begun to do so as well, but as such, they are completely dependent upon the Keeper for their sustenance. If we can kill Aecleton, we may be able to destroy the Shadows as well. Perhaps we might finally see some good come from the foolish mistakes of the past."

Ericahs had the strange feeling that Lismella wasn't just talking about the Lumidian as she referred to the foolish mistakes of the past.

"The Keeper has grown too strong and either it must die or we must die," said Lismella. "We can no longer exist together."

"But where did Aecleton come from?"

"That is an answer people have spent the last three hundred years searching for. No one knows, Ericahs, just as no one knows why Selene is misshapen. It's something that happened just after the Lumidian was built. I doubt if even the original Guardians knew why. Perhaps it was something the Guardians themselves did."

"Why do you always blame the Guardians for everything?"

Lismella pierced him with her blue eyes. "Whom else is there to blame? The Guardians are the very reason I guard my secrecy so deeply. Do not let your faith within them be misplaced. They are still just men and woman, the same as you and I. They are not all seeing and they are not all powerful. If I told them all the things I know, they would think me an evil witch and kill me without giving me a moment to explain myself."

"You have a rather cynical way of looking at the world."

"I have looked at the world long enough to know that it's true. I can't trust anyone with the knowledge that I have."

"Then why trust me?"

"I don't. I have only told you what you needed to know. The rest is mine. I have the knowledge and you have the sword. The magic I imbued within its blade shall allow you to strike the beam of light into the heart of the darkness."

"And at last kill the man that took my family," said Ericahs looking at his sword with determination.

Lismella looked at Ericahs strangely. "What makes you so sure the Keeper is a man?"

# Chapter Seventeen

## ESCAPE

"We need to raise the alarm!" Kelgar panted as he reentered the temple through the secret door. "Now!"

"What do you want me to do?" asked Milessandra.

"Touch it," said Kelgar. "I need you to touch the light field as a diversion while I make ready to grab Enira in the chaos."

Milessandra nodded. "How long."

"I need to be right up beside the front door. When you think I am there, touch it."

"Good luck."

"No, we're going to need more than luck," said Kelgar. "We're going to need magic and plenty of it." He slipped back out through Raede's force field.

Milessandra stood alone, counting the minutes she knew it would take Kelgar to reach the front of the temple. Other than having her sound the alarm, Milessandra had no idea what Kelgar was planning to do. She could only hope it wasn't too late to save Enira. As the seconds passed, she made ready to touch the field.

Kelgar stood amidst the darkness in front of the temple, slowly making his way toward Enira. He could see her; he was almost there. The alarm hadn't sounded. It should have sounded by now. Kelgar looked around, but neither Raede nor his men gave any indication that Milessandra had been caught. The archers raised their bows at Enira. Why hadn't the alarm sounded yet?

117

Suddenly there was a scurrying of soldiers running out of the palace toward Raede. Kelgar smiled. This was the moment he'd been waiting for. Waving his arm he quickly extinguished all fire and obscured the light of the moon.

Kelgar could hear of the screams of panic in the confusion around him, but he paid it no heed. His only thought was to get Enira to safety. He quickly scaled the front of the temple and released Enira from her bonds.

"There!" one of the archers shouted, letting go of his arrow.

Kelgar tried to pull Enira out of the way, but he was too late. The archer's arrow sunk itself deep into Enira's skin. She cried out in pain as Kelgar dragged her down the steps of the temple.

Once he was at the bottom, Kelgar glanced quickly at Enira and was relieved to see that the arrow was only in her shoulder. While it no doubt pained her, it was likely that it had not hit anything vital. The important thing now would be to remove the arrow before Enira bled to death, and then hope the wound did not become infected.

The citizens of Argentum ran back and forth in the chaotic darkness Kelgar had created. They did not know it was a simple trick of the Guardians. As far as they knew, the Keeper of Darkness itself had descended upon them to wreak havoc on their lives.

Someone banged into Kelgar in the darkness. Enira winced as the man jostled the arrow in her already painful shoulder. The man looked up and recognized both Kelgar and Enira.

"It's the Guardians!" the man shouted to those around him. "Get them!"

Even in the darkness the people began to swarm like insects toward the sound of the man's voice. Kelgar lit the man up like a torch. In the confusion and darkness, the people mistook the glowing man for a Guardian. Kelgar slipped away unnoticed, bearing Enira's weight upon him. He was well out of the way before the people realized they'd been fooled.

Kelgar chose a spot in the trees where he knew they would be unseen. He waved his hand in the direction of the temple and the moon's light reemerged from the darkness. The people were still running in circles like a group of hornets whose nest had just been disturbed. Raede was nowhere to be seen. Presumably he had retreated into the safety of the temple's confines to begin plotting his next move.

"Has the entire world gone crazy?" Kelgar muttered under his breath.

"They seemed so willing to turn on us," said Enira in a shaky voice.

"They're frightened, Enira," Kelgar replied. "People do crazy things when they're frightened; even try to kill Guardians. Raede is remaining calm, so they are looking to him."

"Kelgar?" a voice sounded behind them.

Kelgar pulled a knife and turned around to see Milessandra.

"It's just me," said Milessandra quickly.

"What are you doing here?" asked Kelgar.

"I came to find you after raising the alarm," Milessandra replied. She was confused as to why Kelgar seemed so put out by her presence.

"Good," said Kelgar relaxing a bit. "I just wasn't expecting you to find us so easily. I hope you're the only one." He resheathed his knife.

"I wasn't followed," Milessandra reassured him.

Kelgar nodded and looked at Enira. "She's safe, but she's wounded. Can you take care of her?"

"Of course," said Milessandra, "but where are you going?"

Kelgar didn't answer.

"You're going after the gypsy aren't you?" asked Milessandra.

Kelgar didn't answer.

"You should go, Kelgar," said Enira.

"It may already been too late," said Kelgar.

"I'll be fine," Enira pressed. "You need to save the gypsy. She's rumored to have powerful magic. It may be power that we can use."

Kelgar still seemed to be hesitating.

"Don't feel guilty about leaving me," said Enira. "The kitchen maiden can take care of me." She motioned to Milessandra.

"A fine way to talk about your cousin," Kelgar chided.

Enira looked confused.

"I told him," Milessandra confessed.

"Oh," said Enira looking relieved. "Then that's all the more reason you know you're leaving me in capable hands."

"Very well, maybe you're right," Kelgar agreed. "Raede has receded to the temple and we've no way to get at him. It's nearly impermeable and we can't use the secret door anymore. They'll be watching it."

"What about your moon pendant?" asked Milessandra. "Can't you just get into the temple again with that?"

Kelgar shook his head. "I'm afraid I lost it in the confusion while trying to save Enira. It's a loss for us, but at least Raede can't get his hands on it either. Raede can be dealt with later. Right now the Shadows are the real threat and there is not a moment to lose. With each passing night they grow in strength and soon we'll be unable to defeat them. I'll save the gypsy and then meet with Notelcea. Together we can stop the Shadows and bring down Raede as well. His power over the people will be greatly weakened once their fear of the Shadows has been abated."

"Where is Notelcea?" asked Enira.

"You don't remember do you?" asked Kelgar.

Enira shook her head.

"Poor child, they must have hurt you more than we thought. I sent Notelcea to the palace library just before Raede sieged the temple."

"I thought you didn't know where she was?" asked Milessandra, feeling somewhat betrayed.

"I didn't until just recently," Kelgar admitted. "She never went to the library."

"That must be why Raede kept trying to tell me no one knew where she was," said Enira. "If she didn't go to the library, then where is she?"

Kelgar smiled. "She's gone east to Delarue," he replied. "I've only just received a message from her telling me so."

"Delarue?" asked Enira. "That's nothing but a wasteland and a seven day's ride besides."

"Yes, it's a seven day's ride," Kelgar agreed, "but it's far more than a wasteland. There is a large group of powerful sorcerers who live there. Notelcea is enlisting their help and they'll soon return to storm the temple and remove Raede. As long as Raede doesn't come upon them in surprise, they'll be safe. Everything will go as planned."

Enira smiled. "I am glad to hear it. Go now and save the gypsy. We'll keep watch for Notelcea."

"I shall. I'll return as soon as I can." Kelgar spoke more to Milessandra than Enira. "I plan to steal a horse as soon as I am on the outskirts of the kingdom. Raede's soldiers will have horses and I'll need one if I wish to catch them. I'm sorry I have to leave, but it's something that has to be done."

Milessandra nodded, not sure if there was some additional message there that she was missing. She watch as Kelgar slunk away, moving expertly in and out of the darkness like a true street child. She only hoped he was doing the right thing. She turned her attention to her cousin.

Very carefully she broke off the end of the arrow. She tore off a piece of her dress and wrapped it around Enira's shoulder. "That will have to do for now until we find somewhere to hide."

"You have the touch of a healer," said Enira. "Well done. My thanks to you."

"Come on," said Milessandra, "We've got to get you someplace safe."

"Oh, I'm sure I'll be fine," Enira replied, her demeanor changing slightly. "It's not the first time I've been struck by an arrow."

"It's not?"

Enira smiled a strange smile.

"Enira?"

Enira picked up a large branch and began inspecting it, ignoring Milessandra's questions.

"What's wrong with you?"

Holding the branch in one hand, Enira reached into her dress and pulled out a moon shaped object. "Do you recognize this?"

"Kelgar's pendant!" Milessandra gasped.

Enira swung the branch, hitting Milessandra hard against the side of the head. "Did you really think we'd make it that easy?" Enira hissed with a grin.

# Chapter Eighteen

# FEAR

Ericahs awoke to a sensation of heat washing over his body. He sat up with a start. It was a feeling he knew all too well. Many years of living alone on the edge of the law had sharpened his senses well beyond those of ordinary men. He was particularly adept at picking up another nearby presence. That was the feeling now awakening him from his slumber.

Ericahs glanced over at Lismella lying beside the fire. She seemed to be honestly asleep and Ericahs knew it was not her presence he'd felt. There someone else. There was someone out there amidst the trees, probably watching him at that very moment.

Ericahs felt the hair on the back of his next prickle and he knew that whoever, or whatever, it was out there was moving in closer. Very slowly he began to slide his sword out of its sheath. He was so quiet Lismella did not even stir. Keeping his eyes glued to the grove in the surrounding darkness, he wrapped his fingers around the cold steel of his hilt and jumped to his feet.

No sooner had he done so when a darkly cloaked figure struck at him with its own sword. Ericahs' quick reflexes parried the blow, but he quickly realized that he was no match for his opponent. The cloaked figure's skills of swordsmanship were far superior to those of his own.

Lismella, having been awakened by the commotion, stood watching. She wasn't sure whether to stop the fight or let it progress. Perhaps Ericahs needed the latter. Seeing the cloaked figure beginning to get the better of Ericahs, however, Lismella made to interfere.

"No!" said Ericahs quickly, continuing his fight.

The cloaked swordsman seized advantage of Ericahs' moment of distraction to strike a hard blow, knocking Ericahs' sword from his hands. Even though Ericahs' attention had been elsewhere, he was still shocked. Having lived by his sword for most of his life, there were few people who could vanquish him.

The swordsman held the point of his sword to Ericahs' neck and turned to Lismella. "Move and he dies."

The voice was firm, but it was not that of a man. It was a female's voice, one that Ericahs knew well.

"Ikeara?" he asked in disbelief.

"Ericahs?" The girl replied.

She lowered her sword and pulled down her hood, letting her long, blond hair blow in the night wind. She was as surprised to find Ericahs as he had been to find her. Perhaps even more so.

"What are you doing here?" Ericahs demanded.

"Guarding Renieman," Ikeara replied matter-of-factly, referring to one of the nearby villages. "What are *you* doing here?"

"I…uh…I'm just…" Ericahs stumbled over his words trying to come up with a good excuse that did not disclose too much of the truth. He noticed Lismella, still there staring at the two of them, and quickly directed the conversation town her. "This is Lismella," he explained.

Ikeara nodded at the sorceress.

"Lismella, this is Ikeara," said Ericahs. "She is an old…friend of mine."

He looked back at Ikeara, knowing that the look did not go unnoticed by Lismella. He knew Lismella could see that Ikeara was a bit more than an "old friend." He knew he wouldn't even need to explain it to Lismella. He was sure she could practically read the entire story in his body language.

"Perhaps it was a bit more than friendship," Lismella replied coldly.

Ericahs glared at her.

"Why are you wandering around this part of the woods at this hour?" asked Ikeara, not noticing the exchange between Lismella and Ericahs. "Are you mad?"

Ericahs looked at Lismella.

"You may as well tell her the truth," said Lismella.

"Very well. We're on our way to destroy the Keeper," Ericahs admitted.

"The Keeper of Darkness?" asked Ikeara in disbelief. "You *are* mad."

"I'm not crazy, Ikeara. If we don't stop Aecleton he'll destroy the entire world," Ericahs defended himself.

"And what's it to you? You've never been one to take another's noble cause."

"It's different this time. You know Aecleton took my family; this is my chance for revenge. And there is a prophecy that said I would be the one to–"

"A prophecy? Really?" Ikeara wasn't convinced. She motioned to Lismella. "And I suppose she told you that."

"Yes, but–"

"What happened to you, Ericahs? This doesn't sound like you at all. Believing some strange woman and–"

"She's seen the sun, Ikeara."

"What?" Ikeara glanced at Lismella again, who stood stoic, betraying no emotion in her face. Ikeara shook her head. "She's not old enough."

"I am older than I look," said Lismella joining the conversation.

"Yes and Aecleton has gilded fairy wings," Ikeara scoffed sarcastically. She turned back to Ericahs. "How can you really believe this?"

"I don't know. I just do." Ericahs couldn't explain why he believed Lismella either. Her stories were exactly the sort of thing he wouldn't believe, but Lismella was just different. Maybe it was simply that when he looked into her eyes, they looked back at him with three hundred years worth of wisdom. He didn't know why he believed Lismella, he just did.

"Well," Ikeara put her hood back up, "so long as I've established that you two are not intruders bent on destroying Renieman, I'll leave you to your fairytale."

She began to walk away.

"Wait!" Ericahs called after her. "Wait! Maybe you can help us."

"What?" asked Ikeara.

"What?" asked Lismella as well.

"She's a good swordsman," said Ericahs. "She could help us."

"I already told you, mere swords aren't going to destroy the Keeper of

Darkness," said Lismella.

"She could still be of use to us."

Lismella cocked her head. "Could I speak to you for a moment?"

It was more a demand than a question. Despite the sweet sound in Lismella's voice, Ericahs could hear the undertones dripping with disdain. He knew Lismella was furious, but he wasn't entirely sure he cared. He didn't see why she was making such a big deal about the situation. Ikeara wasn't going to make or break the mission one way or the other, so what did it matter if she joined them?

"What?" Ericahs demanded when they were out of earshot of Ikeara.

"You think I don't know what's going on here, Ericahs?" asked Lismella. "I saw the look you gave her, the lust in your eyes."

Ericahs grew defensive. "She's a fellow swordsman. I enjoy her company and I respect her."

"You should know by now that you can't hide anything from me," Lismella replied. "You're not merely enjoying her company. You're smitten with her. Your own stupid stubbornness prevented you from admitting it to her before, and now you think can fool yourself again into believing it's nothing more than a friendship."

"That's all it is."

"Your heart doesn't play by the same rules as your mind, Ericahs. You can control one, but you can't control the other. Though you may say in your mind that you feel nothing for her, your heart says otherwise. Perhaps you are already so afraid of losing her that you won't even allow yourself to care for her, but you do care for her. Your heart cares for her very deeply even if you won't admit it to yourself. When I met you Ericahs, I thought you were alone, someone without attachments, but it seems I was wrong. Being apart from her for so many years has only made your heart long for her more."

"And what would you know about it?" Ericahs demanded. "My grandfather was probably still bouncing on his mother's knee the last time your heart felt a flutter! Maybe I don't want to end up cold and alone like you."

"You'll end up dead!" Lismella was losing her composure. She took a deep breath trying to regain her calm and began to explain. "Even if you won't admit it, you are in serious danger of falling in love with that girl. The longer we keep her here, the more likely that is to happen. Deep in your heart, you're already in love with her. You can't let it grow any more than that."

"Why not? Why is that so terrible?"

"Because you will lose all your power against the Shadows. The only reason you have a chance to defeat them is because you have nothing left to lose, and so you are fearless. If you keep that girl here, you will have something to fear losing. That fear will leave you prey to the darkness. And no matter how tightly you hold onto her, you won't be able to keep her from slipping away."

"You don't know that for sure," Ericahs challenged.

"Yes, I do," Lismella replied. "If there is one thing that I know with certainty, it is that. Aecleton doesn't know you're on your way to defeat the Shadows right now. Aecleton hasn't yet perceived you as a threat, but it will eventually. Once it does that girl will surely be the first thing it will strike to wrench your heart with pain and make you utterly incapable of fighting. If you're afraid of losing her, you may end up losing everything."

Ericahs didn't answer.

"Do you know what I see when I look into your eyes now?" asked Lismella. "Fear. And not just the fear of fear, but real fear."

"I'm not afraid!"

"Yes you are! And that fear is only going to grow if you keep her here."

Ericahs looked back toward Ikeara. Perhaps it was the "stupid stubbornness" that Lismella had mentioned within him, but he was now feeling more defiant than ever. He knew that Lismella wasn't just using him, that she was actually intent on saving the world, but he got the feeling that there was something more.

It just seemed as though Lismella had other deep secrets that she wasn't revealing. He got the feeling that in addition to saving the world, she had some sort of personal agenda as well. He knew there was more information she was keeping from him. Perhaps he was so determined to keep Ikeara simply because Lismella was so vehemently opposed to the idea. Ericahs didn't like being challenged, and he wanted to keep Ikeara if only to prove to Lismella that she was wrong.

"Ikeara stays and that's final," said Ericahs. "If you want me to help you stop the Shadows, that's my decision. Take it or leave it, you paranoid old hag. *You* are the one who keeps holding me back, not Ikeara. I'm ready to fight Aecleton."

At Ericahs' last words, Lismella seemed to snap. She waved her arm and directed a large force of energy at Ericahs. He couldn't see it, but he could certainly feel its power as it slammed him backward into the ground. Lismella leaned down close to his ear.

"You're not ready until I say you're ready," she hissed. She stood up and walked away.

Ericahs looked back toward Ikeara who had pulled out her sword. Ericahs shook his head and waved her down. He knew Ikeara's swordsmanship would be of no use against Lismella's powers and would probably only further infuriate her.

Ericahs had just learned a very valuable lesson; Lismella was far more powerful than she had been letting on. She had been speaking lightly of her powers since she'd first met him, but now he was beginning to understand just how easily she could take him apart. As he watched her stalk away in anger, Ericahs began to wonder exactly what else Lismella's magic was capable of.

The breeze began to blow and Ericahs looked up at the sky. The clouds were rolling in heavily. He watched the sky closely as the glowing orb of Maan's light disappeared, consumed by the darkness. He sighed realizing that another moon had just been taken. Aecleton was getting stronger.

# Chapter Nineteen

## THE GUARDIAN'S DECEPTION

Kelgar reined his horse to a halt. He'd snatched the animal from some unsuspecting dupe near the edge of Argentum and had been riding quickly ever since. Fortunately the man hadn't recognized Kelgar as a Guardian or there might be a serious price to pay later. The last thing people needed to believe was that the Guardians were thieves.

Kelgar reached into his pocket and pulled out his moon pendant. He gave a small grin. Did Raede really think the Guardians would make it that easy?

As soon as Kelgar had rescued Enira, he'd realized something was wrong. It had just felt off and he soon perceived that Enira was not really Enira at all. She was an impostor hoping to steal the moon pendant and possibly information as well. Kelgar had let her think she'd gotten both.

Kelgar had felt it when the false Enira had snatched his pendant, but he was no ordinary sorcerer. As a former street child, Kelgar had a little bit of pickpocket in him as well. It had served him in the past during times of desperate need and it had served him this evening. He'd taken back his own pendant and used his magic to replace the one the false Enira had. Little did she know, all she would be bringing to Raede was a sparkly stone.

As far as the real Enira was concerned, Kelgar was back to square one. If it hadn't been the real Enira on the platform about to be executed, then it meant the real Enira was still somewhere within the Temple of Aurora. Once again Kelgar had no way of getting Enira that didn't risk getting her killed as well.

Of course the temple was not really as impermeable as Kelgar had told the fake Enira. That was just what he wanted the woman to go back and tell Raede. Let Raede get comfortable with the idea that he was safe and secure within the temple. Let Raede think that Notelcea had gone east to raise a sorcerer militia. If all went as Kelgar hoped, Raede would send his army on a wild goose chase looking for Notelcea and her imaginary sorcerers in Delarue.

Of course Kelgar had no idea where Notelcea really was. Other than a few scattered words sent by firelight, he'd been given no indication of her condition or whereabouts. He knew with certainty that she would not be in Delarue, however, for it truly was nothing but a vacant wasteland. All the more reason it would be the perfect place to trick Raede's army into going.

The nearest shelter was almost two leagues from Delarue. Raede's men would be sitting ducks if Kelgar led a band of sorcerers to destroy them. They'd have nowhere to run. And with Raede's forces having vacated the Temple of Aurora, it'd be nothing for a group of sorcerers to storm the stronghold and retake the temple from Raede. With their combined magic and the absence of Raede's army, they should have little trouble getting Enira out alive. Of course part of that plan depended on finding Notelcea.

Kelgar didn't know why Notelcea hadn't trusted him enough to tell him where she was going, but he couldn't deny that it irked him a bit. Kelgar knew she was older than he and he should respect her wishes for privacy, but wherever she was, he hoped she really knew what she was doing. The window of time they had in which to defeat the Shadows was getting dangerously small and Notelcea's help would be of great value at the present time. Especially with the real Enira still trapped in the Temple of Aurora. At a time when he could really use Notelcea's help, the eldest Guardian was nowhere to be found.

Kelgar knew he might as well try to save the gypsy if it wasn't already too late. He knew the soldiers Raede had sent to the forest to kill the gypsy would be waiting to set a trap for him. He was sure that was why the fake Enira was so insistent that he depart and try to save the gypsy. What they didn't realize, however, was that Kelgar already knew they would be waiting for him, and he was making a few plans of his own.

While Kelgar knew that Raede's men would reach Silverwood long before he did, he had faith in Mordrelina's powers. She already knew Raede had tarkweed and therefore she would not be caught off guard trying to use magic that wouldn't work. Kelgar hoped that would be enough to save the gypsy. By the time he got to the forest, he would know one way or the other. In any event, he had to try.

The one thing he regretted about the situation was Milessandra. He hadn't planned on Milessandra finding him. They'd made no arrangement to meet up after she sounded the alarm. After he'd realized that Enira was a fake, he certainly wasn't going to return to the secret side door of the temple. It had never occurred to him that Milessandra would so easily locate him. It had forced him to slightly alter his plan.

Kelgar had felt guilty as he ran away into the darkness leaving an unsuspecting Milessandra with an agent of Raede. It had been the lesser of two evils, however. As long Kelgar pretended that he thought the woman was truly Enira, then she would take the false information about Delarue back to Raede. If Kelgar had divulged the truth by telling Milessandra what was really going on, that golden opportunity to deliver fake information to Raede would be gone.

It had not been an easy decision, but it was one that Kelgar had been forced to make. He hoped Milessandra would not begrudge him too deeply when she learned Enira was a fake. More importantly he hoped that having revealed Milessandra to be the real Enira's cousin, that Raede might think Milessandra was of some value as well. Kelgar didn't want to think about what would happen if they deemed Milessandra of no value. He knew he would never forgive himself if anything happened to that girl.

# Chapter Twenty

# READY

Ericahs woke up quickly. He could feel that the wind was blowing strangely. The moon Ngame should have been glowing above him by now, but when he looked up in the sky he saw nothing except the darkness of the Shadows rolling in.

The campfire was dying. Ericahs seized a torch and Ikeara awoke with a start. It was too late. The blackness swirled in snuffing out all the firelight. Ericahs looked around, but Lismella was nowhere to be seen, hidden somewhere in the blackness.

"Ericahs?" Ikeara called with a note of fear in her voice.

Ericahs grabbed her. "Stay close!" he shouted rekindling his torch. "I don't think they can harm me, but they may harm you if you let them. Don't believe in them. Don't fear them and you'll be invincible."

The wind blew harder and a whistling sound emanated from the gusts. Sparks flew from Ericahs' only torch as the wind began to overpower its light. Ericahs held tighter to Ikeara and tried to shield the torch from the wind, but it was of no use. The torch was dying and Ikeara's fear was growing.

The torch suddenly went out and Ikeara began screaming as the Shadows drew in closer. Ericahs knew the screams, he'd heard them before. He held Ikeara more tightly, but somewhere is his head he could hear a voice echoing: *No matter how tightly you hold onto her, you won't be able to keep her from slipping away.*

"Don't fall to them, Ikeara!"

Ikeara seemed not to hear him as her screams became more high pitched.

"No!" Ericahs shouted into the night above Ikeara's screaming. "Spare her! Spare her and take me! Don't do this to me again! Don't do this to me again! I hate you! Take me!"

There was a familiarity about the situation as Ericahs remembered the night his brother was taken by the Shadows, but there was something different as well. Ericahs was far too busy trying to hold onto Ikeara to think about it, but subconsciously it just felt strange. Ikeara was screaming, but her screams were not being feasted upon by the demons. They seemed less spirit and more material than Ericahs remembered.

Ericahs could actually feel the energy force of the dark shapes as they swooped in around him. It was all very different. Suddenly he felt Ikeara's form leave his grasp. Her voice was silenced and she was gone. Ericahs looked around as the Shadows receded into the darkness of the forest. Once again something he loved had been taken from him while he was left to bear the grief.

It was not so much grief, as anger that he was feeling now, however. He didn't understand why the Shadows never took him, but left him powerless to save those around him. Perhaps that was his curse; perhaps that was the Shadows' way of tormenting him. Since he himself had no fear for them to feed upon, they punished him by reminding him that they were still in control. Whatever the reason he was still alive, it infuriated him.

The next moon was emerging from the cover of darkness and the black cloud was retracting, but Ericahs was too angry to let it go now. He tore out through the trees chasing the blackness, but it floated away much too fast for him to follow. At last Ericahs had to stop out of sheer exhaustion.

"If you want me then take me!" Ericahs shouted into the forest. "Just take me! Come and find me; I am ready!"

Ericahs received no reply from the night. The only echo he did hear in the darkness was the shuffling sound of feet coming up behind him. He turned to see Lismella, her white gown glowing eerily in the darkness.

"Yes, Ericahs," she said, "I believe at last you *are* ready."

Ericahs just stood there breathing hard, wondering where she had been when he needed her help.

"Perhaps this was what it took to make you ready," Lismella continued. "I tried to make you relive it in your dreams."

"The powder," said Ericahs in realization.

Lismella nodded. "Yes. I thought if you relived the death of your brother at the hands of the Shadows it would make you ready. But perhaps this was the only thing that could truly ready you. Perhaps the Shadows themselves have given you the very weapon you need to fight them."

"Did you have anything to do with it?"

"With what?"

"With Ikeara's death."

"No."

Ericahs knit his eyebrows. "How do I know you're not just lying to me?"

Lismella pierced him with her sapphire gaze. "Look into my eyes, Ericahs. I swear to you that I didn't kill Ikeara."

Ericahs nodded. Her knew it was true for he was looking into the depths of her eyes and there was not an ounce of untruth within them. She had not killed Ikeara. It made Ericahs hate the Shadows all the more.

"I believe you," said Ericahs, "though I almost wish I didn't."

Lismella nodded. "The Shadows are trying to make you weak, but it is their own downfall. Every stroke they take against you may in fact make you stronger."

"So what happens now?" asked Ericahs. "Where do we go from here?"

"Nothing has changed," Lismella replied. "We proceed just as we previously planned. We make for the Valley of the Shadows."

# Chapter Twenty-one

# SHADOWY ATTACK

With two moons gone, the trees were black as pitch while Lismella and Ericahs slowly made their way to the Valley of the Shadows. It had been almost an entire day since Ikeara's disappearance and Ericahs had said very little to Lismella. The Silverwood underbrush was thick in this part of the forest. It made their going all the more slow and noisy.

A twig snapped to the right. Ericahs turned quickly, his sword raised, though he knew not whether his foe be man or Shadow. It was neither. It was nothing more than a little old woman, walking alone in the dark of night.

"What are you doing wandering around here by yourself in the darkness with the Shadows so soon to be about?" Ericahs demanded, pointing his sword at her.

Lismella already knew who the woman was, however. She carefully touched Ericahs' arm making him lower his sword. "She's the Silverwood Gypsy."

The old woman nodded. "I am." She looked at Lismella. "I've seen Kelgar."

"Kelgar? Kelgar?" said Lismella, running the name around in her head as if it sounded vaguely familiar. "He's one of the Guardians isn't he?"

The gypsy nodded. "Yes." She stole at a quick look at Ericahs and then returned her gaze to Lismella.

"And what information did you give him?" asked Lismella slowly.

"Only what he needed to know," the gypsy replied.

Lismella seemed to relax a bit.

"Kelgar is coming here even now," the gypsy continued. "He is coming to warn me of something he thinks I haven't already foreseen."

"Raede?"

"Yes. He is sending his men through Silverwood. They will soon be here to kill me."

"Then why are you still here?" asked Ericahs, knowing that he was well out of the loop in whatever the two women were discussing.

"It is not Raede's men who frighten me, boy," the gypsy replied. She turned to Lismella again. "Kelgar is looking for you, you know."

Lismella hung her head. "I know."

"You know?" asked Ericahs. "I thought you said you didn't know the Guardians."

Lismella looked up sharply. "I never said that. I said they would kill me if they knew what I know."

Ericahs was growing suspicious. "Then why would they be looking for you?"

Lismella ignored Ericahs and instead spoke to the gypsy. "Tell Kelgar to go to the library, to the section in the far east corner. It will tell him everything he needs to know."

"Everything?" asked the gypsy.

Lismella nodded. "Everything. And may he one day forgive me for what I have done."

The gypsy gave a small smile. "He is not one who forgives easily."

"I know," said Lismella, "but by the time he understands, all this will be over."

The gypsy nodded. "You know how to kill the Keeper, don't you?"

Lismella looked at Ericahs. "I think so."

Ericahs couldn't stand it anymore. Whatever Lismella and the gypsy were talking about, they were deliberately trying to keep him out of it. He didn't like being kept in the dark, especially when he was the one risking his life.

"What are you not telling me?" he demanded. "What is it this Kelgar will find in the library that you haven't told me? What does he need to forgive you for?"

"Ericahs, I–" Lismella began, but she was abruptly cut off by the sound of approaching horse hooves.

Lismella, Ericahs and the gypsy turned to see Raede's men, torches in hand, riding toward them.

"There she is!" one of the men shouted, pointing at the gypsy.

"Raede's men!" Ericahs shouted.

"They've come for me," said the gypsy.

"Well they're not going to get you," said Lismella determinedly. "Ericahs, beside me!"

Ericahs stood beside Lismella, blocking Raede's men from reaching the gypsy. The lead rider fingered his crossbow.

"Out of the way you fools or you'll be killed along with this traitorous witch," he said.

"You're not killing anyone here," Lismella growled.

Ericahs tightened his grip on his sword. He fought for a living, but he wasn't sure that he and Lismella would able to stop that many men. He glanced at the gypsy, fairly confident she would soon be dead. The man with the crossbow smiled and raised his weapon.

Without warning a blinding bolt of white light suddenly shot through crowd. The man with the crossbow dropped his weapon to cover his eyes. The men behind him shielded their faces. Their horses reared in fright, dumping their riders and fleeing into the forest. Even Ericahs had to turn away.

The light subsided and everyone turned to see Lismella, panting hard, staring at them with a look that could kill. Ericahs gasped in shock as he saw a moon-shaped pendant hanging around her neck, having worked its way out of her dress during the display of magic. Only the gypsy did not seem surprised.

"Light magic! She's one of them!" the leader yelled. "Get her!"

The men charged toward them on foot with bows and swords, but Ericahs and Lismella were ready. Ericahs fought off anyone with a sword, being only momentarily distracted as Lismella pelted off bursts of light. The gypsy stayed back against the trees, not wanted to be on the wrong side of either fighter.

It was a losing battle for Raede's men and they knew it. While they might have been able to hold ground against Ericahs alone, they were no match for Lismella's magic. Ericahs was just beginning to enjoy the sensation he always felt as victory approached, when the hairs on the back of his neck suddenly prickled.

He felt his blood run cold and looked up at the sky to see dark clouds beginning to roll in. He knew what was coming.

"The Shadows," he whispered under his breath.

"Ericahs!" Lismella shouted, tossing him a torch. Lismella had obviously felt the Shadows' presence as well.

Ericahs ducked a blow from the man he was fighting and rolled across the ground to catch the torch. He jumped to his feet quickly, holding the torch in one hand and using his other hand to run his sword through his opponent. He turned to look at Lismella.

Ericahs could see Lismella and he could also see the leader of Raede's men. The leader had regained his crossbow and was standing back behind a tree, taking careful aim at Lismella's head. Lismella seemed oblivious.

"Lismella!" Ericahs shouted.

Lismella looked up at Ericahs just as the man with the crossbow released his arrow. What happened next occurred so fast that Ericahs couldn't even be sure he was seeing what he thought he saw. Ericahs seemed to be watching in slow motion as the arrow cut through the air toward an unaware Lismella. But the arrow never made it.

The shaft was suddenly pushed off course, never even grazing Lismella. Ericahs couldn't be sure, but he thought he saw a dark shape block the arrow just before it hit Lismella. Probably some magical shield she had set up, he supposed. Whatever it was, it had just saved her life.

Lismella spun toward the fallen arrow in surprise and looked up to see the man with the crossbow. He was even more surprised than Lismella and couldn't understand why his perfectly aimed arrow hadn't hit her. Lismella didn't wait for him to figure it out. As he raised his crossbow to fire again, Lismella picked up the fallen arrow and sent it back to him with her magic.

It wasn't light magic. It was something else entirely. Ericahs couldn't say what sort of magic it was, but he knew what it was fueled by; rage. Having been fed by the fire of its power so many times himself, he knew what rage looked like when he saw it. Lismella was angry. The question was, why? Yes, a man was trying to kill her, but so was every other man and woman in the forest at the moment. There was something else behind Lismella's rage, Ericahs just didn't know what.

Ericahs suddenly sensed the trees around him growing very dark. It was as if a thick, black fog had suddenly permeated the woodland, obscuring his vision. He could barely see Raede's soldiers around him. This was different than what he had experienced the previous night with Ikeara. This was how it had felt the night his brother had died.

"Ericahs! Fall back!" Lismella shouted.

Ericahs looked up and saw Lismella holding her torch. It wasn't a fog; it was the Shadows. The wispy demons were choking the air around him. They were hungry and they had come to feed. Having sensed a multitude of people in the forest, they were seeking the nourishment of human lives. The only barrier between them and their prey were the burning sticks the people held tightly in their hands.

Ericahs ran toward Lismella, who was already beside the gypsy. The two of them stood bathed in a halo of torchlight as the dark forms of the Shadows swirled around them like a sea of midnight. Ericahs cut his path through the blackness. The curtain of Shadows opened before him as their mass was parted by the glow of his torch.

"Hold on!" Lismella commanded.

She turned toward Raede's men cowering in the darkness, clinging desperately to their own sources of light. With one swipe of her hand Lismella magically extinguished all their torches, leaving them in darkness, completely at the mercy of the Shadows. They could be heard scurrying in the underbrush.

Some were trying to run toward the haven of light provided by Ericahs and Lismella's torches. Others were simply trying to relight their own lost light sources. Neither attempt was of any use. The Shadows were already upon them, knowing that their prey had no escape.

And then Ericahs heard the screams. All the men and women in the company Raede had sent began to shriek and curse aloud. Ericahs knew what it was before he even ventured a glance. He'd heard the sound before, many years ago. The Shadows were taking them.

The screams were terrible, bloodcurdling. They were the same horrible screams that had sounded as Ericahs' brother slipped into the darkness of the Shadows' hold. It was a call that Ericahs had hoped he'd never have to hear again, but here it was sounding once more. It was that same desperate sounding plea. A final, pathetic attempt by a hopeless soul to wrench some measure of mercy from those who would give none. The Shadows knew nothing of mercy, and they cared little for their victims' cries.

Even though Raede's company had just tried to kill him, Ericahs could not help feeling a small pang as he listened to the Shadows consume the company's very essence. No one should have to die like that, not even the murderers who worked for Raede. In truth, death would have been a far finer fate. The men and women of Raede's company now faced something worse.

They weren't merely being killed by the Shadows; they were becoming part of the Shadows. The dark presence was finding that bit of fear, no matter how small, within each person there and feeding upon it. The Shadows were making those little spots of fear grow and grow, filling up their human bearer, until at last the fear was everywhere within them.

The fear spilled out of their very beings, until they were utterly consumed by its power. And then they were no more themselves. They were part of the black mass of otherworldly destruction. They had become part of the Shadows. Ericahs turned his head away, unable to watch. All he could think of was his brother.

Then suddenly it was over. The screams had stopped. The Shadows still hovered on the air, swarming over the spot where they had just taken so many lives, but those lives were now gone. There was no trace of any of the men or women who had stood there only moments before. They were completely gone; absorbed by the realm of the Shadows.

Ericahs, Lismella and the gypsy were crouched beside a thick cluster of small trees. The orange pool of radiance surrounding them was the only barrier between their lives and the dark forms that roiled around them. The wind blew fiercely, driven by the Shadows in their attempt to break down the wall of light. The flickering flames of the torches danced wildly in its powerful breath. Any ordinary fire would have been doused by now, but Ericahs had a feeling Lismella's magic was keeping their present torches alight.

The Shadows clustered around them, just outside of the torchlight, but only for a few moments. They were not yet strong enough to penetrate the light and so they floated off through the land to go find other, more accessible victims. With two moons gone, they now had even more hours of darkness during which to partake in their endless hunt. They were growing stronger with every moment, with every life they took.

"We have to go," said Lismella, "now."

Ericahs nodded and stood up. Lismella handed her torch to the gypsy. The gypsy took it without question.

"What about you?" asked Ericahs.

"I don't need a torch," Lismella replied without explanation.

"Kelgar comes even now," said the gypsy.

"We can't wait for him," said Lismella, "nor would I want to. Tell him of the library; that is all. Ericahs and I must travel a different road."

Lismella said no more. She simply motioned to Ericahs and the two of them ran off through the forest. When they were a good way from the gypsy, Ericahs stopped and turned to Lismella.

"Those men of Raede's, they recognized you," he said slowly, "and I think there's something you've been keeping from me. You're a Guardian aren't you?"

Lismella looked at him without changing her expression. "No, Ericahs," she replied, "I am *the* Guardian."

# Chapter Twenty-two

# AFTERMATH

Kelgar could see the glint of steel in the pale light of the rising moon. It seemed that everywhere he looked upon the ground was another ownerless weapon. Their masters were strangely absent. No dead bodies and no blood, just the cool gleam of forsaken blades scattered through the forest.

Kelgar reined his horse to a halt as he took in the aftermath. Something very grim had transpired here and Kelgar had a pretty good idea what. He was sure it had been the Shadows, but what he didn't understand was how. There were torches lying amongst the swords. Obviously Raede's company had been armed against the Shadows with light, so how had they all been so easily overpowered by the Shadows?

There had to have been something else that happened. Kelgar knew the Shadows were not yet strong enough to extinguish fire, so there must have been another presence at play. Kelgar couldn't begin to image what. He simply hoped that whatever had destroyed Raede's company, had not also destroyed the gypsy they had been sent to kill.

"You're late," said a voice in the darkness.

Kelgar smiled, his worry easing away. He turned to see the gypsy standing behind him in the darkness. "Mordrelina," he breathed.

"You sound relieved," she said in an amused tone of voice. "You didn't really believe a simple company of Raede's men was going to get the best of me did you? Especially not when I foresaw them coming."

"No. I wasn't worried until I got here and saw all this." Kelgar motioned to forest floor around him. "Surely the Shadows are not yet capable of darkening Raede's torches?"

"No," Mordrelina replied, "but there are other powers that can."

"What? What could cause all this?"

Mordrelina smiled. "You who are yourself capable of creating and quenching light cannot find the answer to that question?"

"A Guardian?" asked Kelgar not registering it at first. Suddenly he gasped. "Notelcea!"

"Yes," the gypsy nodded. "She was here."

"So she's not gone crazy and abandoned us."

"She's not crazy," Mordrelina agreed, "but I cannot say for certain that she's not abandoned you."

"What is that to mean?"

"There is something very unusual about her youth, Kelgar."

"This from the woman who aged me decades before my time?"

"Do not mock my admonition," Mordrelina warned. "I saw Notelcea with my own eyes and I could not read what lay within her. Most people open before my eyes like a book just waiting to be read, but not Notelcea. Some form of magic was cloaking her deepest thoughts and emotions from me, and it was every bit intentional. I think there may be more to her than meets the eye."

"You and everyone else who's ever met her," Kelgar sighed.

He knew well enough that Notelcea was a mystery, but he also knew that he didn't have time to dwell on it now. There was too much at stake to waste time wondering what Notelcea was hiding as far her personal mysteries. It was, however, of great importance to find out what Notelcea was hiding as far as her secret endeavors during such a time of crisis. She still had not truly told Kelgar where she was and honestly he was beginning to grow a bit irritated with her. She'd taken the time to chat with the gypsy; she could have at least dropped Kelgar a small message.

"I don't suppose she left you with any life-altering piece of information that might possibly resolve our tiny problem of the impending end of the world, did she?" asked Kelgar sarcastically. "She hasn't so much as given me the direction of her whereabouts."

"Nothing except that she wanted you to go to the library," the gypsy replied.

Kelgar snorted. "What is that? A vengeful suggestion of relation against me for sending her on a pointless excursion to the library? An excursion that she never undertook anyway, I might add. She simply ran off into the gathering darkness and left us with no guidance."

"I can hear the anger building in your voice, Kelgar."

"Wouldn't you be angry?"

"I think perhaps your anger is misplaced."

"Don't play the mind games with me now, Mordrelina. I'm in no mood for it. I've had a very long several days and I've only just left a young girl to what may in fact be her death. I can't image what she'll think of me when she realizes that I knew full well I was doing it."

"Very well, if you want it plainly, I suggest to you go to the library. Notelcea spoke to me and I saw no lie in her eyes. She asked for you to check the far east corner of the library."

"That's where the texts of ancient histories are kept," said Kelgar in confusion. "She must just be trying to keep me out of her hair. What does she really expect me to find in that dusty heap of papers?"

"The history in that corner is very old, Kelgar. Perhaps there is something Notelcea knows that she did not feel safe divulging aloud. She also asked that you could someday forgive her."

"Why, what's she done?"

"I don't think she's done anything yet, but perhaps as you fear, she has abandoned you. She was using a fake name and traveling with a ruffian of the woods. Her methods seemed to be for her own purposes, not for ours."

Kelgar shook his head and looked around in despair. The scattered blades of the ownerless swords were just a further reminder of how bad things were. He just couldn't understand why Notelcea would be shirking her responsibilities as a Guardian. She'd held that position longer and with more fervor than any of the others. Why run away now just when she was needed the most?

Mordrelina watched Kelgar closely. She didn't have to read his mind to know what he was thinking. She already knew him well enough to see it on his face. She glanced at the swords in the forest around her and knew his thoughts were turning to Raede.

"Even if the key to saving the world does lie within those books, Raede's never going to let a Guardian into the palace library," said Kelgar. "I managed to slip in there once already. I'm not sure I'll be able to do it again so easily. I've sent his men on a wild goose chase, but I doubt if he's fool enough to leave his palace entirely unguarded."

"You won't know until you try," Mordrelina advised. "There is one other alternative, you know."

"I have an inkling of what's running though your mind," Kelgar replied.

"Do you plan to simply kill Raede?"

"I don't know," Kelgar admitted. "I've had far too many problems to deal with for that to even be a possibility. I'm only here now because I sought to save you from his men."

"You know what killing Raede means," Mordrelina pressed. "You would be forced to ascend the throne."

"No one knows of my birthright except you and that's the way it stays."

"As a Guardian you don't have the authority to remove the king. He is the rightful heir and not even a Guardian can remove him. You know this. Only someone of his house can challenge his wrongdoing...someone like a cousin."

"I'm not taking the throne, Mordrelina; I'm not a king."

"You've always run away from your problems, Kelgar, and while it has served you well in the past, you can't run from your destiny forever."

"Destiny?" Kelgar scoffed. "Until a few nights ago we didn't even know who my mother was. Now I'm suddenly supposed to act like I was raised in the royal palace?"

"It wasn't my idea to find out who you were. I was actually quite hesitant because I know that new information always changes everything, no matter what it is. A new path is always created. You're the one who asked me to scry her."

"And I'm beginning to wish I hadn't!" Kelgar hissed angrily. He wasn't actually angry with Mordrelina, he was angry with himself.

"Well it doesn't matter because whether you would wish it again or not, we do know now, and knowledge is a powerful thing. A little knowledge can change everything."

"You know very well the only reason I had you scry in the first place is that I wanted to be sure Raede was not my brother. And even had he been, I know I would still have to kill him."

"If you merely remove Raede in a time like this, there will just be someone else to take up his place. Sheep always need a shepherd."

"I am not that shepherd."

Mordrelina gave him a reproving look. Kelgar knew the look well. It was the look that all mothers give their children as they silently scold them without words. The look that tells their children they're behaving in an unacceptable manner. Kelgar was in no mood for it.

"Mordrelina, I am not a king! You've seen what's happened out there; the people will never follow me. From their point of view I wasn't even any good as a Guardian, having let the moon slip away under my watch. I'm just a street-running gypsy child who ascended to the rank of Guardian. In truth I'm nothing more than the bastard child of the king's aunt."

"You can't be a street child forever, Kelgar."

"You're the one who raised me that way!" Kelgar shot back. "Setting a bit of a double standard aren't we?"

"Did you come back for a reason, or are you only planning to argue with me?"

Kelgar sighed. Mordrelina could always get the better of him. "I just can't take the throne, Mordrelina, and you know very well why. It would open too many doors for those who follow in my place. You know I would never be corrupted by that power, but there are many who would be.

"There is a reason that the Guardians and the king are never the same person. The ones with authoritative power should never be the ones with magical power. It would be too easily abused. As the Guardians, our magic is there to keep the authority in check. If I were to take the throne it would destroy everything.

"You've seen what can happen when people follow a fool. Can you imagine what would happen if a foolish Guardian were to follow in my footsteps? Those who have the magic that we have should never be given the power to rule as well. It's too much power for any one person. If we open the door to allow Guardians the throne then where will it end? How long will it be before the world falls under the power of an evil king or queen? We might as well let the Shadows take everything now.

"Raede is merely a common sorcerer with a few magic tricks that he learned at the knee of his mentor and you've seen what's happened to him. It's already gone to his head. His rule is living proof that the Guardians can never be on the throne, no matter what blood flows within my veins. We can't merely trade one dictatorship for another."

"This time, Kelgar, we may have to. There was a reason that I never looked into your past, because some things are not meant to be known. But you wanted to know and now you do, so you must take responsibility for it. You looked into the future; now face the consequences."

Kelgar knew there had to be another way. He shook his head, firm in his resolve. "No," he replied simply.

# Chapter Twenty-three

## SIDES OF DARKNESS

"What do you mean you're *the* Guardian?" asked Ericahs.

"My name is not really Lismella," she confessed, "it is Notelcea, and I have more knowledge of darkness and light than all the other Guardians combined."

"Notelcea?" asked Ericahs in surprise.

Notelcea nodded. "Yes, Ericahs. I am the leading Guardian of the Temple of Aurora."

Ericahs felt betrayed. He knew that Lismella, or Notelcea as she was now revealed, had been keeping secrets from him, but he couldn't have imagined they would go so deep. It was one thing to hide the fact that she was a three hundred year old sorceress, but it was an entirely different matter to hide the fact that she was a Guardian.

The Guardians of Light were supposed to protect the people from the Shadows and yet here was Notelcea with seemingly no more idea than any common man of how to defeat them. She had plucked Ericahs from the wild and was hoping to make him the savior of the future. It left a stale taste in Ericahs' mouth and he could not hide the venom in his words as he spoke to her.

"So you lied to me," he accused her. "You lied to me about everything."

"Not everything, Ericahs, just some things."

"Why?"

"Why do you think?" Notelcea shot back. "You don't trust anyone; how can you really expect anyone to trust you? I'm a Guardian. I'm supposed to protect the world from the plague now seething to consume it and you expect me to just reveal three hundred years worth of protected magical secrets to a man I pulled from the rough lands? I didn't even know you, Ericahs, and you were as stubborn and defiant as any person I'd ever met. Why would I trust you with that secret information before I was even sure about you?"

Her words were passionate as she spoke. There was no lie in them; it was the open truth she was now presenting. Her usually cool composure was unraveling in the light of truth. The entire world was upon her shoulders, for she was older and knew more than any of the other Guardians. Her human vulnerability was exposed as she revealed her true feelings of helplessness.

"Why would I trust you?" she added under her breath. "I can't even trust myself."

"What's that supposed to mean?" asked Ericahs.

"Nothing," said Notelcea quietly, as though she hadn't meant for Ericahs to hear that last part.

"So you're the one then, the one who ranks higher than all the others?"

Notelcea nodded. "Yes. I am the senior Guardian of Light now, but it's even more than that. I am far older than even Kelgar and Enira know. I was there at the beginning, one of the original Guardians. There were three of us that first night."

"Three? I thought you said you were one of many sorcerers."

"Sit down, Ericahs."

Ericahs looked at her suspiciously. "Why?"

"Well, I assume you know little about the history of the light. There are few who do. So this may take a while."

"Very well." Ericahs sat down.

"Yes, there were many sorcerers that night, but there were three of us who would become the Guardians. Three of us who would wield the light magic. I was one of those three. My name is on the hidden tablet in the hall of records. I helped build the Lumidian that first encased the dreaded Shadows in their Valley of Darkness so many centuries ago. We needed the multitude of sorcerers to bring down the sun, but it was the three of us, myself, Lunella and Celmidian, who first changed the world. From that day there have always been three Guardians. I was the youngest of the three at the time; powerful, but foolish."

"Why foolish?"

Notelcea gave a small smile. "Because power and intelligence are not the same thing as wisdom. The other two were older and far wiser than I. I shouldn't even have been in their company, but they needed a third to help build the Lumidian and I was the best choice at the time. They knew I would outlive them and pass the knowledge of the light onto the next generation. I am sure they never dreamed I myself would be that next generation for so many generations."

"How did you build the Lumidian? How did you build a trap for the sun?"

Notelcea drew a circle in the dirt, then another circle inside that, and another until she had seven circles. "Layer by layer," she said, "piece by piece. We just kept building it, pouring layer after layer of magic into it. It's not something that can be explained in words. It's not something that can even be understood with the eyes. It's simply something that has to be experienced. We built the Lumidian layer by layer and then we pulled the sun into it."

"But something must have gone wrong," said Ericahs.

"Why do you think that?"

"Because of Aecleton," Ericahs replied. "You said he was created when the Lumidian was. It must have been something that got lost in the magic when you brought down the sun."

Notelcea shook her head, the far away look glazing over her eyes as she remembered that distant time so long ago. "No. I said Aecleton was almost as old the Lumidian. Almost, but not quite. The sun was already concealed within the Lumidian by the time Aecleton was born and entwined itself with the Shadows. Right after the Lumidian was built, something happened to the moon Selene. No one is entirely sure how, but the perfect moon crystal of Selene was broken. A sliver of the crystal was gone and a small piece of the moon disappeared. That is why Selene has always been misshapen. Whatever happened in that moment is what created Aecleton.

"I am sure that is why Selene was the first moon that Aecleton took; the weakest moon of the five. It was the moon with the broken crystal. None of that matters now, however, for we are fast approaching the end of this. Soon it shall all be over and Aecleton will be dead, and if we are lucky, the Shadows with it."

"How can you be sure we are so close to success? As far as I can tell the world just keeps getting darker."

Notelcea smiled. "That's exactly how I can tell. The night is darkest before the dawn. The world grows black around us, but soon the sun shall rise."

"You mean the real sun?"

"No. I meant it only in a manner of speech. Releasing the real sun would be far too dangerous. We lost enough people when we first captured it. To release it now would be like opening a volcano beneath the world."

Ericahs looked at her face. It was still difficult to believe that she was centuries old, old enough to have seen the sun, but he had no reason to doubt that. While she may have lied about her true identity, he was fairly certain she was speaking the truth now. Having himself already lost anything he'd ever loved, he couldn't image hundreds of years of watching those around you die.

"How is it no one noticed that you never aged?" asked Ericahs.

"Oh they noticed," Notelcea replied, "but I was a sorceress. Once Lunella and Celmidian had passed, I was the senior Guardian, the most powerful sorceress in the Temple of Aurora. Everyone simply assumed I used magic to remain young looking. No one thought twice about it. One by one I watched the Guardians grow old and drop away while I remained young and alive. I knew that if it went on too long, people might begin to wonder about me, so something had to be done.

"As senior Guardian it was within my power to make temple laws, and so I did. I created the law of Guardian silence. I am the reason we never speak of the Guardians before us. I didn't want anyone to learn my secret, so I made the rule of silence. I made it so no would ever know the true identities of the former guardians. So no one would know it had always been me from the beginning. From that day onward, for all those who followed in our footsteps, being a Guardian meant forsaking your own identity. The Guardians' names would not be remembered in tales or songs, for there were no individual identities. There were simply the three, as always, and their place of honor.

"Initially I told people it was out of respect for those Guardians who had passed, but after a time legend grew that it was bad luck to speak of the former Guardians. Even the townspeople feared to speak their names. It was all nonsense of course. There was no bad luck associated with speaking their names, but I let the rumor spread because it did well to protect my secret."

"But what about the history books?" asked Ericahs. "The library in the palace holds everything doesn't it? How did you manage to keep people from reading what the historians no doubt recorded somewhere within a book?"

Notelcea didn't answer, but Ericahs saw her sapphire blue eyes turn downward.

"You destroyed them," he said, answering his own question. "Didn't you?"

Notelcea met his gaze. "Yes," she nodded, "in a manner of speaking. I committed sacrilege to protect myself. I erased the names from the history books. I rewrote what was written within them, leaving Lunella, Celmidian and even my own name as nothing more than a memory. Soon they were all but forgotten, as was I. We were simply referred to as the 'The First Three,' and no one remembered our names. My secret was safe. The true history I kept within a text that I have hidden, waiting for the right moment to pass it on to the one who follows me on the day that I am lucky enough to die."

"The far east corner," Ericahs breathed.

Notelcea nodded.

"That's why you told the gypsy to send Kelgar there."

"Yes," Notelcea nodded again. "He will soon know the truth; the truth about everything."

"What did you want him to forgive you for?"

Notelcea sighed. "I've done many things in my life, and not all of them wise. Sometimes there are repercussions to our mistakes and sometimes those repercussions can hurt others."

"What did you do?"

Notelcea looked away. "Something that I of all people should have known better." She looked back at Ericahs. Seeing the confused look on his face, she explained. "It's simply that when you spend so many years keeping secrets from the Guardians, they will probably tend to resent it later on. They have no idea how old I really am. I am older even than Aecleton and I remember the days before the Keeper of Darkness. The days of sun and the terrible nights of Shadows."

"That's one thing you haven't yet explained to me. How have you lived for so long?"

Notelcea walked around behind Ericahs, refusing to face him. "I won't say that I don't know, because I do, but only in part. Right after the Lumidian was created, something happened to me. I just stopped aging, frozen in time. There was a lot of magic flying around in the air at that time. It was a new world with the loss of the sun and we sorcerers were changing the lifecycle of plants and animals. We were altering the world's very existence so everything could survive in the new land of night and moon that we had created. It made us feel almost invincible to wield such power.

"As I said, I was the youngest and by far the least experienced and least wise. I got caught up in that magic and it caught up with me. Something was changed within me forever and I knew there was no going back. All I could do was use my long life to prevent the Shadows from ever returning. And I seem to be failing even in that."

Ericahs looked at her. He watched as she picked up a large branch off the ground, fiddling with it as though she were trying to use it to change the present topic of discussion. There was still something she wasn't telling him. Something she'd done that she wasn't yet ready to divulge. Kelgar seemed to be the target of the forgiveness she sought, so Ericahs wondered if she had done something to him. Being so old, she could have been interfering in Kelgar's life from the time he was born.

That was just a theory, however. Ericahs obviously had no way of knowing what Notelcea was truly keeping. She was well adept at guarding her secrets. She'd been practicing that skill for the last three hundred years. So unless she decided to openly tell Ericahs what she was hiding, he wasn't likely to find out. And judging from her expression, Ericahs could see that she had no imminent intentions of revealing anything.

"So what are you doing here with me in Silverwood?" asked Ericahs at last. "If you're one of the original three, then you have more knowledge than anyone. Why aren't you out helping the other Guardians save the world? Why haven't you told them where you are? Or is that what you want them to forgive you for?"

"I built the Lumidian," Notelcea replied simply, "and I am the only one who can stop Aecleton."

"What about me?" asked Ericahs.

"I may have been mistaken about you."

"What? What is that supposed to mean?" Ericahs was beginning to grow angry with Notelcea. "You've been dragging me all around Silverwood, nearly getting me killed by the Shadows and suddenly you think you may have been mistaken about me?"

"Something has recently come to my attention and it may require a slight change in plans," Notelcea admitted. "There is something else that makes me different from everyone."

"What?" Ericahs demanded furiously. "What else haven't you told me?"

"The Shadows feed on the fear in a person's dark side, but I'm unique in that I don't have a dark side."

Ericahs shook his head, feeling that Notelcea was just stalling now. "You said everyone has a dark side," he accused.

Notelcea shrugged. "I lied."

She quickly brought up the branch she'd been holding and swung it with all her might, hitting Ericahs in the back of the head. He dropped like a stone, out cold. Notelcea dropped the branch beside his motionless body and ran off through the darkness. Her white dressed billowed behind her in the moonlight as she left Ericahs lying there alone on the forest floor.

## Chapter Twenty-four

## THE HIDDEN LIBRARY

Kelgar stood in the far east corner of the library staring at wall upon wall of papers, illuminated by the light of his palm. Despite his trepidations concerning the library guards, he'd been able to sneak in practically unnoticed. Save for a few unfortunate lower-ranking palace guards, Kelgar had not run into anyone on his way in.

He'd not killed the palace guards, but he couldn't help using them as subjects upon which to vent his frustration. He'd spent so much time running back and forth to and from Silverwood, so many times in the past few days, and yet he'd accomplished so little. Raede still had control of the temple, Enira and Milessandra were still prisoners there, and the Shadows were still growing stronger by the minute. Now Kelgar stood in the foretold place of the library and wondered how in the world he was to find the texts Notelcea had referred to in this huge mess of information.

It could take him hours or even days to comb through those books and papers. It was a lot of time to be wasting when time was something that was currently in such short supply. He'd been here thousands of times. What was he supposed to see now that he'd never seen before?

As if in answer to his silent question, a grating noise suddenly sounded from somewhere in the dark room. Kelgar made his way through the shelves of books, around the stacks of papers, and over to the very furthest corner of the room. The sound was coming from that corner he just couldn't see it.

The library was so dark in this corner that mirrors had been strategically placed along the walls to enhance the light of a person's torch. Kelgar had his palm light instead of a torch, but even with the mirrors, it was not bright enough to comfortably light the black corner. Glancing around to be sure no one had entered the library without his notice, he cautiously enlarged the sphere of white light in the palm of his hand.

Kelgar searched to locate the source of the grating sound and found it in the outline of the wall. It almost looked like a box taking shape from the stone. He'd never noticed it before and he was sure it hadn't been there previously.

He scanned the outline of the box, but there seemed to be no handle with which to pull it from the wall. He resolved to try prying it from the wall with his fingers. He knew it was probably a futile attempt, but he could think of little else to do at the moment. Whatever was in that box, he was sure it was what he needed to get.

As soon as he touched the box, it suddenly sprang away beneath his fingers. It slid out of the wall by its own will without any further help from his hands. A radiant light poured forth from the interior. Kelgar knew it was no accident. It was magic and could have been done by only one person; Notelcea. He leaned over to examine the contents within.

There were two items in the box; a stone tablet and an ancient book. The book looked old, very old, somewhere in the vicinity of three hundred years old in fact. The pages were worn and tattered, yet preserved by the layers of dry sand that someone had the foresight to put in the box with it. He gingerly lifted the book and the tablet from the box.

The stone tablet had three names carved upon it; Lunella, Celmidian and Notelcea. Kelgar had no idea what it meant. He wondered if perhaps Lunella and Celmidian were relatives, possibly even parents of Notelcea. Notelcea's own family had rarely been spoken of, so it seemed plausible. Why their names, along with Notelcea's, would be carved on an ancient stone tablet made no sense all, however. He wondered if perhaps the Notelcea he knew had been named after the Notelcea whose name appeared on the tablet.

Kelgar turned his attention to the battered book. It was the dustiest piece of writing he'd ever seen. It was so dilapidated it was falling apart at the seams. Whatever it was, it had never been recopied. This was some piece of a historical account still bearing the pen marks of the original author. It had to be something important.

Kelgar carefully peeled open the initial pages and began to read. The writing was smudged and faded in places, but there was enough to make out what was being said. It was not at all what Kelgar had been expecting, however.

Kelgar was reading the history of the Guardians of Light in the old book, but unlike any version he'd ever read before. Whenever he'd studied the history of the light, the names of the original Guardians, or any who followed, had always been absent. He knew it was a rule of the land to never mention the names of the Guardians, for they were to be merely Guardians, forsaking their own personal identities in their service to the light. Here, however, were those very names, plain for all the world to see. Kelgar wondered just why he'd never seen this text before. He read the words with ravenous hunger.

The book told of the Lumidian, how it was built layer upon layer. It told of the night the sun was drawn down into the Lumidian and turned into the five moons. It told of the magic that was used to alter the seasons and the growing of plants so people would have food all year round. And each time it mentioned the name Notelcea as one of the Guardians, Kelgar could not shake the feeling that it was the same Notelcea that he knew. The description of the youngest Guardian seemed to fit Notelcea perfectly, but he had trouble believing that Notelcea could really be over three hundred years old.

Of course Kelgar had always known that Notelcea was older than himself. He knew that she used some sort of magic to keep herself looking young. But having been himself aged in appearance by use of magic, he'd never thought to question Notelcea's magical youth. The possibility that she could be three hundred years old had never occurred to him, however. The real question was, why had she never told him?

If Notelcea had been one of the original Guardians, she of all people could make or break the traditions of the temple. Kelgar knew it would have been by her doing that the names of the former Guardians were never mentioned. It made sense to create the code of silence if she were trying to hide the fact that she'd been there at the beginning, but why exactly was she trying to do that? Why would she stay so many years in the temple and go to such lengths to hide it?

Kelgar continued to read, unable to tear himself away from this newfound treasure trove of information. Had the book not been so obviously old, he might have doubted the validity of the story within. It was clearly old, however, and Kelgar had the strong feeling that Notelcea had intentionally hidden this book to keep the world from ever knowing the true history of the Guardians of the Light. As the Guardian names were never to be mentioned, once that generation had passed on, Notelcea's secret would have died with them.

The book was written in several different hand strokes, three to be precise. Kelgar had never been a great scholar of penmanship, but he was sure he recognized one of the three sets of handwriting as Notelcea's. The original three Guardians must have shared the task of writing the history. It seemed only to give further credence to Kelgar's suspicions.

There was a break after the general history of the light. The next section of text was about Aecleton itself. According to the text Aecleton had come about shortly after the creation of the Lumidian, somehow damaging the moon crystal of Selene in the process. The text gave no explanation as to *where* exactly Aecleton had come from; simply that it *had* come.

*Perhaps we made a mistake in darkening the sky*, the passage read. The tone was different from the above accounts. Whereas the previous writing had been a simple recording of the factual events, this set of text had a more drear underlying tone to it of what seemed to be almost misery.

This block of text was entirely in Notelcea's hand, Kelgar was sure of it. She had been there when Aecleton was born and she was still in the world now. Kelgar suddenly realized why Notelcea had been keeping him in the dark so long, and why she had only now sent him to the library.

He shook his head. "She thinks she can stop the Keeper on her own," he sighed to himself in the darkness. He was beginning to understand her secrecy.

Kelgar knew that if Notelcea had really been there at the beginning, then she was even older than the Keeper. She might even have some knowledge of where

Aecleton came from. As such, she probably thought she knew something that could stop the Shadows. And rather than risk the lives of the other Guardians, she was trying to do it on her own.

"That's why she hasn't told us where she is," Kelgar whispered. "She's still trying to be the mother Guardian and protect us all while she risks her life alone. She probably doesn't even know Raede has Enira."

Kelgar wasn't talking to anyone. He was alone in the library. He was simply muttering his own musings to himself. It was a habit he'd created many years ago, finding that when he spoke his thoughts aloud, he was better able to put them in order. It didn't seem to be helping much at the moment, however.

Whether Notelcea was trying to protect the other Guardians or not, Kelgar still felt she was being foolish. No matter what ancient knowledge she possessed, there was still a possibility that she could be wrong. Her plan could fail. She could even be killed in the process. If that happened, where would it leave the Guardians then?

"It would leave us in deep trouble," Kelgar answered his own question. It would leave the other Guardians in *very* deep trouble, and far less powerful without Notelcea's help. What could she possibly have been thinking running off alone, Kelgar wondered.

"Who's back there?" a voice suddenly sounded from the doorway of the room Kelgar was skulking in.

*Oh great*! Kelgar thought to himself. Some nosy little member of the palace guard must have noticed his palm light as he read Notelcea's ancient books. That was all he needed at the moment.

Ever so quickly Kelgar doused the light in palm and slunk around a pile of books, heading toward the door. The man had a torch which illuminated the room a bit. The light was dim, but still plentiful enough to see. Unless the guard was blind, he would have little trouble spotting Kelgar as he edged toward the door.

Kelgar gazed at the torch providing the faint orange glow. He studied the guard silhouetted in the doorway and grinned. With a quick sweep of his hand, Kelgar extinguished the man's torch.

Now it was dark. The guard would be unable to see Kelgar, but Kelgar had little trouble seeing the guard, as he was now backlit by the torches out in the hallway. Kelgar quickly moved in on the confused guardsman.

Before the guard even had time to readjust his eyes to the darkness, Kelgar had crept up behind him. Grabbing the nearest large book he saw, Kelgar brought it down hard on the man's head. The guard fell to the floor senseless.

Kelgar dragged the man behind a pile of old texts where he wasn't likely to be found right away. He waved his hand relighting his palm light and picked up the book he'd used as a weapon. *War Tactics* was scrawled across the front cover.

"How apropos," Kelgar chuckled to himself as he returned the book to its pile.

Glancing at the man he'd just knocked unconscious, Kelgar suddenly had an idea. Here he was wondering how he was going to get into the Temple of Aurora unnoticed, and the answer was lying on the floor in front of him. He could take the man's uniform, and as long as he didn't run into anyone of any rank, he could probably pass for a palace guard.

It was a long shot, but at this point it was one Kelgar was willing to take. He now had Enira and Milessandra being held prisoner in the temple, and spirits only knew what Raede was doing to them at that very moment. He still lamented the fact that either of them could be killed, but he saw no other way around the matter. Notelcea obviously wasn't coming back any time soon to help him. For now at least, he was on his own.

The one bit of consolation was that perhaps Notelcea really did know something about how to stop Aecleton and the Shadows. If that were so, then perhaps the demise of the Shadows was near. Raede would be momentary caught off guard by the return of the moons, and it might be just the window Kelgar would need.

"Perhaps Notelcea can still help me that way," Kelgar muttered as he stripped the guard of his uniform. He was just about to leave when he remembered the corner. Best to close the enchanted box back up, lest unfriendly eyes were to stumble upon it.

He ran back to the corner. He picked up the book and placed it gently in the bottom of the box, then grabbed the stone tablet. One of the mirrors reflected his movement and that was when he suddenly saw it, something he hadn't noticed before. He'd never realized just how few times he'd actually seen the names of the Guardians written, and certainly never in a mirror's image.

Kelgar looked again, turning the tablet toward himself just to be sure, running each letter of the name over his tongue. He didn't want to believe it was true, but it was. The cold hard reality was carven in stone upon that tablet. There was no denying it and it couldn't merely be a coincidence. The question was had it been on purpose or was it merely a subconscious slip? Was it a secret guilty confession or perhaps even a heavily cloaked cry for help that had been ignored for the last three hundred years?

Whatever it was, it was staring him right in the face. For when he reversed the letters of the last name on the tablet, they spelled a single word. It was a single word that had more meaning than almost any other. A name of complete and utter darkness. Kelgar couldn't believe it.

"Spirits above us," he gasped. "It's Notelcea!"

# Chapter Twenty-five

## THE FINAL CONFESSION

Ericahs awoke with a throbbing pain in his eyes. He sat up woozily, rubbing the spot where Notelcea had hit him. A large bump was already forming and it was very sore to the touch. Ericahs glanced around.

"Lismella!" he shouted into the night. Then remembering he'd learned her real name, he added, "Notelcea!"

Neither name elicited any response. Ericahs wasn't exactly surprised. If he'd walloped somebody with a tree branch, he probably wouldn't wait around until they woke up either. The one thing Ericahs didn't understand was why.

If Notelcea had wanted to get rid of Ericahs, why had she asked him to come with her in the first place? He checked his belongings, but they were all still there, so Notelcea obviously hadn't been hoping to rob him. He was also fairly certain she hadn't been trying to kill him. If she had been, Ericahs was confident he'd be dead now instead of nursing a heavily bruised head.

"Demon-spawn wench," he muttered under his breath.

Ericahs didn't care if she was a Guardian. He didn't care if she was over three hundred years old. He didn't even care if she had seen the sun. None of that gave her the right to knock him out and then run off into the darkness with no explanation. He couldn't begin to image what had suddenly changed her mind.

Ericahs looked up at the sky. The moon was out, but he couldn't tell which one it was, having no idea how long he'd spent lying there. He fashioned himself a new torch, but didn't light it. He was simply going to save it for when the moon set. Then he set out in search of water to ease his throbbing head.

Eventually he heard the telltale sound of trickling coming from somewhere in the underbrush. He followed the noise and came to a small creek, gleaming silver in the moonlight. It was a welcome sight. He bent down beside the creek and began soothing his head with the ice-cold water.

A twig snapped behind him and he turned around quickly with his sword drawn. He couldn't believe what he was seeing. It was Notelcea with her white gown glowing in the moonlight. He was sure she'd be miles away by now.

"Ericahs," she called quietly.

"What do you want, demon witch?" he asked venomously.

Notelcea ignored the insult. "It won't kill me," she said plainly.

"What won't kill you?" asked Ericahs, still holding his sword. At this point he'd be more than happy to do that job in place whatever wouldn't.

"Aecleton."

Ericahs shook his head. "What nonsense is that?"

"The Shadows won't kill me," Notelcea pressed. "I tried."

Ericahs lowered his sword. "I wondered why you'd attacked me before, now I know. You're just crazy."

"I'm not crazy, Ericahs," Notelcea corrected. "I have just come from the Valley of the Shadows."

Ericahs stared at her. She had his undivided attention now. "What do you mean you just came from the Valley of the Shadows?"

"That was why I stopped you from coming with me. I went there alone because I wanted them to kill me. I could feel them all around me. I could see them with my eyes, and yet the Shadows left me untouched. Aecleton wouldn't let them kill me. Aecleton wants me alive."

"Slow down," said Ericahs trying to play catch up. "You went to the Valley of the Shadows alone?"

"Yes."

"What about the prophecy? I thought I was supposed to be the one to destroy the Shadows and all that?"

Notelcea shook her head wearily. "There is no prophecy, Ericahs, no words of great destiny carven in stone. I etched the words about you in that rock myself.

That prophecy exists only in my imagination."

Ericahs took a step backward. If he had felt betrayed before, he felt doubly so now. It seemed as though everything Notelcea had told him since she'd first met him had all been a complete and utter lie.

"Then why did you pick me?" Ericahs demanded. "Why did you drag me all over Silverwood on some imaginary quest? What was I to you?"

"Expendable," Notelcea replied.

Ericahs couldn't believe it. "So I'm nothing then? I'm nothing to you or all the rest of the world. Just some foolish dupe with a sword who fell for your shiny story."

"Yes," Notelcea answered without emotion. "I didn't choose you because you were special; you're special because I chose you."

Ericahs felt less than special. He felt utterly idiotic. Though he was reluctant to admit it, he'd actually believed Notelcea and her prophecy. He'd seen the words on the stone, and at the time he hadn't realized the magic she'd possessed to carve them. At the time it had seemed so convincing and Notelcea was a much better liar than he'd given her credit for. Then again, she'd been successfully doing it for over three hundred years. Why wouldn't she be a good liar?

"You're not some chosen one," Notelcea continued driving the psychological stake further into Ericahs' heart, "you're just the one I chose. I purposely went looking for an outlander, someone who wouldn't recognize me as a Guardian. I went looking for someone that no one cared about. I needed someone and I found you, you who had almost no connections. You were unlikely to miss anyone, and you were even less likely to be missed."

"I don't understand," said Ericahs.

"I was sending you on a suicide mission, Ericahs."

Ericahs couldn't believe how calmly she'd just said those words to him.

"I needed someone that I could use to drive the light into the heart of darkness," Notelcea explained. "In your case it would be with the sword. There was nothing you loved in this world, so there was nothing preventing you from running head first into the lion's lair if I asked you to; into the Valley of the Shadows itself. You even had a grudge against the Keeper. What more could I ask of my weapon? I always knew that whomever I chose wouldn't be coming back."

"And who died and made you a goddess?" Ericahs shot back. "What do you think gives you such a right to use and manipulate people to your own end?"

"I've been doing exactly that for three hundred years, Ericahs," she replied. "Nothing's changed. I'll not pretend to be a perfect human being. I've done such terrible things, but in this case I was honestly trying to choose the lesser of two evils. By sacrificing your life, I could save all the rest."

"Why didn't you just do it yourself? With all your high and mighty ideals, why didn't you make yourself the tool the defeat the Keeper instead of looking for another to do the job? If you have enough power to bestow upon someone else, you should certainly have enough to use yourself."

"I couldn't risk the possibility of not being here if it didn't work. If something happened and I were killed before I'd reached the heart of darkness, the world would fall without me there to stop it. I was there in the beginning and I know more than anyone else. It seemed safer to first send someone else while I stood watch to be sure that it worked. If it didn't, I could always go in myself the second time."

"My life isn't yours to sacrifice," Ericahs growled, "and neither was Ikeara's."

Notelcea almost laughed. Ericahs glared at her, not finding Ikeara's death a very humorous subject. He turned away and began packing up his things, eager to leave the dark and spiteful woman behind him.

"You still really believe she's dead don't you?" asked Notelcea in amusement.

Ericahs turned toward her, knitting his eyebrows in suspicion. He wondered if Notelcea was simply trying to bait him.

"I though you would have figured it out by now."

"Figured out what," Ericahs demanded angrily.

"She was never here, Ericahs," Notelcea replied. "Ikeara was never here."

"What?" That didn't even make sense. He specifically recalled the memory of her being taken by the Shadows. It was what had so enraged him and made him more ready than ever to stop the Keeper. He didn't see how it was possible that she'd never actually been there.

"You didn't think it was a bit coincidental that your long lost love, whom you haven't seen in years suddenly shows up here in Silverwood?" asked Notelcea.

"Well…"

"You didn't question the fact that she seemed so willing to shrug off her guard duty to come and join you on some dangerous mission to the Valley of the Shadows?"

"I guess–"

"You didn't think it was a bit strange that the Shadows rolled in faster than ever before? That you were not even touched by them, but Ikeara was deftly destroyed? Or that I was suddenly nowhere to be found during the attack? Perhaps you're more gullible than I thought."

"But if it wasn't all real, then how? How did you do it?"

Notelcea gave a small grin. "I'm a *very* powerful sorceress, Ericahs. Given enough time I could put any number of things into your head and make you believe they were real."

"What about the moons?" asked Ericahs. "I saw them disappear. That was real wasn't it?"

"Yes, that was real, unfortunately," Lismella replied, "but nothing about Ikeara's presence here was in truth."

Ericahs didn't understand her purpose behind it all. "But then why the show? Why all the anger about me wanting to bring her with us?"

"It was your dream, Ericahs. I made sure the Shadows took her, but it was still your dream. Your own mind took it to where it went. It was your interpretation of how I would react to your wanting to bring her. I suppose it was probably brought about by that ever-present stubborn streak within you. Even in your dreams you feel the need to rebel against me."

"So she's still out there somewhere then?"

"Yes, somewhere. Perhaps you'll find her again someday when this is all over. For now I simply needed you believe that she was dead; that the Shadows had taken her from you."

"But why! What was the point of it all? If her being here was all just a dream then why did you have to put me through that and make it feel so real? Or are you just so bored after three hundred years of life that you now delight in tormenting people for your own personal enjoyment!"

"Because I needed you to believe it," said Notelcea. "I needed you to be angry at the Shadows. I tried by making you dream of your mother and your brother, but I soon realized that their deaths were too long ago. There had to be something new to rekindle that anger within you once again, so I gave you Ikeara's death.

"It was something fresh to renew your hate of the Shadows. I knew that hate would drive you and prevent you from quaking within the valley of the dark ones when I sent you to drive the sword into their midst. You were my weapon, my one hope for saving the world, the transport vessel for my power. I needed to be sure your courage would be strong."

"So why the big change now?" Ericahs asked. His voice sounded broken and he could do little to disguise it. He was tired and just wanted to know the whole truth. "If you were so confident that you'd made me your perfect weapon, why did you suddenly decide to knock me over the head and run off to valley yourself? Why are you suddenly so determined to die?"

"Because when we were with the gypsy, I noticed the Shadows were actually protecting me."

Ericahs thought back to that fight. He remembered the dark shape that had crossed in front of Notelcea. At the time he'd simply thought it was magic, but now he was realizing what it had truly been.

"The arrow," he said. "The Shadows blocked that arrow from hitting you."

Notelcea nodded. "Yes. That was when I knew. It wouldn't matter how much power I put into that sword of yours. If the Shadows were protecting me, it must be because they needed me alive for their own survival. I had to die."

"Why? What do you have to do with them?"

Notelcea sighed. "I have one final confession to make, Ericahs."

"And what is that?"

Notelcea pierced Ericahs with those hypnotizing blue eyes of hers. "I am Aecleton's mother."

# Chapter Twenty-six

# THE WHOLE TRUTH

"You really expect me to believe that you're Aecleton's mother?" asked Ericahs. "Aecleton isn't even human. You are."

"Well, I've always preferred to say that I was Aecleton's mother because it made it seem that much more distant from me," Notelcea explained. "In truth, I guess you might say that I am Aecleton herself."

Ericahs shook his head. "Ok. Now I know you're insane." He turned away and resumed packing up his belongings.

As the prophecy had just been revealed to be a fake, the world wasn't actually riding on his shoulders, so he saw no reason to stay with Notelcea any longer. If she was really three hundred years old, and for some reason he still believed she was, then maybe she'd just spent too long living alone in that tower of the Guardians. In any event, Ericahs was washing his hands of her.

"You remember how I told you that I was different, that I don't have a dark side?" asked Notelcea.

Ericahs didn't answer. He ignored her completely.

"It's because Aecleton *is* my dark side," Notelcea finished, knowing Ericahs could still hear even if he wasn't purposely listening. "I know it sounds crazy, but it is the truth."

"The truth!" Ericahs shouted, throwing his water gourd at Notelcea in anger. She blocked it with her magic as he shouted, "I've been listening to your versions of the truth for nights on end now, and honestly I don't want to anymore!"

He glared at her. The look of surprise on her face was evident and it just made him even angrier. She had quite the nerve to assume she could knock him out, go her own way, and then show up again and expect him to be sympathetic.

"You obviously came back here because you need my help for some reason," Ericahs continued. "I can't imagine what, but I know it's true. The world doesn't depend on me anymore, however, so I see no point in staying unless you tell me absolutely everything. No more half-truths, no more lies, no more withholding secrets. You're going to tell me everything right here, right now or I'm leaving!"

He saw Notelcea's hand move ever so slightly.

"And don't think for a moment that your sorceress powers can frighten me into submission. As you so insensitively pointed out, I don't have any connections, so I don't have anything to fear losing. I'm just expendable, remember? Killing me won't make me help you."

Notelcea stared at him for moment. Ericahs wondered if she was actually contemplating turning him into a toad or something along those lines. At this point he really didn't care, however. If she'd rather kill him than give him the truth, that was fine as long as he didn't have to help her.

"Alright, Ericahs," Notelcea said at last. "I'll tell you everything."

Ericahs watched her closely as she began.

"You already know I was the youngest of the Guardians," said Notelcea, "and as I said, there was a lot of magic in the air after we built the Lumidian. That was what frightened me."

"Frightened you?"

"Yes. Magic is an intoxicating thing. I could feel it even in myself and I didn't want it to consume me. I didn't want that power to turn into a lust for more power. I was afraid the magic would call to my dark side, so I removed it."

Ericahs shook his head. "How do you just remove your dark side?"

"I wasn't a peasant, Ericahs. I was the youngest of the first three Guardians, but I was still a very powerful sorceress. I developed in secret a way to remove my dark side. I of course mentioned none of it to the other Guardians. I knew it was morally wrong on so many levels, but I was so afraid of being tempted by the great power surrounding us. It was only later that I realized everyone needs their dark side just as much as their light."

Ericahs thought back to their earlier conversations. He repeated Notelcea's previously spoken words, "Without darkness there can be no light, for there would be nothing to illuminate."

Notelcea nodded. "Precisely. It's not our light and dark sides that make us good and evil, for we need both. It's which one we choose to follow."

Notelcea lit a sphere of white light in her palm. She twirled it in her hands for a few moments, saying nothing. It glowed brighter and brighter until Notelcea suddenly closed her palm over it, snuffing out the light. She closed her eyes as she did.

"Of course once I'd removed my dark side, that was when the real trouble began." Notelcea opened her eyes. "I hadn't thought ahead enough to know what to do with it once I'd removed it. In a moment of desperation, I did something even more foolish than removing my dark side. I thought back to the teachings of the temple. Remembering that light can permeate darkness, I severed a small sliver from one of the light crystals."

"Selene," Ericahs breathed.

"Selene," Notelcea nodded. "I put the sliver of the light crystal into my dark side. I had hoped the power of the light would destroy it, but I couldn't have been more wrong. It was only a short time before I realized that my greatest hope was fast becoming my greatest curse. In putting the light within my dark side, I had given it a small piece of what it needed to survive on its own.

"I tried to fix what I'd done, but it was too late. I couldn't undo what I'd already set into motion with my own stupidity. My dark side was no longer my own. It had everything it needed to become an entirely separate entity from me, and so it did. But it was disproportionate.

"The Selene crystal was only a tiny fragment of light in a being comprised entirely of darkness. The creature used that bit of light to make itself its own being, but it was a being of nearly pure evil. It continued to grow until it was completely out of my control and there was nothing I could do to stop it. It set out on its own with its own intentions, entwining itself with the Shadows. With their help it could feed on fear and darkness, sustaining itself forever."

"And no one ever knew?" asked Ericahs.

"No one, not even my fellow Guardians," Notelcea replied. "That was why I made the rule of never mentioning the Guardians. I couldn't let anyone know what I had done. If anyone knew I had been there since the beginning, they might grow suspicious and eventually put everything together. I couldn't have that. The thought of a Guardian who created darkness would be so terrible it would utterly destroy our civilization.

"So I kept my secret, just waiting for the day when I would die. Waiting for the day when I would be freed of all the sins I had committed. Hoping only that I would die before the secret was revealed. But that day never came. I watched the other Guardians grow old and die, but it didn't come for me. People began to think I was a witch who used my powers to keep myself young, but they had no idea just how old I truly was. I bore the secret alone and silent, as it gnawed away at me for three hundred years."

Ericahs stared at Notelcea, her unnaturally young face twisted with pain. He believed she was telling the truth. It was not that she acted any more earnest than she had before; it was simply that he didn't believe anyone could make up a story like that. Besides, if it was true, it explained a great many things.

It explained why she'd always been so secretive. Why she would try to go to the Valley of the Shadows herself. And why the gypsy had seemed so interested in her. Ericahs could only hope it was all true because if it wasn't, he couldn't begin to imagine what was.

"So it's Aecleton that keeps you young then?" he asked.

Notelcea nodded. "Yes. I've not aged a day since I created that monster. We are still connected even if we are apart, for we were once part of the same being. Aecleton keeps me alive through that one connecting strand. I've known it for a very long time. I even knew I would probably die once Aecleton was dealt the deathblow. What I hadn't realized is that I was keeping Aecleton alive just as much as it was me. As soon as I saw it stop the arrow at the gypsy's, that was when I knew that my own self was still feeding life to my dark side. The Shadows have probably been protecting me from the moment I first breathed life into Aecleton with the Selene crystal."

"So why is it only now a threat to us?"

"It's always been a threat to us, Ericahs, it's just taken Aecleton this long to grow strong enough. I had quite the conniving mind when I was younger. I think a large portion of that must have stemmed from my dark side, for once I removed it, I seemed to have lost quite a bit of the deep thought process. That of course can only mean one thing; Aecleton has it.

"Knowing how well the wheels in my head used to turn, I am sure Aecleton has been plotting this nearly since its inception as a separate being. It must simply have taken this long for it to develop the strength to carry out whatever plan its mind has hatched. And with that part of my mind being held by Aecleton, it's nearly impossible for me to outplay the monster. So at last after three hundred years of near quiet, my greatest folly has returned to haunt me."

"One more question," said Ericahs. "Where did it get the name Aecleton?"

"That is what I began calling it," said Notelcea. "Everyone knew it was not the Shadows. They knew it was something else far more powerful, though just as sinister. It needed a name, so I called it Aecleton. If you reverse the letters of Aecleton, they spell my name. They spell Notelcea."

"Why would you do something so foolish as to name it with your own name in reverse? Didn't you worry that someone would notice?"

"Actually no. You would be surprised at how few people think to reverse the letters in a given word. I knew no one would notice. People only see what they want to see. They believe whatever they want to believe and that is their truth until they decide to believe otherwise. No one would want to believe a Guardian was the mother of the darkness, so no one even noticed.

"Besides, it was more for myself than anyone else. I gave it my name in reverse to remind myself that though it had once been a part of me, it was no longer me. It was a creature of darkness, my exact opposite. I also wanted to be sure I never forgot my own foolishness. Aecleton was a reminder that would always be there. I am in control of everything…except myself.

"I created that darkness and only I can destroy it, because it is truly a part of me. The only destiny a person has is the one they make for themselves. Fate did not create Aecleton, I did."

Ericahs looked at her. "I think you're right to a point, but I also don't believe that fate is a complete myth. You created Aecleton of your own accord, but look at how fate has allowed us the opportunity to destroy the Shadows all together. You said that because Aecleton is entwined with the Shadows, if we kill Aecleton, we can destroy the Shadows as well. Maybe there's still a little of you within Aecleton too and that little bit is giving us this window of opportunity. Maybe it's true that we make our own fate, but maybe sometimes fate makes a little of us too."

Notelcea nodded. "I think you're right, Ericahs. So let us finished it."

"How?"

"Kill me."

Ericahs took a few steps back. "What?"

Notelcea stepped toward him. "I need you to kill me."

"I thought you said you already tried."

"No. I tried to have the Shadows kill me and they won't because I am what is keeping them alive. I need *you* to kill me."

"I'm not going to kill you, Notelcea. Why don't you just kill yourself?"

Notelcea sighed. "I dare not try. I've no idea what effect suicide would have on the magic that binds me to the Shadows. It could be the wrong choice and end up making them immortal. It might only increase their strength. I might simply become one of them, giving them my other half. Monsters never die by their own hand, they have to be killed, and a monster is exactly what I have become. That is what I created and it can only die if I die. You must kill me, Ericahs."

"What if you're wrong? You chose poorly before; what if you're doing the same thing now? What if we kill you and the Shadows are released to run rampant throughout the cities?"

"I don't think I'm wrong. I was young and impulsive before. Now I've had three hundred years worth of learning, three hundred years of watching the workings of the world. I think I'm in more of a position than anyone else to decide what will happen here. I know they're protecting me, and why should they be if not to protect themselves? I am what's keeping them alive in the same way they are keeping me alive. To kill them, you must kill me."

"But how can you be absolutely sure that the Shadows will be gone?" asked

Ericahs. "If I kill you, there's no way to undo that deed."

"There will always be shadows, Ericahs, for in life we make our own shadows, but the only power they have is that which we choose to give them. Your shadows won't harm me, because I don't fear them, just as my shadows won't harm you. They have no power. They're not real, but your mind makes them real.

"Like your mother. There were no real Shadows tormenting her. She did that to herself. The difference is the Shadows in the Valley of the Shadows are true demons. They are real and they do have the power to harm anyone within their path. But killing me can put a stop to them once and for all. I beg of you to strike me down."

"Notelcea, I can't. I can't just kill you."

"Please, Ericahs."

Ericahs looked away and ran a hand over his head. He'd never felt so conflicted in his entire life. He knew he should kill her, but he just didn't feel right about it. He'd killed people in self-defense before, but never someone who wasn't fighting him.

He glanced at his sword gleaming in the moonlight and looked back at Notelcea with the almost pleading look on her face. He knew she was in earnest. She truly wanted to die, and he was fairly confident that she truly believed her death would destroy the Shadows as well.

He closed his eyes and shook his head. "Alright," he agreed at last. "Alright, I'll kill you if that is what you truly want."

"It is," Notelcea replied.

Ericahs nodded and picked up his sword. He slowly paced over to Notelcea who stood waiting. He couldn't believe what he was actually about to do, and he couldn't shake the feeling that it was all very wrong.

His hands shook and he felt sweat beading on his brow. He raised his sword trying to steady his hands. Notelcea nodded and closed her eyes waiting for Ericahs to strike. Ericahs looked at her heart, hoping that it would not be too painful of a death for her after he plunged his sword into her body. Ericahs took a deep breath and pushed his sword toward her chest.

# Chapter Twenty-seven

# BARGAINING

"I can't do it!" Ericahs shouted bringing his sword down at the last minute. "I can't just kill an unarmed person."

"Would it help if I fought you to the death?" asked Notelcea.

"Don't mock me, Notelcea. I can't just kill you. It just doesn't feel right."

"But it is right, Ericahs."

"No, it's not," Ericahs protested. "Not yet at least."

"What are you saying?"

"I'm saying I need *your* help this time."

Notelcea stared at him. "What could you possibly want with my help?"

"I need you to help me set the world right," Ericahs replied. "We need to dethrone Raede before you're dead."

"Ericahs, what do you think will happen to the world if I continue to live?"

"What do you think will happen to the world if you don't?" Ericahs countered. "You've heard the news as well as I have. You know what's been happening in Argentum. Raede is running rampant and he's poisoned the people against the Guardians."

"You're an outlander. When did you start caring so much about the Guardians being in power?" Notelcea asked suspiciously.

"I don't," Ericahs admitted. "But if the people are against the Guardians, then it means they're siding with Raede. That is something I do care about."

"So this isn't so much a concern for the world's well-being. It's a personal grudge against the king because his road taxes are responsible for getting your family killed?"

"That's only part of it," said Ericahs. "I'm not going to deny that I hate him. I hate him at least as much as the Shadows, but there's another reason. I can't imagine what would happen to Argentum and beyond if Raede stays in control. He's power hungry and will no doubt seek to expand his empire, even if it means coming to Silverwood. That's the one place I thought I could escape him. Besides, he's using the Shadows to torment people, and I of all people know that no one should have to die like that."

"You've gotten very idealistic all of a sudden."

"Yes, I suppose I've been consorting with you too long. I hope you're not starting to rub off on me."

Notelcea grinned at his jest.

"Maybe that imaginary version of Ikeara you put into my head made me remember there are things in this world that are worth fighting for," Ericahs continued. "If I kill you now and the Shadows die, there will be nothing to stop Raede from gaining control of everything. The people will follow him without question because it'll look like he saved them all from the Shadows and the Guardians will be overthrown completely. Raede will take the glory for the demise of the Shadows and that would be almost as bad as the Shadows themselves. He'll be able to do whatever he wants. The people will blindly follow him and any who oppose him will surely be executed."

"Then what do you suggest?"

"We go into Argentum and dethrone Raede."

Notelcea shook her head. "You can't just dethrone him, Ericahs, he is the king. You'll never be able to prove that he is using the Shadows to his advantage. No one is going to believe that whether it's true or not."

"Then we have to find a way to *make* them believe it!" Ericahs shouted. "The people have to know it was the Guardians, not Raede who saved them. I won't bear for anyone to live under that man's rule. Raede is the one who implemented the road tax that killed my family. I'm not going to let him sit upon the throne as well."

"I hope you have a plan to go along with this burning desire for revenge."

"Well, I have part of a plan, anyway," said Ericahs. "The Shadows won't harm you, which is more than Raede can say. Perhaps we can use that to our advantage. If the people see you immune to the power of the Shadows, it might renew their faith in the Guardians."

"No one will notice I'm immune to the Shadows, Ericahs; they'll all be too busy running for their own lives."

Ericahs let out a sigh of exasperation. "Then we'll have to find some way to do it. You have the power of the Guardians and you're the only one the Shadows can't kill. That's got to be worth something to the people."

Notelcea looked at Ericahs for a moment before answering. It was a look of mixed emotions. On the one hand it was a look of pity that Ericahs was so passionate about the situation, yet seemed to have so little of an understanding about it. On the other hand, it was a look of faith. A tiny of flame of desperately wanting to believe. In the end, the latter won out.

"Alright, Ericahs," Notelcea agreed. "I'll bargain with you. I will help you find a way to dethrone Raede as long as you will make me a promise."

"What promise?"

"That when this is over, you *will* kill me."

Ericahs still didn't like the thought of killing Notelcea, but he knew the agreement was fair. He couldn't expect her to help him without giving her anything in return, and it seemed that death was the only price she was willing to take. So as it was obviously her greatest desire, he would do as she asked and kill her once Raede was gone.

"Agreed," said Ericahs. "You help me kill Raede and then…I'll end your life."


Ericahs and Notelcea tramped back through the thick forests of Silverwood. Having initially been on their way to the Valley of the Shadows, they were already nearly through to the far edge of the woodland. As such, they had a long walk back now that they were turned around.

They were heading back toward a world to which neither of them wanted to return. Argentum meant something different to both of them, but the conclusion was the same. Neither of them wanted to go back there.

For Notelcea, returning to Argentum meant facing the sins of her past. That was something she'd been trying to avoid for three hundred years. Even Kelgar knew the truth now, and Notelcea was less than thrilled at the prospect of having to see him once again. She'd planned to be dead already, never having to face him. She could only imagine what he thought of her now.

For Ericahs, Argentum was a return to civilization. That was something he'd hoped never to return to if he didn't have to. He'd left towns and cities behind him long ago, taking refuge in the emptiness of the outer lands, the more lawless lands. That was where he fit in because that was where he was alone. Being with people was something he didn't do well.

No matter what their reasons were, however, Ericahs and Notelcea had no choice. If they wanted to stop Raede, they would have to return to that place once more. Even Ericahs, with as few morals as he had, could not bear the thoughts of Aecleton or Raede winning. If returning to civilization was what he had to do to prevent that, then so be it.

They were following the roads instead of cutting across country now. It was faster traveling and at this point neither of them were very worried about being seen anymore. Raede's men had tried unsuccessfully to kill them multiple times now and Notelcea was sure she could overpower them again if need be. Besides, they weren't likely to be recognized heading back toward Argentum. Raede would be expecting them to go the opposite direction.


At length a shape began to appear in the darkness on the road ahead. As they drew closer, it began to take the shape of a small building with a very wide fence running out from either side of it. It wasn't just any building, however. Ericahs knew as soon as he saw it; it was a toll booth. Notelcea realized what it was as well and looked at Ericahs, knowing his particular hate for road tolls.

"Let's just go around," said Notelcea. "It may take a bit longer, but perhaps it's worth it. Neither of us is carrying any toll money."

"No," said Ericahs firmly. "We're not going around anything."

Notelcea nodded.

Ericahs listened to the sound of the wood beneath his shoes as he stepped up onto the platform. He listened to the gate in the little house open as the toll taker came lumbering out. He watched as the man extended his palm expectantly waiting for payment. Ericahs stopped, trying to control his rage.

"Toll," the toll taker demanded dryly.

That was enough to break Ericahs. He grabbed the toll taker, slammed him to the ground, and held a sword to his throat. He glared in the face of the man who would ask money for something as trivial as use of the road.

"Do you know how many people can't afford this toll?" Ericahs demanded. "Or how many people have died because of it! The king starves the people, over taxes their harvest, and then demands payments for crossing on a road! And you, you are the little weasel who stands there and collects it from all the people who can't afford it."

"Please," the toll taker squeaked. "It's just my job."

Ericahs was breathing hard. It was all he could not to pull his blade across the man's neck. "I suppose you never considered any honest work! Hunting, farming, some sort of a trade. No, you'd rather sit here idly doing nothing until some poor traveler comes along and you can leach money from their pockets!"

Ericahs made to move his sword hand.

"Ericahs!" Notelcea shouted.

His hand stopped moving. He looked at Notelcea, then back at the man who lay at his mercy.

"Ericahs, you've made your point. Let him up."

Ericahs didn't move.

"Ericahs!" Notelcea called again.

Ericahs didn't look at her, but he did remove his sword from the man's neck. He pulled the man to his feet and leaned in close to his ear.

"You'll not get a shilling from us," Ericahs hissed.

He threw the man back against the wall and walked on by. Notelcea watched with understanding. She looked for a moment at the toll taker who stood unmoving against the wall. Then she followed Ericahs across the platform knowing she was wasn't the only one still being haunted by demons from the past.

Ericahs had a set all his own.

# Chapter Twenty-eight

## THE MARK OF THE OUTLAW

Kelgar stood in the woods for a moment, contemplating his situation. Raede had sent his soldiers on the imaginary goose chase that Kelgar had been hoping for. They wouldn't be able to make it back for several days. The Temple of Aurora was now probably as empty as it was ever going to be. Still there was one thing that kept nagging in the back of Kelgar's mind; Notelcea.

Despite the fact that this was probably the most ideal time to try and save Enira, his gut feeling told him he should try to find Notelcea. If there was one thing he'd learned being raised by Mordrelina, it was to never ignore a gut feeling. And there was still the man that Mordrelina had mentioned traveling with Notelcea.

Kelgar didn't know anything about that man. Was it some poor fool that Notelcea was using for her own ends, or worse, was it a dark sorcerer she'd found to help her? A new thought entered Kelgar's mind. What if she wasn't trying to protect the Guardians? What if this had been her plan all along?

Kelgar's blood ran cold at the thought of it. If Notelcea truly was Aecleton, as her name in reverse suggested, perhaps she had merely sent Kelgar to the library as her way of bragging. If that was the case, then she was far more dangerous than even Raede now.

Kelgar's logical side told him that it was probably just the adrenaline of the situation making him think such dire thoughts. Even Guardians were not immune to panic. The other side of his mind, however, was indeed running wild with thoughts of Notelcea's betrayal. In the end, the less logical side of his mind won out.

He decided it was his duty to save the world from whatever malicious plan Notelcea had in store for it. Raede may be using the Shadows to his advantage, but if what Kelgar had just read in the library was true, then Notelcea might actually have the power to control the Shadows. If she decided to use that power against the world, what force could possibly resist her?

It didn't take Kelgar long to find Notelcea and her traveling companion. They were only a short way outside of the city limits, walking along the roads as though nothing were amiss. They certainly weren't hiding.

Kelgar reined his horse to a halt and glanced up at the sky. The moon was still out and that at least was in his favor. If Notelcea truly had betrayed the temple, the one thing Kelgar didn't want to do was fight her in the darkness.

Notelcea suddenly caught sight of Kelgar. Kelgar lit an orb of white light in his palm, ready to attack if need be. "Notelcea!" he called out.

Notelcea said nothing until she and Ericahs drew close enough for Kelgar to hear them. "You know my power exceeds your own, Kelgar." She motioned toward the light in his palm. "I don't suggest you try it."

Kelgar didn't lower his hand. "You expect me to sit idly by in the face of your betrayal?"

"Betrayal?" Notelcea scoffed.

Ericahs looked from Kelgar to Notelcea, and pulled out his sword. He pointed it at Kelgar. It was still infused with Notelcea's light magic, so Ericahs hoped it might provide a bit of a shield if the need arose. If not, he knew there wasn't much he could do during a battle of sorcerers anyway.

Kelgar looked at Ericahs. "I don't know what she's told you, boy, but it's lies all of it. Don't believe anything she's said."

"I don't think you know what she's told me," Ericahs shot back in his ever-defiant tone of voice. "I probably know more than you."

"And did you know that reversing the letters of her name spells–"

"Aecleton?" Ericahs finished Kelgar's sentence. "Yes, I already know that. I know everything."

"Then you're helping her. What did she offer you to betray the world?" asked Kelgar.

"Is that why you think I sent you to the library, Kelgar?" asked Notelcea. "Do you really think I would have shown you all that if my only intention was to destroy the world? What would I gain if the Shadows run free? I'd be nothing more than the queen of a barren wasteland with no one but the demons to keep me company. Who would strive for that? Even Raede doesn't understand that such is what he's headed toward if he continues to try and befriend the Shadows."

Kelgar lowered his hand a bit, knowing that she had a point. "Then why *did* you show it to me?"

"Because," said Notelcea, "I thought you deserved to know the truth."

"The truth that you're Aecleton!"

"I'm only part of Aecleton, Kelgar. I'm not going to pretend I'm not, but neither did I intend for this to happen. I was young and stupid and made a terrible mistake that I've been running from ever since. I thought it was time for you to know."

Kelgar shook his head. "Why only now? Why have you waited over three hundred years to reveal it?"

"Because this is the the first time Aecleton has begun to grow stronger than me," said Notelcea. "And because when I am gone, you will be the senior Guardian at the Temple of Aurora. I felt it was important that you know what really happened."

"When you're gone? What do you mean when you're gone?"

Notelcea sighed. "I'm only immortal as long as Aecleton is alive, and the same is true of Aecleton. The only way to kill Aecleton is to kill me."

Kelgar dropped his hand completely and extinguished the light in his palm. He was beginning to realize how wrong he'd been about Notelcea. She wasn't trying to take control of the world, she was trying to save it. What was more, she was ready to die in order to do so; a true Guardian still.

"The Shadows won't kill her," said Ericahs. "I've seen it."

Kelgar looked back at Notelcea. "Is this true?"

Notelcea nodded. "Yes. I've only just learned it myself, but it is true. The

Shadows and Aecleton know that I am keeping them alive as much as they are me."

"But the Shadows were here before you."

"Yes, but Aecleton has become one with them. If we kill Aecleton, we may very well rid the world of the Shadow demons as well."

"Right now we can use Notelcea's immunity to our advantage," said Ericahs. "Even Raede can't withstand the Shadows, but if Notelcea can, then we can overpower him."

Kelgar looked at Notelcea. "This is the plan you've thought of?"

"No," said Notelcea. "I was foolish enough to think I could kill Aecleton with a sword. Aecleton got the conniving and clever part of my mind when my sides were split. I think Aecleton has been playing my weakness for a very long time. It was actually Ericahs who thought of this, and I think it does have a very practical application."

"What's that?" asked Kelgar.

"I didn't think of it," Notelcea replied. "Therefore, Aecleton is not as likely to be able to out think us on it."

"Raede has Enira," said Kelgar. "Spirits only know what he's been doing to her."

"Or what she's told him," Notelcea gasped.

"The sooner we get her out the better," Kelgar agreed. "I haven't tried yet myself for fear of getting her killed, but with your help, we just might be able to get her out safely."

"She could still get killed, even with our combined magic," said Notelcea.

"Yes, but I've sent the majority of Raede's men on a wild goose chase into the badlands. They'll be gone for days. The temple is as empty now as it's ever going to be and it may be our only chance."

Notelcea looked at Ericahs. "Well, I suppose you and I could find a way to sneak in while we send Ericahs out front to scout danger or create a diversion if needs be. No one would recognize him in a crowd–"

"Before you get too far with this little plan of yours," Ericahs cut her off, "I think there's something I should probably tell you. I can't just walk through town as though everything is fine."

"What do you mean?" asked Notelcea.

Ericahs sighed. "I have a small confession of my own to make. I bear the mark of the of the outlaw." He rolled up his sleeve revealing a royal emblem burned into his skin. "If I try to walk through the main gates like an ordinary citizen, they're going to check me for this. They'll probably even recognize my face as much as yours. We're going to have to go in stealthily or not all."

Notelcea stared at Ericahs. He was sure he could see the anger welling behind her eyes. He didn't really think she had a right to be mad at him, however, not when she had kept so many secrets herself. It seemed a bit hypocritical.

"And when were you planning to tell me this?" Notelcea demanded.

"A fine companion you've got here, Notelcea," said Kelgar sarcastically.

"Stay out of it, Kelgar!" Notelcea snapped. She turned back to Ericahs. "When were you planning to tell me this!"

"Never, if I didn't have to," Ericahs replied. "I didn't know anything about the other Guardian being kept by Raede. I assumed you could pretty much light-blast your way through any problems we might meet on the road. I didn't know the plan involved getting their permission to enter the city."

"You should have shown this to me and you know it."

Ericahs bristled. "It's not exactly something I feel compelled to publicize. Half the people in Silverwood have already guessed it anyway, seeing as how I always wear my sleeve long, even on the warmest of days. I can't believe you didn't figure it out actually. Besides, you weren't exactly forthcoming about the fact that you're a Guardian and part of Aecleton."

"That's different," said Notelcea. "That was something that could affect more than just myself."

"Well maybe it's different to you, but not to me. I'm sorry I'm not someone of high rank like you, but this is a big deal to me and it was something I wanted to keep secret if I could."

"What did you do?" asked Notelcea.

"I tried to kill Laede," Ericahs admitted.

"You what?" asked Kelgar in surprise.

"I was a depressed and hot-headed fourteen year old boy," said Ericahs angrily. "I'd lost everything familiar I'd known in the world and I'd turned to the sword to survive. I was getting fairly good with it and I saw an opportunity to kill the king, the man who was responsible for the road tax that ended up being the death of my family."

"The road tax killed your family?" asked Kelgar.

"I'll explain later," said Notelcea.

"Needless to say I failed," said Ericahs. "Raede wanted to have me executed, but I guess Laede's heart was a bit bigger than his brother's, because he made a different decision. He didn't want to kill me because I was only fourteen. Instead he had me locked in the dungeon for three years and then branded me with the mark of the outlaw so I could never again enter the royal land. So now you know."

"This doesn't help us," Kelgar sighed. "We're just standing here arguing pointlessly about the past while the Shadows draw ever closer. We need a plan, and we need it now."

Notelcea stood thinking for a moment. Even she hadn't foreseen this, but she realized there were many things she hadn't been able to foresee, not the least of which was the demon cloak now spreading throughout the land. This was going to take some thought, a skill which had unfortunately been getting less and less useful to her as of late.

"The two of you are sorcerers. Can't you just use your magic to mask the mark?" asked Ericahs.

"No," said Kelgar.

"Yes," said Notelcea.

Kelgar looked at her.

"Well, not exactly. It can be done, but we don't have time for it. That mark was made by magic specifically so someone couldn't just wave their hand and make it disappear. The king certainly wouldn't want outlaws to just run out and find some renegade sorcerer to remove such a mark. I do have the magic to remove it, but it would take weeks."

"Something we don't have," said Kelgar.

"Well they're not just going to let a couple of Guardians and a royal assassin walk into the Temple of Aurora unannounced!" Ericahs was becoming frustrated.

Kelgar motioned toward Ericahs with his head and said to Notelcea, "We could always leave him behind. You and I can at least cloak ourselves somewhat, but we're never going to get anywhere with him."

"I'm standing right here, Kelgar; you don't have to talk around me," said Ericahs becoming annoyed.

Notelcea shook her head. "No matter what we do, we risk getting Enira killed. We need a very good plan. We need something so crazy that Raede would never expect it."

Ericahs suddenly looked up. "I have an idea."

# Chapter Twenty-nine

## TARKWEED

Ericahs made his way toward the city of Argentum alone. He could see the gate in the distance, heavily guarded. Now that he was here, however, he couldn't help having second thoughts. There was no telling if the soldiers of Raede would do what he wanted.

"Hold up," said a large man when Ericahs reached the gate.

Ericahs stopped and threw his sword to the ground to show he meant no harm. "I've not come for trouble," he said.

"Well, we'll see about that won't we," said the man.

Ericahs wasn't sure if the man recognized him as an assassin, but he could tell by the man's tone of voice that he certainly suspected it.

"Why don't you roll up your sleeves for me," said the man.

"I would," said Ericahs with a slightly smart-mouthed pitch to his voice, "but if I do so, you're likely to see that I'm bearing the mark of the outlaw. You're likely to realize that I tried to kill the king when I was fourteen, and you're not likely to let me into the city."

"So you're the brat who tried to off Laede, aye?" The man aimed a crossbow at Ericahs' head. "You're right, we're not going to let you into the city, so you might just as well go back the way you came while you still have a head to walk away with."

"Well as I said, that's why I wouldn't roll up my sleeves, because that's what would happen if this were any ordinary night."

"And this isn't an ordinary night?" asked the solder, not lowering his crossbow.

"Not for you," Ericahs smiled. "This is your lucky night."

"In about three seconds it's not going to be so lucky for you if you don't turn around and head back to whatever dung heap you crawled out of, boy."

"Alright," said Ericahs. He began to turn around as though making ready to leave before adding, "Then I guess you're not interested in learning the location of two Guardians who lie unsuspectingly sleeping not more than a league from here."

"Are you speaking the truth, or are you merely trying to get passage through the gate with false stories. You're well outnumbered here."

"No, I'm not trying to get passage through the gate with false stories," said Ericahs. "I told you this was your lucky night. You get to be the soldier who tells Raede that the other two Guardians have been captured. That is assuming you're smart enough to take the opportunity that's now presenting itself to you."

"What makes you think a few soldiers can capture the Guardians?" asked the man lowering his crossbow. "Many have already tried and failed. The elder Guardians are powerful sorcerers."

Ericahs glanced around and leaned in close, dropping his voice to a whisper. "Yes, but I hear even *they* are powerless against tarkweed. If we were to get some of that around them, they'd have no more power than you or I. Less in fact, because we are warriors."

The soldier stood straighter. Ericahs could tell he liked the sound of the idea. Being the officer who brought in the two missing Guardians would certainly have its perks. Perhaps even a promotion would be in order.

"So what is your price for this information?" asked the soldier.

"My price?" asked Ericahs. "My price is simple." He rolled up his sleeve. "I want this mark removed."

The man narrowed his eyes at Ericahs.

"You can keep all your gold. All I want is the mark of the outlaw taken off my arm," said Ericahs. "I want to be able to travel freely without people running in fear from me. Laede is dead now anyway; it's not as though I'm going to try and kill him again. Give me a promise of freedom from this mark and I'll give you the

Guardians."

"I'll need to ask Lord Raede," the man replied.

"That's quite acceptable," Ericahs nodded with a grin. "I would suggest you do it soon, however, for I've no intention of revealing the location of the Guardians without a guarantee."

"Assuming I send one of my men for tarkweed and the king's word," said the man, "what then is your plan for capturing the Guardians with it?"

"Easier done than said," Ericahs smiled again. "You might say I've *befriended* them both. They trust me. I can easily get close to them and get the tarkweed around them. They'll never suspect it. Even now they think I'm out hunting. Keep your men back until I've used the tarkweed to subdue their powers, and then you can bring them to Raede like the trophies they are."

The man looked thoughtfully at Ericahs.

"All I want is the mark of the outlaw removed," said Ericahs trying to drive the point home. "For that I'll give Raede the world. I guess it just depends on how badly he really wants it."

"Skellen," said the man without removing his eyes from Ericahs.

"Yes, sir?" replied a man behind him.

"Ride to the Temple of Aurora. Tell the king we're bringing in the last two Guardians in exchange for removing the mark of the outlaw from this man." The solder grinned. "And bring back some tarkweed."

"Yes, sir," said Skellen. He disappeared from view and Ericahs could hear horse hooves running away in the distance.

"For your own sake, I do hope it's as easy to catch the Guardians as you say it is," said the soldier.

Ericahs smiled darkly. "Believe me, it will be."


It did not take Skellen long to return with a pleased look on his face and a bag. Ericahs was sure it contained tarkweed. Ericahs smiled. Apparently Raede had seen fit to grant his request. Things were going well.

Skellen and the superior officer, whom Ericahs had learned was named Fallah, exchanged a few words. Skellen handed the bag to Fallah. Fallah nodded and Skellen went back to his post. Fallah turned to Ericahs.

"Well, the king has granted you an audience," said Fallah.

Ericahs smiled. "I am pleased."

"You should be," Fallah replied. "Not everyone is awarded such an honor. The deal is simple; you bring the Guardians to us and Lord Raede will have the mark of the outlaw stricken from your skin. You'll be a free man."

"All I want,"said Ericahs.

Fallah held out the bag. "You'll need this. It's the tarkweed."

Ericahs took the bag and looked inside. Therein lay several ropes of greenish hue, twisted from the magic-numbing leaves of the tarkweed herb. Ericahs swallowed nervously, knowing that what he held in his hands would make Kelgar and Notelcea completely powerless.

"Follow behind," said Ericahs looking up, "but not too closely. Wait until I've subdued them with the tarkweed before moving."

"Lead the way," replied Fallah.

Fallah signaled with his arm and a dozen soldiers fell into line behind him. They were heavily armed, but their weapons would be nothing against sorcerer magic if the tarkweed didn't work. If the tarkweed did work, however, the sorcerers would be so easily captured, the soldiers wouldn't even need their weapons.

Ericahs nodded. "This way," he said and began moving out.

Fallah and the dozen soldiers followed behind him single-file. Ericahs was impressed by just how quietly they moved. Even with that many feet and so many pounds of armor, they weren't much louder than Ericahs himself. He swallowed nervously again. There was only one shot at this plan working. He could only hope things wouldn't go badly.

Ericahs stopped a little way from where he knew Kelgar and Notelcea lay waiting for him. He motioned silently to Fallah to wait for him there. He dug into the bag and tied a slipknot in two pieces of rope, aware that Fallah was watching him closely.

Ericahs pointed into the trees ahead and Fallah looked to see. There lay Kelgar and Notelcea, apparently sleeping in the light of the moon. Notelcea's white gown just barely glowed in the pale light. Fallah nodded. Ericahs took one deep breath and quietly walked toward Kelgar and Notelcea, holding the knotted tarkweed behind his back.

Notelcea sat up as Ericahs drew near. "Ericahs?" she called.

"Yes, it's me," said Ericahs, still holding the rope behind his back. He knew that Fallah was within earshot as well.

"Did you bring back anything for dinner?" asked Notelcea.

"No, I didn't see any game around," said Ericahs. "They must all be in hiding."

Ericahs drew closer to Notelcea.

"Well, that's alright," said Notelcea. "I'm sure we'll see something before long."

She leaned over to rouse Kelgar.

"Now!" Ericahs shouted.

Ericahs quickly threw one of the knotted ropes around Notelcea's wrists, pulling it up tight. Kelgar was roused almost immediately and Ericahs threw the other rope around him. Fallah and his men came rushing in. Notelcea raised her hands, but nothing happened.

"It won't do you any good,Guardian," said Fallah. "These ropes were woven from tarkweed and prevent you from using your magic."

A look of fear crossed Notelcea's face.

Fallah smiled. "What? You think Raede doesn't know the sorcerers' weakness?" he asked. "How do you think he kept the young Guardian for so long?"

"Our bargain?" asked Ericahs.

"Ericahs, what are you doing!" Notelcea screamed.

"Seizing an opportunity," said Ericahs coldly.

"You'll regret this, boy," Kelgar growled, struggling against his own tarkweed bonds.

"Quiet, both of you," Fallah commanded. "Neither of you are going anywhere so long as your power is neutralized by the tarkweed." He turned to Ericahs. "As for you, you truly told no lies. Well done. The Guardians have been captured and you shall have your freedom. Accompany us to the Temple of Aurora and Lord Raede will remove the mark from your arm."

"That's it?" Notelcea shouted. "You've betrayed us merely to remove the mark on your arm! I could've done that for you. Think about what you're doing!"

"I am thinking about what I'm doing," Ericahs replied. "The Guardians have lost their status, so it seems to benefit me more if I choose to serve Raede rather than a few sorcerers soon to be without magic."

"The boy is wise," Fallah smiled darkly.

"You're going to regret this, Ericahs!" Notelcea continued screaming at him. "You mark my words!"

"Unfortunately you won't be around to see it," Ericahs shot back.

"Move out!" Fallah commanded. He glanced up at the sky, seeing the moon would soon be setting. "And better make us some light."

Fallah's soldiers quickly assembled a few torches. They sparked a fire and the orange light blazed forth as each solider lit a torch for the next, one by one. Now they had a light in the darkness and the final two Guardians as prisoners.

Fallah tightened the ropes around Kelgar and Notelcea's wrists. He didn't want them coming loose and giving the sorcerers the advantage of magic. He grinned. Right now the two most powerful sorcerers in the world were nothing more than a couple of helpless prisoners. A small woman and an old man. Neither likely to put up much of a fight without their magic.

Notelcea stole a quick glance at Kelgar before she was jerked forward by the soldier holding onto her rope. Kelgar was jerked forward as well. The two sorcerers followed quietly behind their captors. Ericahs took up the rear, falling into line behind everyone else.

"This is the beginning of the end," Kelgar hissed as he walked by Ericahs.

"Silence!" Fallah commanded.

Everyone proceeded to the temple without another word.

# Chapter Thirty

## NO RETURN

"So at last we have the mighty Notelcea and the slippery Kelgar," Raede grinned from the balcony as he watched the small procession leading them to the temple. Raede turned to the man standing behind him. "You sent word for our men to return from the wastelands?"

"Yes. As soon as we learned that the information had been false, we sent word for them to return. They should be here within four nights. What shall be done with the Guardians, My Lord?" asked Darak. He was a lower-ranking officer, but he was head of the guard while the higher-ranking officers were away.

"Bind them with Enira," Raede replied. "I want them all to watch as I wipe their position from our world forever...just before I wipe *them* from our world forever."

Darak nodded and scurried away to meet Fallah leading the procession. Raede smiled knowing that Argentum was his at last, as it always should have been. Now he knew nothing could stop him.

Darak waited at the door of the temple. Fallah slowly marched his prisoners up the stone steps of the Temple of Aurora. It was a bit ironic that the temple, once the haven of the Guardians, was now their own personal dungeon. Perhaps they should have thought twice before defying the king, Darak reasoned.

"Behold the two missing Guardians," said Fallah proudly.

"Well done, Fallah," Darak congratulated him. "A fine meal awaits you and your men once the prisoners have been taken care of."

Darak looked at Ericahs. Ericahs looked back. He knew Darak was nothing, just the guard left in charge when the others were gone. As soon as the others returned, Darak would go back to being just another nameless soldier in the crowd. Ericahs found it amusing that he was trying to present himself as such a high officer now.

"And this is?" asked Darak.

"This is the man who led us to the Guardians," Fallah replied.

"Ah, the mark," said Darak.

"The mark from long ago," Ericahs replied, slightly defiantly. "So where is Raede?"

"Lord Raede to you, boy," Darak replied.

"Raede or Lord Raede; it makes no difference to me. I live in Silverwood. But we have a bargain and I expect it to be kept."

Darak turned to Fallah. "Feisty one isn't he?"

"He's merely a soldier of fortune, Darak," Fallah replied carefully. "He doesn't have the honor that you or I have."

"Clearly," said Darak.

Ericahs narrowed his eyes.

"However, as a soldier of fortune, he's wise enough to realize that being with Lord Raede will benefit him more greatly than being against him," Fallah continued. "His qualm was with Laede. It doesn't matter anymore. And he did receive the king's word that the mark would be removed in exchange for delivering the Guardians."

Darak nodded looking at Notelcea and Kelgar. "Which he has most certainly done. Very well. Let us take care of the Guardians and then we shall call upon Lord Raede."

Darak led the procession through the twisting halls of the temple. They went up several flights of stairs and through more halls until they came to a door with a slash mark across it. It was not even locked and Darak easily pushed it open.

Inside the room stood Enira, her hands tightly bound to a pillar with tarkweed. In the corner was Milessandra. Her hands were bound as well, but she lay unconscious, a small line of blood streaming from her head where someone had hit her.

"Milessandra!" Kelgar shouted when he saw her.

"Silence!" Darak shouted, striking Kelgar in the head.

He fell to the ground as blood began to flow from his own head wound. He quickly sprang to his feet, surprising everyone in the room with his agility. His breathing was being fueled by anger.

"Kelgar!" Notelcea shouted.

Kelgar turned to meet Notelcea's eyes. There was a deadly look within them, as if Kelgar would very shortly regret it if he didn't draw back. Kelgar turned away, but he made no further reaction. He simply stared at Milessandra lying in the corner.

"You're quite spry for an old man," Fallah grinned.

"But you're probably wise to listen to your friend," said Darak.

Enira hadn't said a word, but a look of terror was pasted upon her face. She couldn't believe that Kelgar and Notelcea had been so easily caught. She'd been sure they were out somewhere trying to save the world from the plague of Shadows. That at least had made her torment somewhat more bearable.

Now, however, Enira was seeing that there was no hope. Kelgar and Notelcea were just as much prisoners as she was, subdued by the properties of the tarkweed that bound them. There was little hope of the Shadows being stopped now, and even less hope of being rescued. With all the Guardians held prisoner, who could possibly help them now?

"Bind them to the posts," Darak commanded.

Kelgar and Notelcea were dragged to the pillars supporting the temple. Their hands were tightly bound to the pillars with more tarkweed. No amount of pulling was going to free them. Notelcea stole one last look at Ericahs as he and the soldiers began to head for the door.

"This is your last chance, Ericahs," she said.

Ericahs looked at her, then smiled. "No, it's yours."

Darak and Fallah laughed. Fallah slapped Ericahs on the back, enjoying his insubordinate tone. In a way, Ericahs reminded Fallah of himself when he was a younger man, and he couldn't help but be amused by it. He liked the way Ericahs didn't fear the Guardians. Still laughing, Fallah led everyone out of the room and Darak slammed the door behind them, not bothering to lock it. There was no way the Guardians were getting through the tarkweed.

As soon as the door was closed, Enira began having a breakdown. "How did you let yourselves get captured? Now there's no hope for the world! Raede doesn't know what he's doing. He's foolish enough to think that the Shadows will bend to his will and without us to stop him–"

"Shhh!" Notelcea whispered sharply.

"Calm down, Enira," said Kelgar. "Everything is fine."

"Fine!" Enira shrieked. "You're crazy, Kelgar!"

"Shhh!" said Notelcea again.

Enira was silent this time.

"Just be quiet for a few minutes, Enira," said Kelgar. "I have to wait until the soldiers are far enough from the door that they don't hear or see me."

"Far enough for what?"

"Magic."

Notelcea looked at her own bonds, then turned to Kelgar. "You're sure this will work, Kelgar?" she asked. "I don't have any magic right now; I can feel it."

Kelgar nodded. "The tarkweed isn't affecting me at all."

"I'm glad of that."

Kelgar looked at Enira. "We got ourselves captured on purpose, Enira."

"You what?"

"It was the only way we could get in here without getting you killed in the process. Ericahs is with us. It's all part of the plan, but he's very good at convincing the guards otherwise."

"What about the tarkweed?" asked Enira. "I've been trapped here for ages by it. Raede says it numbs our magic."

"It does numb your magic, and Notelcea's as well," Kelgar agreed, "but I'm different. I am immune to it."

"How is that possible?"

Kelgar grinned. "I was raised by Mordrelina," he said. "That's how it is possible. I'm not as old as I look, Enira. When I young, Mordrelina made a special concoction, which included tarkweeed, and had me bathe in it. It was her own personal spell to protect me from the powers of tarkweed."

"Did it work?"

"Yes, it worked. I still have have every bit of magic I ever possessed," said Kelgar. "What she hadn't expected was how it would age my appearance, but I think now I can forgive her for that."

Kelgar looked at the door. There was no sound coming from beyond it and he didn't see any change in the light flowing beneath it, meaning there was probably no one standing outside of it. He looked at Notelcea and Notelcea nodded.

Kelgar took a breath, closed his eyes, and released a blinding ray of white hot light. It cut through the bonds securing his wrists, leaving him free. He quickly cut down Notelcea and Enira as well, then ran to Milessandra.

Enira was weak, barely able to stand on her own after Kelgar cut her down. Notelcea caught her as she was about to fall. Enira leaned on Notelcea for support, watching as Kelgar rolled Milessandra over.

"They brought her in like that," said Enira. "She hasn't woken up since. Someone hit her very hard."

"That's because she was helping me," Kelgar sighed.

"What?"

"I'll explain later. Notelcea, can you heal her?"

Notelcea nodded. "Yes."

Notelcea and Kelgar changed places. Kelgar stood beside Enira to support her weight while Notelcea bent down beside Milessandra. Enira looked on in wonder. She was learning a lot she'd never known about the Guardians.

"What are you doing?" asked Enira. "That's not Guardian magic."

"I have much more than Guardian magic, Enira." Notelcea replied without looking up.

Slowly the color came back into Milessandra's face and she began to stir a little. She opened her eyes groggily to find someone sitting over her. She jumped a little before she realized it was Notelcea.

"Guardian!" she shouted gratefully.

Notelcea quickly clapped a hand over Milessandra's mouth. "Shhh!" she cautioned. "We can't have anyone hear us."

Milessandra nodded understanding.

"Are you alright?" asked Kelgar.

"Yes," Milessandra replied.

"I'm sorry I had to leave you," said Kelgar.

"I know why you did," said Milessandra.

Notelcea stood up looking at Enira and Milessandra. "They're weak, Kelgar, too weak to help us."

Enira shook her head. "I'm not too weak," she protested.

"You don't even have your moon pendant now and you can hardly stand on your own, Enira," Notelcea replied. "You're not going to be much use in a fight."

"She's right, Enira," Kelgar agreed.

"Get them out of here," said Notelcea.

"What are you talking about?' asked Kelgar. "You can't do this alone."

"I'm not going to," Notelcea replied. "You're going to help me, but not from here. You've worked this long to keep Enira alive; let's not get her killed now."

"I can't just leave you here, Notelcea."

Notelcea looked away. "Yes, you can. You know I'm not coming back anyway."

"What does she mean?" asked Milessandra.

"I'll explain later," said Kelgar.

"Go," said Notelcea. "You're immune to the tarkweed and you can get them out safely."

"And you're not immune to it," Kelgar countered. "What if Raede entangles you with it again?"

"I'll have to take my chances."

"Well I'm not willing to rely on your chances. There's too much at stake." Kelgar looked at Enira and Milessandra. "Enira, if I get you outside of the temple, do you think you have enough strength to create a diversion?"

Enira nodded.

"It's settled then," said Kelgar. "I get them out and I come back to help you."

"I'm not waiting, Kelgar," said Notelcea gravely. "The Shadows are too close."

"I don't expect you to wait, Notelcea," said Kelgar, "but I do expect you're going to need my help."

Kelgar started to pull Enira and Milessandra toward the door.

"Wait! We can't just leave her here!" Enira protested.

"We have to Enira. We can't risk getting you killed. You're the only reason we haven't stormed the temple to begin with. I'm taking you to a safe place. You'll create a diversion and I'll meet back up with Notelcea. Whatever you do, don't let yourself get recaptured." He turned to Notelcea. "That goes for everyone."

Notelcea nodded.

Kelgar picked up a piece of tarkweed just before he reached the door. He lit a sphere of light in the palm of his hand. Notelcea did the same.

Kelgar grinned. "Let's show them just what the Guardians are capable of!"

# Chapter Thirty-one

## HEIR TO THE THRONE

"My Lord, this is Ericahs," said Darak.

Raede look up from his chair at Ericahs. He smiled and settled back against the cushion, apparently very pleased with what he was seeing. It was all Ericahs could do not to try and kill him at that moment. He was smart enough to know, however, that he needed to wait for Notelcea. He'd never overpower Raede's magic with a sword.

"So, the would-be assassin," said Raede smoothly.

Ericahs made no reply. He knew how slippery Raede was and he was sure the king was just trying to get a rise out of him.

"Perhaps not having you put to death *was* actually the best way to serve the city," Raede continued. "I suppose my brother was wise in some ways, though I doubt he would've foreseen something as this."

Ericahs still made no reply.

"Let's see the mark then," said Raede.

Ericahs rolled up his sleeve. Raede was still on the other side of the room, but Ericahs knew he could tell what mark it was. Raede nodded in confirmation.

"Very well," said Raede rising at last and slowly walking toward Ericahs. "You have kept your end of the bargain, therefore I shall remove the outlaw mark."

Raede put one hand on either side of Ericahs' forearm. Ericahs could barely contain his hate and he was hoping it wouldn't show too much on his face. Raede started muttering some magic words as he rubbed Ericahs' arm. Within a few moments the mark on Ericahs' arm had become several shades lighter.

Raede stepped back looking very pleased with his own skills. "That should start it," said Raede. "It will continue to fade on its own now and after several days shall be gone entirely. You're a free man now, Ericahs–"

An explosion suddenly sounded from down below, followed by the shuffling of footsteps and several bouts of shouting.

"What's going on!" shouted Raede.

The torches in the room suddenly went out.

"Somebody bring me a light!" Raede commanded.

Ericahs knew he was supposed to wait for Notelcea, but he couldn't help himself. The opportunity was presenting itself now. Raede was confused and in the dark. What better time to strike?

Ericahs pulled his sword off his back and swiftly moved toward the place Raede's voice was coming from. He raised his sword high in the air and swung. It was dark so he couldn't see what he was swinging at, but he felt his blade contact something solid. His stroke was followed by the sound of Raede crying out in anger as the sword tore his flesh.

"You killed everything dear to me!" Ericahs hissed.

Ericahs suddenly felt himself flying through the air. His body slammed against the far wall and his sword flew from his grasp. A torch was lit, followed by several more and Ericahs could see throughout the room again. Raede's arm was bleeding, but it was no more than a graze.

"Find out what's going on!" Raede shouted to the others in the room as they scurried to do his bidding. He turned his attention to Ericahs. "So you thought you could kill me like you tried to kill my brother did you?" he hissed. "Well you have failed once again, boy, and this time Laede is not here to save you from the sentence I would have given you before."

Raede held out his hand and began muttering words in a magic language. Ericahs didn't know what he was saying and didn't really care to have them translated. He was far too concerned with what those words were doing to his body.

Ericahs felt his body temperature rise as if he had a fever. He began to sweat but the heat kept rising. Ericahs tried to turn away, but there was nowhere he could run to. The heat was surrounding him, it was within him, burning him from the inside out.

The pain began to grow intolerable and Ericahs was unable to prevent himself from crying out in pain. Raede laughed at Ericahs' pain. Ericahs fell to the ground writhing in the inescapable heat.

"Ericahs!" Notelcea's voice sounded.

The pain Ericahs was feeling suddenly stopped. Ericahs looked up just in time to see Raede flying across the room, smashing into a wall on the far side of the temple. Notelcea stood there breathing hard.

Raede pulled himself to his feet, his hands up and ready to block any spells that Notelcea might send his way. Ericahs had a feeling it wasn't going to matter. Notelcea was a far more powerful sorceress with three hundred years worth of magic at her command. Besides, if Raede somehow managed to get the upper hand, he'd kill the Shadows by killing Notelcea, which was what she wanted anyway.

"How did you get out of there?" Raede demanded.

"Magic," Notelcea hissed.

"You're lying!" Raede shouted. "Magic doesn't work through tarkweed!"

"Well then I guess you'll just have to keep wondering," Notelcea toyed with his mind, "because I'm never going to tell you."

Raede gave a signal to his men and they slowly began to move in as Raede started casting spells at Notelcea. Notelcea deflected Raede's spells with ease and sent Raede's men flying backward against the wall. Raede glared, but continued to throw spells at her.

Ericahs meanwhile recovered his sword and began to go after the other men in the room. Every now and again he had to duck as a spell or a web of light went flying over his head. He had a feeling that Notelcea could have easily taken Raede out, but she was trying to get him to kill her. She was trying to get him to kill her without letting him realize that she wanted to die. Ericahs only hoped that Raede would die too if he killed her. If not, Notelcea would have broken her word to Ericahs.

Ericahs dodged a sideswipe from the man he was fighting. He spun around and dragged the sword across the man's neck, watching as the soldier tumbled to the ground lifelessly. Ericahs turned around just in time to see a soldier creeping up on the occupied Notelcea, a piece of tarkweed in his hand.

"Notelcea! Watch out!" Ericahs shouted.

He tried to run toward her, but another man with a sword barred his way. Ericahs was forced to fight his way through the man, watching as Notelcea turned around. But it was too late. The man with the tarkweed latched the rope onto Notelcea's arm before she had time to react and her power was muted.

"No!" Ericahs shouted still trying to fight his way through the soldier.

Raede smiled at Notelcea. "Where are your powers now, Guardian?" he asked evilly. "Apparently you are not quite as immune to tarkweed as you claim."

"But I am!" said Kelgar suddenly appearing in the doorway.

Kelgar was holding a knife in one hand. He glared at Raede. Notelcea quickly rolled out of the way, trying to free herself from the tarkweed entangled on her wrist. Kelgar stepped into the room.

"I challenge you!" said Kelgar fiercely. "I challenge you as king."

"Only one of royal blood can do that," Raede hissed in response.

"I have royal blood," said Kelgar.

"What?" said Raede.

"What?" said Ericahs.

"What?" said Notelcea staring at him.

The other men in the room exchanged glances nervously, wondering if that was true, and if so, how it could be possible.

"I am the unclaimed child of your aunt," Kelgar explained. "I have the same blood as you, and I challenge your claim to the throne."

"You're going to have to prove that," Raede shot back, not believing Kelgar for a moment.

"Oh I shall," said Kelgar, "right after I kill you."

Before Raede had time to respond, a woman seized Kelgar from behind and wrapped a piece of tarkweed around him. Kelgar spun around, muttered something under his breath and the woman was engulfed in a ball of light. Kelgar threw her across the room.

"I told you it doesn't work on me," Kelgar growled.

He and Notelcea lit their palms with light and aimed them toward Raede. They sent the blast toward the king with the greatest of speed. Raede quickly muttered a spell and put up a shield to lessen to the blow before diving out of the way.

Raede knew he was outmatched by the two Guardians and their magic. No amount of his soldiers would be able to help him if Kelgar was immune to tarkweek. Kelgar and Notelcea would pick them off like flies. Without waiting for the Guardians to send another blast of magic, Raede ran out the door of the room. Kelgar tossed the knife at him on the way out, nicking his shoulder.

Kelgar, Notelcea and Ericahs hurried to follow Raede, but Notelcea suddenly stumbled and fell. She gasped, holding her chest as she collapsed to the ground. Kelgar and Ericahs grabbed her as she went down.

"Notelcea!" shouted Kelgar.

Notelcea looked up. "They're here! The Shadows are here!"

Ericahs stood up and looked out the window just in time to see the setting moon disappear beneath a veil of black clouds. A murmur began to sound from the crowd that had gathered outside the temple, quickly followed by shrieks of fear.

"Aecleton has swallowed the fourth moon," Notelcea breathed. She turned to Ericahs. "You have to kill me now."

"Raede's not dead yet!" Ericahs protested.

"He has no more magic," said Kelgar. "The blade I hit him with had been coated with tarkweed. It'll take at least three days for it to be washed from his bloodstream. Until then he has no magic."

"There's not going to be another three days!" Notelcea shouted. "There won't even be a tomorrow! Aecleton is only moments away from taking the final moon!"

Ericahs looked at Kelgar.

"Kelgar can't kill me," Notelcea hissed. "I can't have a Guardian kill me. I don't know what it would do. You have to kill me, Ericahs!"

Ericahs still seemed to be hesitating. He couldn't help thinking that if he killed Notelcea now, something could go wrong. Raede could somehow survive and then Notelcea would already be gone, unable to help them remove the evil king.

"If you don't kill me now, the fifth moon will never rise!" Notelcea screamed. "We'll all be dead! You have to kill me now!"

Ericahs looked at his sword, the faint glow of Notelcea's light magic still emanating from it. He suddenly heard footsteps on the stairs above him. He knew it was Raede.

"He's heading for the seventh tier!" Kelgar gasped, wondering what Raede planned to do in the temple's most sacred room.

"Well he's not going to get there!" Ericahs shouted grabbing a torch off the wall and running for the door.

"Ericahs, no!" Notelcea shouted.

Ericahs barely even heard her, however. His hate for Raede was too strong for him to stop now. He ran out of the room with his sword and torch, heading for the direction of the footsteps. Ericahs meant to kill Raede tonight, even at the cost of his own life.

Kelgar made to run after Ericahs, but Notelcea grabbed him. "No!" she shouted. "Get out of here, Kelgar!"

"What?"

"Go!" Notelcea shouted again. "Enira is weak. She can't hold the Shadows back for very long alone. She needs your help. We are still Guardians and our duty is still to protect the people, even from the evils that we ourselves create."

"What are you going to do?" asked Kelgar.

"Nothing that shouldn't have been done a long time ago," Notelcea replied.

"You're going to bring down the temple borders," said Kelgar in realization. "You're going to let the darkness in."

Notelcea nodded. "I can help Ericahs...and then he can help me."

"You're really not coming back are you?"

"You know I'm not, Kelgar. This is the curse that I laid upon myself. It's time to finish it."

"What are we going to do without you, Notelcea?"

"You're wise, Kelgar. You'll find the way," Notelcea replied. "Go!"

Kelgar nodded and headed toward the door. He stopped briefly and looked back. "It has been an honor, Guardian."

He said no more and ran out the door to the crowd below. Notelcea looked out the window to see the white light was growing brighter and she knew Kelgar had reached Enira. The people would be safe as long as they stayed near the Guardians. It would all be over in just minutes.

A few tears began to form in Notelcea's eyes, but she rubbed them away. She didn't have time to be emotional now; there was too much at stake. She'd spent the last three hundred years making mistakes and missing the opportunities to make them right. She was not going to miss this one. She took a deep breath and raised herself to her feet.

# Chapter Thirty-two

# THE SEVENTH TIER

"Raede!" Ericahs shouted into the darkness.

Ericahs was on the seventh tier, alone in the Lumidian room. The device's own light making a barely perceptible glow within the room. The light itself was pale, as though it were sick, and it might as well have been. Where once there had been five moons revolving around the center point, now there floated only one. The last moon, alone.

"Raede!" Ericahs shouted again holding his torch higher to illuminate the dark room.

A shadowy shape sudden leaped from behind one of the stone pillars in the room and attacked Ericahs. Ericahs' torch and sword went flying across the room as he turned to see his attacker. It was Raede, just as he'd hoped.

"I'm going to kill you!" Raede hissed as he clobbered Ericahs' face with his fist.

After taking a few punches, Ericahs managed to spin around and roll Raede off of him. The king may have had the initial element of surprise, but he possessed barely half the strength of Ericahs. Now that Ericahs was off his back, he'd have little trouble getting the upper hand.

Ericahs drew back his fist and drove it hard into Raede's face. Raede fell backward against the ground covering his face where Ericahs had hit him. Ericahs jumped to his feet to meet Raede clumsily climbing to his. Blood was streaming from the king's right eye.

"Not before I kill you!" Ericahs growled in response to Raede's threat.

Raede made no reply, nor did he cast any spells. Ericahs smiled knowing that the tarkweed must be working as well on Raede's magic as it had on Enira and Notelcea's. He was getting a taste of his own medicine for a change.

"What's the matter Raede?" asked Ericahs taunting the king. "Not used to having your own weapon used against you?"

Raede glared at him and looked toward Ericahs' sword laying on the floor in the dim glow of Lumidian light. Ericahs caught the gaze and took off at the same time as Raede. They both raced for the sword, reaching it almost simultaneously.

Raede's fingers contacted the hilt first, but Ericahs was right behind him. He barreled into the king's body, knocking him away from the sword. Without magic Raede was no match for Ericahs and he knew it.

Raede gave Ericahs a quick right hook for good measure then scrambled to his feet. He fled from the room like a frightened dog. Ericahs jumped to his own feet, but had the good sense to grab his sword and torch off the floor. He relit his torch from another in the hall before chasing after Raede as fast as he could. He had no intention of letting the king get away again.

Ericahs raced out of the room and around the corner. He could hear Raede's footsteps on the stone floors ahead of him and he followed the sound. Rounding another corridor, he found Raede in a room with no exit, save for the one Ericahs was standing in. He had the king cornered at last, but in Raede's hands was a bow with an arrow nocked and ready. He was pointing it straight at Ericahs.

Meanwhile several tiers below, Notelcea was waging a war of her own. However, where Raede and Ericahs battled one another as opponents, Notelcea was fighting only herself. It was time to find out exactly what she could do with the dark magic surrounding her.

Notelcea moved to the very center of the room The power of the Shadows was all around her and she sensed their presence creeping closer. They drew in near to her, Aecleton in part trying to regain contact with its human form.

Notelcea did not try to resist. Instead, for the first time in her life, she embraced it. She embraced the darkness and became one with it, letting its deep power flow through her. She could feel the magic coursing in her veins thicker than her own blood and she knew how to use it. Closing her eyes, Notelcea brought down the barriers.

The walls of the temple began to shake and the wind began to rise. Its dark breeze swirled throughout the hall like a liquid poison obeying Notelcea's every command. She called upon the wind to blow harder, snuffing out the light of the temple torches one by one.

The magic barriers of the tower fell to Notelcea's power piece by piece. With its magical boundaries breached, the Shadows poured through the walls of the temple like a plague. The physical stone construction of the tower gave no resistance as their presence infiltrated the Temple of Aurora, infecting every square inch of it with their malice.

Notelcea stood there in the midst of those Shadows encircling her like their mother. They would not kill her. They could not kill her, for it was she who had brought them the Aecleton they were now entwined with. It was she who had given them more power than they'd ever before possessed. It was she who had created new life for them and it was her life that kept them alive.

In that circle of darkness where most people would have been afraid, Notelcea floated in ecstasy. It had been so long since she'd felt such power that she'd forgotten just how intoxicating great magic could be. How easy it was to get swept away by its power. But now that she was feeling it once again, she reveled in it, drunk with the exhilaration it gave her.

Even so, it was not the same intoxication that had latched hold of Notelcea three hundred years earlier. While that had been an overwhelming sensation of power that had frightened Notelcea and threatened to consume her very essence, this time it was a most welcome invocation. There would be no world-altering mistakes this time. This time Notelcea knew exactly how to use the immense power that was being bestowed upon her.

Notelcea took in that magic, absorbing it in its entirety, darkness and all, letting it fill itself up within her. She drank in the sheer magnitude of the power it gave her riding higher and higher into the air. She froze there for one solitary moment, letting the magic gather in the surrounding silence, and then she sent it slingshotting throughout the rest of temple, watching as it consumed all light in its path.

Up on the seventh tier Ericahs stood at the doorway of the room in which
Raede had cornered himself. Ericahs still held his sword and torch, its orange light
illuminating the room and the bow within Raede's hands. Raede's arrow was
trained on Ericahs' head.

The walls of the temple suddenly began to shake and a cold wind blew
throughout the room. Ericahs looked around knowing he had felt all this before.
As he glanced at Raede, he saw the realization cross the king's face as well.
Notelcea had unleashed her power and the Shadows were coming.

The non-material essence of the demons melted through the solid walls as
though the stone wasn't even there. The Shadows surrounded Raede and Ericahs,
their dark forms twisting and writhing just as they had in the gypsy's woodland.
They swirled around the room, tightly encircling the men, kept at bay only by the
fiery glow of Ericahs' torch bathing them both in its light. Every other torch in the
temple had gone out.

Ericahs looked at the torch in his hand. It was his lifeline, the one thing
keeping him alive at that moment, but Ericahs was also unintentionally keeping
the man he hated alive with that same torch. All he had to do was douse the light
and Raede would meet his demise at last.

Of course extinguishing that light would mean destroying Ericahs' only
beacon of hope as well. Everything else was dark save for that single torch. If
Ericahs smothered that tiny flame of life, he would be as vulnerable to the
Shadows as Raede.

Ericahs glanced up at the king. Raede had not moved a muscle since the
Shadows arrived. He knew as well as Ericahs that the torchlight was the only thing
that stood between him and sudden death. He had no intention of doing anything
that would eliminate it.

Raede was without magic and without anywhere to run. He could not loose
his arrow for fear that the torch would fall from Ericahs' dead hand, therefore
extinguishing that one light keeping him alive. The two men were in a stalemate as
the dark Shadows continued to pour in around them.

As Ericahs stared at the cowering king and the Shadows beside him, a wave of insane hatred washed over him. Raede was in part responsible for killing everything Ericahs loved. He glanced at his torch and then at the Shadows one last time and he knew it was worth it.

"It seems we're at a standstill, boy," said Raede. "We're in the same predicament."

Ericahs nodded, knowing that Raede spoke the truth, but not caring anymore. He wanted Raede dead badly enough that he was willing to give up his own life to achieve that goal. He stole a quick look at the hall behind him.

Ericahs knew Raede would shoot him dead before he'd gotten two steps if he tried to run. If that happened, Raede might still be able to ward off the Shadows with the torch. Ericahs couldn't have that. He couldn't risk the chance that Raede might live. There was only one thing to do.

"If you drop that torch, boy, we're both dead!" Raede shouted sensing Ericahs' thoughts.

Ericahs grinned evilly. He knew it was a sacrifice worth making. "Then so be it!" Ericahs shouted in defiance. He tossed the torch into the air, letting it go to the darkness.

"You fool!" Raede shouted in horror abandoning the bow and running for the torch.

It seemed to go in slow motion before Raede's eyes as he futilely tried to grasp it. The torch spun circles in the air, its light waving to-and-fro on the current as it slid back toward the ground. It crashed to the stone floor just as Raede's fingertips graced the wood of its handle. It was too late. The flame died upon contact with the floor and Raede's last hope for salvation disappeared before his eyes.

The Shadows swooped in to devour them just as they had taken so many others before. Ericahs closed his eyes, giving himself up to it. He could feel them all around him, writhing across his skin and in that chaos and he could hear them. Whispering and hissing they roiled, wrapping their poisoned claws around him.

Not far away Ericahs could hear them attacking Raede as well. It was Ericahs' only comfort in that darkness as he felt himself becoming one of the demons that now consumed him. Even with his own death taking him, he could still feel a small smile spreading across his lips as he realized what a fitting way it was for the king to die.

Raede was the man who had implemented the road tax that caused Ericahs' family to be taken by the Shadows. Raede was the man who had murdered the king through use of the Shadows. Raede was the man who had tried to overthrow the Guardians. He was the man, a mere mortal, who had been arrogant enough to think himself capable of controlling the demonic force of the Shadows. It was fitting that he now met his demise at their hand.

Raede was dying and it gave a Ericahs a sense of peace, a closure. He took a deep breath and released himself to the Shadows. He was ready and he had no need and no intention of screaming. Raede however did.

It was the scream that Ericahs had already heard too many times before. The scream he had heard when the Shadows took his brother. The scream he had heard at the gypsy's tent in Silverwood. It was the scream that was unique to someone being consumed by the Shadows. That final, bloodcurdling cry of desperation in a last plea for help that would never come. That was the scream that Raede made and then suddenly all was silent.

Ericahs opened his eyes. He looked up. The wind was still blowing and the Shadows were still swirling all around him, but he was alive. He didn't understand how it was possible, as he had felt the Shadows clawing at his skin with their otherworldly venom.

He gazed deep in the midst of the Shadows and began to stand up. He was still holding his sword and that was when he noticed the glow. The blade of his sword had a milky-white hue; a coating of a light like an endless torch that would never cease to burn. It was the light magic, still burning fiercely within his blade.

"Notelcea!" he gasped.

Ericahs ran from the room and headed toward the stairs, his sword lighting his way. The magic Notelcea had permeated within his sword was potent as ever and it glowed even brighter as he ran. He knew it was the only reason he was still alive.

Ericahs ran through the Shadows with his sword. It was different than carrying a torch for there was no orange sphere of light between himself and the demons. They could reach him, they could touch him, but they could not take him; not so long as he held tightly to his light-imbued blade.

Ericahs burst through the door of the room where he had left Notelcea and found her still there. She was surround by the Shadows. The entire room, the entire temple was filled with them. They rubbed against Notelcea without harming her as she sat in deep concentration.

"Notelcea!" Ericahs shouted.

Notelcea looked up. "Ericahs," she breathed.

"Raede is dead," said Ericahs.

"Then there is only one thing left to be done," Notelcea replied. "I can't hold them much longer, Ericahs. I've been expanding the magic in that sword to keep them from destroying you, but my power is waning. You have to kill me now, before it is too late."

Ericahs nodded and slowly moved in toward Notelcea. The Shadows bounced around, furiously trying to get at him as he approached their mother, but they were unable to. The woman who kept them alive also kept them from harming the one who would kill her.

Ericahs raised his blade to Notelcea's throat. He met her sapphire eyes with his own, looking deeply into them. Notelcea's eyes began to well as she pulled her moon pendant from around her neck. She placed it into Ericahs' free hand, holding his hand within her own to avoid breaking contact with it.

"The Lumidian should never have been built," said Notelcea in a shaky voice, her blue eyes glistening with tears. "We were never meant to control the light."

Ericahs held tightly to her hand, knowing that if Notelcea let go of the pendant they both held, the Shadows and the light would be out of her control.

"This is the only way, Ericahs," she whispered as her tears began to flow freely down her face. "I am the one who made the mistake and I am the one who must pay the price."

Ericahs nodded. "Thank you for helping me to redeem myself," he whispered.

"No," Notelcea whispered back. "Thank you for helping me redeem *myself.*" She smiled even through her tears.

Ericahs nodded. There was nothing left to say. Without another word, he slid his hand sideways, dragging the blade across Notelcea's throat.

# Chapter Thirty-three

# THE TOPPLING OF THE LUMIDIAN

Outside the temple, Enira and Kelgar were surrounding the people with their flashes of white light. Kelgar couldn't believe how fickle the people were. Not long ago they'd been trying to capture him, believing Raede's accusations of Guardian betrayal. Now with the Shadows closing in about them, the people were huddling around the Guardians to protect them. It was a bit ironic.

"Take this," said Kelgar slipping his moon pendant around Enira's head.

He could see that she was waning. The strength of the light shield she was producing grew less every minute. Kelgar hoped to extend the young Guardian's power long enough for Ericahs and Notelcea to finish whatever plan they had.

A bone-chilling cry suddenly sounded from deep within the temple. Even through the stone walls, the sound of the cry reverberated out into the night. Even the people standing before the temple knew the sound of that scream. It was the sound of someone being taken by the Shadows.

"Raede!" Kelgar breathed. He was sure of it.

The temple walls were shaking and a dark cloud of Shadows seemed concentrated on the structure. The fifth moon had not yet risen and the temple was still dark. At the rate the temple was shaking, it would only be moments before the walls crumbled entirely and the Shadows within would feast on the people outside. Even Kelgar and Enira would be no match for their strength.

"Get everyone out of here!" Kelgar commanded. "Get the people to the palace and light every torch you can find."

"What's happening?" Enira shouted back in panic.

"She's bringing down the temple," Kelgar replied, referring to Notelcea. "And I'm not sure if she even realizes it."

Kelgar lit his sphere of light in his palm.

"Kelgar!" Enira shouted after him, tossing him back his moon pendant. "You'll need this."

Kelgar caught the moon pendant and slipped it back over his own head. The wind was blowing terribly and Kelgar knew it was no ordinary wind. Something must have happened. Something must have gone wrong. Why else would the Shadows still be killing people?

Perhaps Ericahs had been unable to kill Notelcea. Perhaps he had even been killed and Notelcea was incapable of killing herself. Whatever it was, Kelgar knew he had to get there, and soon. The fifth moon wasn't rising. They had no time and nowhere to run.

Kelgar burst through the door of the temple, keeping the Shadows at bay with his light. He raced up the steps passing several tiers on his way to find Notelcea. The Shadows were everywhere, so thick they choked the air inside the temple. They scoured the space around Kelgar trying desperately to put out his light.

Without warning, the Shadows abruptly froze. Kelgar stopped, staring at the immobile cloud of Shadows. He reached out to touch one of them and the entire cloud of demons suddenly came alive.

Screaming and squawking, the demons tumbled and rolled. Their mass bulged in and out as their awful howling filled the tower. The sound was loud and powerful. Fearing the ear-splitting cries would damage his hearing, Kelgar knelt down and covered his ears with his hands trying to block out the inescapable sound.

Notelcea fell to the ground as her body quickly weakened. Ericahs caught her, lowering her slowly to the floor as the life in her body drained away. The Shadows squealed their high-pitched protests, but there was nothing they could do. Their life-sustaining force was dying before their eyes.

Notelcea closed her eyes, a smile upon her upon her lips. The grip she held upon Ericahs' hand grew fainter and fainter. She was determined to hold the moon pendant until the end to be sure there would be no mistake. At last her hand slid from Ericahs' completely.

A glow of white light suddenly issued from Notelcea's dead body. It surrounded her like a cocoon growing in strength and opacity. Then without warning it shot out in all directions cutting through the Shadows.

The light sliced into the very midst of the darkness, severing what little life the Shadows had left. They had nowhere to run, for the light came from Notelcea, their life-keeper. They fell beneath the white light and vanished, squealing louder and louder as their dark cloud became illuminated. Then suddenly all was silent and the Shadows were no more. For the first time in three hundred years, the Shadows were no longer a threat.

They were dead, as dead as Notelcea. As dead as Raede. As dead as Ericahs' family and all the other innocent victims who had been consumed by their demonic powers. They had chosen to increase their power by aligning their essence with Aecleton and now Aecleton was dead, and so they too had died.

Kelgar burst through the door of the room, having seized the opportunity the moment the Shadows dissipated. He stopped short seeing Notelcea's dead body lying on the floor. Ericahs sat kneeling beside her, a look of emptiness upon his face and his bloody sword laying beside him.

Kelgar ran to Notelcea's body and sat down beside her holding her limp form. He knew it was what had to be done, and he knew there was no way to bring her back. He had no intentions of leaving the room without saying goodbye, however.

"It was what she wanted," said Ericahs quietly.

"I know," Kelgar whispered in reply, trying to keep his emotions from sounding in his voice. "She gave her life to save the rest of us."

Ericahs looked down at the moon pendant in his hand. A beam of light shone through the window crossing the pendant in his hand. He looked up and saw the fifth moon rising over Argentum. *We were never meant to control the light,* Notelcea's words echoed in his head.

Suddenly Ericahs knew what he had to do. He closed his hand around the moon pendant and stood up. That beam of moonlight through the window might as well have been a sign from Notelcea herself for as clearly as it spoke to him. He knew what he had to do and he had to do it now.

"Give me your moon pendant, Kelgar," he said.

"Why?" asked Kelgar looking up.

"Because I need it," Ericahs replied. "Please just trust me."

Kelgar glanced at Notelcea lying dead on the floor, then back up at Ericahs. Notelcea had trusted Ericahs, perhaps it was time he did too. He nodded and stood up, slipping his own moon pendant off his neck. He slowly handed it to Ericahs.

"What are you going to do?" Kelgar asked.

"What Notelcea would have wanted," Ericahs replied. "This may be the only chance."

Ericahs grabbed the moon pendant and picked his sword up from the ground. Without another word he ran from the room heading for the seventh tier. Kelgar watched him go, unable to tear himself away from Notelcea's dead body.

Ericahs took the steps two at time as he raced for the seventh tier. Somehow he knew exactly what to do, though even he couldn't understand how he knew. Perhaps it was whatever essence of Notelcea that still remained which was driving him. It certainly felt as though some force other than himself was guiding his actions. He didn't resist it, however, because he knew it was right, and he knew it had to be now.

He had to make the change before the world acclimated to the absence of the Shadows. He had to do it now amidst the chaos while the balance of magic was unstable. If he waited for the energies of the world to shift it would be too late. It had taken hundreds of sorcerers to entrap the light, but now in the wake of the void created by the Shadows' demise, it might only take one to release it.

Ericahs reached the Lumidian room on the seventh tier. There was the legendary device. Its usual glow was becoming ever-stronger by the moment as the lost moons slowly began to reappear around the Lumidian's center point. With the Shadows dead, the moon crystals were recharging with life. Ericahs knew he had only moments before they reached their full strength. Somehow he knew that if the moon crystals regained their previous life, his chance would be gone forever.

He quickly placed Kelgar and Notelcea's moon pendants on the ground. Taking the hilt of his sword, he pounded on them over and over again, grinding them into a fine powder until they were utterly destroyed. As Raede had been wearing Enira's moon pendant when the Shadows took him, that pendant had already been wiped out as well.

Ericahs scattered the dust of the shattered moon pendants, then turned his attention to the brightening Lumidian. It was the only thing left to destroy. With all the strength he could gather, he pushed against the Lumidian.

The device toppled to the ground, smashing into countless pieces as it hit the floor. Shards of glass, crystal, wood and other materials Ericahs couldn't make out went flying across the room. The five moon crystals exploded like fireworks in the darkness, glittering like diamonds in the sky before the light faded from them completely.

"It's done," Ericahs whispered sliding to the ground in exhaustion. Whether he was speaking to himself or to Notelcea's spirit even he didn't know.

The ground beneath Ericahs feet suddenly began to shake. He looked up and he could see that the walls of the temple had begun to vibrate as well. The tiny pieces of the Lumidian were jumping up and down across the floor and a cold wind began to blow.

The dust from the moon pendants and the crystals began to swirl. It was a very distinct circular motion; a vortex. Even Ericahs, unversed in magic as he was, knew what a vortex meant. It was a door and he knew what would be coming up through it.

"Oh no!" Ericahs breathed.

He grabbed his sword and took off running down the stairs. The force of the wind blew harder through the halls and the shaking increased in strength as Ericahs ran. The walls of the temple were literally crumbling around him in response to the stress of the shaking.

Ericahs' footing on the stairs was nearly impossible to maintain. He made it down two tiers before he finally missed a step in the shaking, lost his balance and slid the rest of the way down the set of stairs. He scrambled to his feet and ran toward Kelgar.

"What's going on!" shouted Kelgar.

"I don't have time to explain," Ericahs shouted back, trying to be heard over the rumbling of the temple.

"What have you done!" Kelgar demanded.

"Just trust me!" Ericahs shouted. "We have to get out of here now!"

Kelgar didn't answer he ran back into the room where Notelcea had died.

"Kelgar!" Ericahs called running around him.

Pieces of the ceiling were falling now as the temple continued to be shaken down. Ericahs knew that if he and Kelgar didn't get out of there immediately, they were going to be permanent occupants of what would soon be a pile of rubble. Ericahs dodged the falling debris trying to catch up with Kelgar.

"Kelgar, come on!" Ericahs shouted grabbing the man and dragging him toward the door.

Kelgar shoved Ericahs off of him long enough to grab a small stone off the floor before turning and following Ericahs down the rest of the stairs. They tumbled awkwardly down several flights before landing on the ground floor and running out the door. They didn't even bother trying to descend the steps at the front of the temple, they just jumped off the side of the platform, rolling as they hit the ground.

Ericahs jumped to his feet and pulled Kelgar along with him. He dragged the sorcerer twenty yards from the temple before he heard a deafening crash. He didn't even bother to look, he just drove himself to the ground and dragged Kelgar with him. Pieces of the falling temple whizzed over their heads.

Daring to venture a look, Kelgar and Ericahs turned to see the temple. It was crumbling to the ground at an astonishing rate. The crashing sound had obviously been the roof of the temple collapsing into itself. As quickly as the temple was disappearing, however, something else was beginning to appear in its place.

A huge orb of light was forming at the bottom of the temple as though it were being born from the ground itself. It grew larger and larger racing up the falling temple until it burst out through the collapsing roof. It soared into the open air growing ever larger as it ascended into the sky. At the same time, the Temple of Aurora suddenly exploded.

Kelgar and Ericahs ducked once again shielding their heads from the danger. Pieces of the temple stones flew every direction landing all around them. They could hear the thuds of the pieces landing in the grass, the cracks of the stones hitting trees, and the grinding of rock on rock as it all crumbled away into nothingness.

At last all was silent and still. Kelgar and Ericahs raised their heads and could not believe what they saw. All around them was light, more light than they had ever seen in their lives. It was sunlight. The first rays of the new rising sun raining down upon the land for the first time in three hundred years.

They had to shield their eyes, unaccustomed to the brightness of the newly released sun. It was so many times brighter than the moons that it actually hurt their eyes look out for too long. They could not resist trying, however, for they had never seen anything like it.

The light went on as far as the eye could see. They could make out details for miles and miles on end. They were seeing features of the land that they had never even known existed until now. And all around them lay the scattered remains of what was once the mighty Temple of Aurora.

A murmur sounded as Enira led the people out of the palace toward the ruins of the temple. They all shielded their eyes against the brightness as well. Most people couldn't believe that they were actually seeing the sun. It had been gone for so long, it had become nothing more than a legend. But there it was above them now, its warm golden light pouring down upon them, just as it had three hundred years before.

"So what happens now?" asked Ericahs, turning to Kelgar.

"I don't know," Kelgar answered staring at the sunlit land around him with the exuberance of a child. "I've never seen the sun either."

# Chapter Thirty-four

## AFTERWARD

In the days followed new changes came across the land. It was a new world and new work had to be done. The seasons had to be changed and put back as closely as possible to the way they had been three hundred years before. Everything had to be changed.

Eventually people grew accustomed to the light of the sun and could walk out in the middle of the day without even having to shield their eyes. At night the sun would set and the land would be covered in darkness, but there were no Shadows haunting that darkness now. There was no Aecleton plotting to destroy everyone in its path. There was no longer any reason to fear the night. The Shadows became nothing more than a legend people would someday tell their children's children.

With the position of the Guardians no longer necessary, Enira became a powerful sorceress. After Notelcea had died, several other secret compartments had opened in the palace library revealing secret texts that Notelcea had hidden. It was some of the magic that the sorcerers had practiced in her time when she was young. She had hidden them away to ensure that not all the magic was lost.

Enira embraced and cherished those texts, memorizing everything within them. She learned the magic well, and she was almost certain that Notelcea was still there in some form, watching with pleasure as the magic of old was revived in someone new. Enira would eventually take apprentices, passing on those ancient secrets, but taking care to make sure it never fell into the wrong hands.

Ericahs took to wandering the roads again for a while. As promised, the mark of the outlaw that had hindered him for so long slowly began to fade away until eventually it was gone. His violent past was erased with the disappearance of that mark and he was free to go wherever he pleased with no protest.

Ericahs took a bit of time searching for Ikeara before he realized it would be a fruitless search. As Notelcea had seen, Ericahs had loved Ikeara once, but had been too stubborn to admit it. He realized now, however, that had been a very long time ago and there was little point in pursuing her now. They were both different people and the Ikeara he had been with in his dreams was exactly that; a dream and nothing more.

Eventually Ericahs returned to Argentum. Though he'd never held much favor for the royal city, it having housed the people responsible for his family's death, he now saw it in a new light. Raede and Laede were gone. There was no ruthless ruler sitting upon the throne anymore. It was as nice a place as any to finally settle down and stop wandering. He knew that someday he would find someone to begin a family with.

Kelgar had perhaps the biggest adjustment of all to make. Having slain the king, he was forced to return to the palace to prove his royal blood and therefore his right to challenge the king's rule. Perhaps it was fitting then that the stone he had risked his life to retrieve from the crumbling temple was the object that saved his life.

That stone had been a truth stone. It was the essence left by Notelcea after she had died. At the time Kelgar had not thought to use it for himself; he had simply been unable to cope with the idea of leaving any part of Notelcea in that falling ruin. When the time came to prove his royal blood, however, it was that very truth stone that cleared his name, showing his words were not false. It made Kelgar smile to think about it. Even after her death, Notelcea was still helping to set the world right.

Despite what most people would have done, Kelgar had no intention of sitting on the throne. Even though the Guardians would be no more, he was still firm in his resolve that no one who possessed such great power should be king. He'd already seen what had happened when Raede was on the throne.

Instead he gave the power to the people to govern themselves. The royal palace became a meeting house where anyone, no matter their status, could come and have a say in what would be done throughout the land. And as for Kelgar himself, he returned to Silverwood.

Kelgar had always preferred life in the woods, living in solitude, always moving. Now that he'd finally forgiven his gypsy mother, he had a lot of lost time to make up for. The Shadows had been broken and he no longer needed to protect the people. After half a life serving Argentum, he felt he was as deserving as anyone to spend the rest of his days leading a quiet life. A quiet life punctuated by bouts of magic-wielding of course. But no matter how many places he moved, or what direction he traveled, Kelgar would watch the sun rise every morning.

Kelgar never tired of marveling at its beauty as many times as he saw it. Every morning after the sun had risen, Kelgar silently thanked Notelcea, wherever she was, for giving it back to the world. Then he would turn and run off through the trees of Silverwood, reveling in the feeling of just being alive.

**The End**

## ABOUT THE AUTHOR

Amber Reifsteck currently lives and works east of the sun and west of the moon in an enchanted gingerbread house that may or may not actually exist outside of her head. She has always been fascinated by the full moon, taking long walks on full moon evenings to get the creative juices flowing. Despite this moon obsession, Amber is not a werewolf...as far as we know. But just in case, you may want to avoid visiting the author's website www.TheWoodlandElf.com on the nights of the full moon...

Made in the USA
Middletown, DE
26 September 2019

70366824R00144